CRIME DOESN'T PAY!

By Kim Hunter

Kim Hunter

Copyright © 2024 By Kim Hunter
The right of Kim Hunter to be identified as author of this work has been asserted in accordance with sections 77 and 78 of the Copyright, Designs and Patents Act 1988.

All rights Reserved
No reproduction, copy or transmission of this publication may be made without written permission. No paragraph of this publication may be reproduced, Copied or transmitted save with the written permission of the author, or in accordance with the provisions of the Copyright Act 1956 (as amended) This is a work of fiction. Names, places, characters and incidents originate from the writers imagination. Any resemblance to actual persons, living or dead is purely coincidental.

AUTHORS OTHER WORKS

WHATEVER IT TAKES
EAST END HONOUR
TRAFFICKED
BELL LANE LONDON E1
EAST END LEGACY
EAST END A FAMILY OF STEEL
PHILLIMORE PLACE LONDON
EAST END LOTTERY
FAMILY BUSINESS
A DANGEROUS MIND
FAMILY FIRST
A SCORE TO SETTLE (BOOK ONE)
A SCORE SETTLED
A DANGEROUS MIND (TWO)
BODILY HARM
SINS OF THE FATHER
GREED
EYE FOR AN EYE

Web site www.kimhunterauthor.com

QUOTES

It is easier to fool people than to convince them that they have been fooled.
Mark Twain

Believe nothing of what you hear and only half of what you see.
Edgar Allan Poe

The loneliest moment in someone's life is when they are watching their whole world fall apart, and all they can do is stare blankly.
F. Scott Fitzgerald

Main characters

Ruby Chilvers, daughter of Harold and Aida, is a kind girl but very naïve and far too trusting. Having mostly failed at school, Ruby's interests lay solely in music and dancing, that was until she discovered boys and in particular Joey Grant. A fumble in Weavers Field after the weekly youth club would result in an unwanted pregnancy and when all of Ruby's troubles would begin.

Aida Chilvers, Ruby's mother had never had it easy. A true cockney she had to fight for everything in life and was the butt of her husband's brutality almost daily throughout her marriage. It was probably the reason she was so hard on Ruby and her younger sister Sadie. Aida was prepared to go to any lengths to stop either of her girls from having to endure such a loveless and violent marriage as she had experienced.

Andy Chilvers was the first of Ruby's children to be born into a proper, though loveless relationship. As soon as he was old enough to understand what his father was capable of he came to loathe the man and at just sixteen years old, had begun to plan his escape.

Shirley Chilvers was the youngest and final child to be born to Ruby. Having taken the name of her father Dennis Tanner even though Ruby never married him, Shirley was a shy girl who watched everything but said very little. She adored her family with the exception of her father and to Shirley her brother was a God.

Konstantin Ivanov, a man of Russian descent who runs the day-to-day operations in England for his mafia bosses. Konstantin is a vicious villain but when Andy first meets him he comes across as a nice man and friend. When Andy's sister Shirley is beaten by her boyfriend, Andy swears revenge but he is forced to promise his sister that he will leave the situation alone. Konstantin, now viewed as a close friend, offers to deal with the situation on Andy's behalf and that's when the problems begin. A favour done is a favour owed and nothing could prepare Andy for what he was asked to do but you don't say no to this man and you most certainly don't say no to the Russian mafia.

CHAPTER ONE
Bethnal Green 1977

The family home on Birbeck Street was a small two-bedroom ground-floor flat. Originally a single terraced home the property had been divided into two units shortly after the Second World War. The Chilvers occupied the ground floor with their two daughters Ruby and Sadie and the Watsons resided upstairs with their only son Thomas. Harold Chilvers preferred to spend his time down the Bishop Bonner supping pints rather than decorating so the house still bore the 1960's gaudy floral paper that had adorned the walls when they first moved in. His wife Aida knew better than to complain as Harold was old school and thought nothing of giving her a backhander if she got out of line or said something he didn't like. The pub called daily to her husband and Aida was pleased when he went out, at least there was some peace even if he did go on and on when he got home, somewhat the worse for drink. Harold was a fanatic when it came to boxing and the Bishop Bonner was a boxing pub with the likes of John Conteh and John H Stacey being frequent visitors. Even Henry Cooper popped in from time to time after retiring in the early seventies.

Music was provided most Saturday nights by the then little-known Chas and Dave and it was standing room only when the duo began to play. Harold never took Aida along, he had an eye for the women, especially the barmaids and as well as reeking of drink, he often smelled of cheap perfume on his return. Again Aida never mentioned this fact; if her husband had managed to get his leg over somewhere else then at least he wouldn't bother her that night.

Ruby Chilvers danced around her bedroom to Stevie Wonder singing 'I Wish'. With a hairbrush in her hand, she tried to mime but she didn't know many of the words so in the end as she applied blue eyeshadow and pink lipstick, she just bobbed her head along to the music. Wednesday was the only night she was allowed out of the house and she was champing at the bit to have some freedom. Dolled up in her one good dress and dancing shoes she had agreed to meet her best mate Gloria Meadows at seven down the youth club over on Goldman Close but as she walked from her bedroom and made her way along the hall things suddenly took a downturn and her chance of going out now wasn't looking too hopeful. Her mother Aida stood at the sink in the small kitchen and glanced in the direction of the hallway when she

Heard her daughter footsteps.

"And just where the fuck do you think you're going, young lady?!"

"Just to the youth club Mum, a bit of a dance and a few lemonades with Gloria."

"Yeah, and pigs will bleeding fly. If your dad sees you dressed up to the nines he'll hit the roof and I really can't be doing with him kicking off tonight and you can get that fuckin' slap off of your face this instant or you'll be going nowhere."

"Oh, Mum please!!!!!"

"Don't oh mum me. Decent girls don't do themselves up like a dock dolly and if your dad sees you like that it will be world war bleeding three and we'll all be made to suffer. Now get it off before I get the tongs out."

The tongs Aida was referring to hung on the side of the old metal boiler that was wheeled out from under the unit on wash days and was used to lift the boiling clothes out and into the spin dryer, a new addition to the Chilvers home and Aida's pride and joy. Held together by a metal type spring, the tongs were the preferred tool of discipline in the house and the mere mention of them saw Ruby instantly return to her room to wipe the slap, as her mother referred to her makeup, off of her face.

Ruby shared a room with her younger sister

Sadie and the six-year-old's toys and games peeved Ruby every time she had to step over them, what she wouldn't give for a room of her own. Ruby wasn't exactly slow but her IQ was low and her interest in education or a career was non-existent. She attended Morpeth secondary school over on Portland Place but the local school had basically given up on her and as she was about to leave, no one really bothered if she attended or not.   The only light in Ruby's life was music and dancing and her old record player continually boomed out the likes of Smokie, Tina Charles and Donna Summer. The Sex Pistols had just had their first number one but Ruby hated them, you couldn't sing and dance along to their music and they seemed to continually spit at people which she found disgusting, not to mention the fact that they all looked so dirty. Thankfully the Youth Club was yet to start playing the Pistols music and for that she was grateful. Re-emerging five minutes later her eyes pleaded for her mother's approval. With a frown on her brow, Aida looked her daughter up and down , which signalled to Ruby that the decision could go either way but at long last she was finally given the nod from her mother. Almost running along the hall she stopped at her mother's next sentence.
"I want you back in this house by ten!"

Slowly Ruby walked back into the kitchen with her head hung low.

"But Mum, the club doesn't finish until ten and it'll take me a good quarter of an hour to get home and that's only if I run!"

"Then you'll have to leave early. If you ain't back in this house by ten Ruby Chilvers, you will never go to that youth club again, do you understand me young lady or do you want me to speak to your dad?!"

Ruby nodded her head, turned and slowly walked towards the front door. Once outside she ran all the way but it still took Ruby ten minutes. When she was almost at her destination all memories of what her mother said had left her mind. The old brick building, which had long ago housed a shoe repair unit and which for some strange reason, still gave off the odd smell of horse glue, had been taken over at the end of the sixties by Tower Hamlets Council. With few places for youngsters in the area to chill and spend time with their peers it had instantly become a success and now in its seventeenth year, didn't look like coming to an end any time soon. As the building came into view Ruby saw her pal leaning up against the wall smoking a cigarette. Gloria Meadows waved and grinned from ear to ear when she suddenly noticed her Ruby.

"Pull your fuckin' finger out Rubes or there won't be any seats left.
Ruby was flushed and while she was still running, fished about in her bag for a tissue to wipe under her arms. As she reached her friend she took a second to sniff under each armpit, happy there was no odour she threw the tissue into the gutter and grinned.
"You manage to get any drink?"
Pulling a couple of small screw-top jars out of her shoulder bag, Gloria winked and at the same time smirked.
"I raided me mum's bar, there's a bit of rum, a bit of Vodka and the last of her latest boyfriends Scotch. Don't look so worried, I topped the mix up with lemonade so it won't taste too nasty."
Smiling, Ruby linked arms with her pal and they entered through the double doors. The modern Hi-fi that had been purchased via a fundraising event was blearing out 10cc 'The things we do for love' and immediately Ruby wanted to dance. Luckily the girls were able to secure seats at a table near to the front and after plonking their bags down so that their seats weren't taken, they hit the small area that was used as a dance floor. Most of the lads who attended stood in groups around the outer walls and eyed up anyone they fancied. Joey Grant had fancied Ruby for weeks but hadn't had the guts to chat

her up, even though he was the head of his own gang and had plenty of bravado. Well, tonight that was going to change as Joey had downed a couple of cans of cider for Dutch courage and now he willed the time to pass and for the slow dances to start at the end of the night. Until recently Ruby had shown little interest in boys but lately, Joey had caught her eye and she had confided in Gloria at lunchtime a couple of weeks earlier while they were smoking at the rear of the boy's gym that she liked him.
"You should go for it Rubes, let him have a bit of a feel up and he'll want you to be his girl."
"Oh no! I can't do that, my dad would have a fit."
"Well, your old man ain't going to be there now is he and what he doesn't know won't hurt him."
By now they had both noticed Joey staring and giggling, they nudged each other as they danced to Rod Stewart singing 'Tonight's the Night'.
"Here Rubes, this song's a message to you."
Ruby could feel herself begin to colour up and she blushed as she slowly shook her head at her pal's words. Remembering that she had to be home by ten she suddenly realised that she would miss the smooches and she wouldn't put it past Gloria to try and take him for herself. Her mum had said if she was late then that would be it regarding the youth club but she wanted to be

his girl so badly that she was tempted to stay.
"What's up?"
"Mum told me to be home by ten, if not I can't come here again."
"Well if you don't want him?"
Gloria Meadows came from a single-parent family, the middle girl of five she practically did whatever she wanted. Her mother Joanie had a string of boyfriends, there were even whispers that she was on the game and as long as her kids didn't get in her way then they could please themselves what they did. Gloria's two oldest sisters were regular shoplifters, especially down Roman Road market and if she cleaned the house after them they would often bring her home the latest clobber that the kids were wearing at the time. Sometimes, if she was lucky, items would be passed on to Ruby so she really didn't want to fall out with her friend.
"Yes I do but…."
"No buts girl, fuck your old mum and just go for it."
"I ain't going all the way Glor, maybe he can feel a bit of tit but that's it."
"I said that at first but once he gets into your knickers you won't be able to or want to stop him. Anyway, you can't get up the duff the first time. I'm lucky, me old lady put me on the pill as soon as I started me monthly's so I can have as

much how's your father as I like."
The hours passed in a whirl with sideways glances passing back and forth between Joey and Ruby. When the first of the love songs began to play Joey swaggered across the dancefloor and taking Ruby's hand, pulled her from the chair. She placed her arms around his neck and he loosely put his hands onto her buttocks. As they swayed to 'Easy' by the Commodores Ruby Chilvers felt as if she was in a dream, a dream she never wanted to wake up from. At five to ten she whispered in his ear that she had to go and as she turned to walk away Joey grabbed her hand.
"I'll walk you if you like?"
Ruby coyly smiled and nodding her head looked in Gloria's direction. Her friend winked, grinned and then made the hand signal for phone me before going back to snogging the face off of a spotty teenager who she didn't even fancy. Ruby nodded but it wouldn't happen as she was never allowed to go anywhere near the home phone. She had only used it once to call Gloria and her dad had walked in and caught her. The thrashing she'd received was extreme even by Harold's standards and from then on Ruby hadn't looked at the device. Heady from the drink she accepted Joey's hand and the two made their way outside. The night was cool and

as she shuddered he placed his arm around her shoulder. Ruby felt warm inside, a feeling she'd never experienced before and she liked it. As they walked they chatted, mostly about music as it was all they had in common but the conversation wasn't awkward in any way. Joey walked Ruby the long route back via Dunbridge Street but she didn't complain and when they passed Weavers Fields he stopped, took her hand again and then gently led her over to a secluded area that was sheltered by a group of trees. As they kissed and it became more passionate he gently pulled her down onto the grass. When his hand caressed her breast through the thin fabric of her dress Ruby didn't try to stop him. Nor did she complain when his hand slid up her thigh and into her knickers. Her body tingled all over and when his fingers began to explore her moist womanhood she groaned with pleasure. Joey released his erect penis, pulled down her panties and took her virginity. It was painful but at the same time the pleasure was immense and now she understood just what Gloria had been talking about whenever she revealed what she had got up to with some boy late at night. The act was over in less than a minute and doing up his trousers, Joey stood up, grinned at her and then strode off into the night. For a few seconds, Ruby lay there

stunned and confused at what she had just let happen. Suddenly thoughts of her mum entered her head and getting to her feet she pulled up her knicker and smoothed down her dress which now felt damp from lying on the grass. Peering at her watch the moonlight allowed her to see the illuminated dial and she gasped when she saw that it was twenty past ten. Making her way home as fast as she could she entered Birbeck Street in just a few minutes. Harold stood in the open doorway and swayed slightly as he waited. The thrashing she received was like none she'd ever experienced before as Harold lashed out with his fists at her stomach and legs. When he was finally spent he fell against the wall but Ruby's ordeal wasn't over yet. It was now her mother's turn and Aida slapped her oldest daughter's cheek several times as hard as she could.
"You dirty little whore!! I told you to be in this house by ten, where have you been?"
Ruby sobbed as she spoke but it didn't gain her any forgiveness.
"I'm so sorry Mum. We were walking and talking and the time just ran away."
"Whoa! We? Who were you with?"
Even though he'd left her, Ruby didn't want to get Joey into trouble so she refused to reveal his name which saw a fresh onslaught of slaps

begin. When Aida was exhausted she at last gave in.
"Get in your room you dirty little bitch!"
Running as fast as her legs would carry her Ruby ran inside and then slammed the door behind her. Her sister was sitting up in bed with the covers wrapped around her neck.
"You alright Rubes, they sound very angry with you."
"Go back to sleep Sadie and don't be so fuckin' nosey."
Crawling into bed Ruby stayed fully clothed. She could feel the sticky residue of cum in her underwear but didn't really know what it was. Gloria used to tell her that boys shot their load, maybe that's what this was. Her whole body ached from the beating but as she closed her eyes all she could see was Joey's sweet face and somehow that made what she'd just been through all worthwhile.

CHAPTER TWO

As soon as Ruby woke up she groaned out in pain. Her ribs hurt like hell and climbing out of bed she stared in the mirror. At least her face wasn't marked, even if it was still a little red from her mother's slaps but that was about it. Gingerly pulling on her dressing gown she slowly opened the bedroom door and took a few seconds to listen for any noise. The alarm clock showed seven thirty so she knew her dad would have left for work by now. The radio was switched to BBC2 and the dulcet tones of Nat King Cole could be heard singing 'Unforgettable'. Knowing that she had to face the music sometime Ruby crept along the hallway and when she entered the kitchen, saw her mother sitting at the old table reading one of the magazines that Mrs Watson upstairs always sent down after she'd finished with them. Aida glanced up and the look of disgust on her face was evident. Ruby took a seat opposite and used the palm of her hand to touch the teapot. It was still warm so she poured herself a cup and still her mother didn't say a word. Finally when she couldn't stand the silence anymore Ruby spoke.
"I'm sorry mum really I am but..."

"Sorry! You don't have the first bleeding idea of what sorry means. I warned you before you went out but still, you defied me. I know you ain't the brightest bleeding bulb in the box Ruby but sometimes I'm at a loss for words as far as you're concerned."

"Is Dad still angry?"

"Luckily for you, he was half-cut when you waltzed in. When he got up this mornin' he was overly nice to me so I think he thought it was me he'd given a pasting to."

For a few seconds, there was more silence before they both started to laugh which forced Ruby to hold her sides as any movement caused her severe pain. Aida Chilvers wasn't a bad woman and unlike a lot of others in the East End she actually loved her girls but her own marriage and how she was treated daily was enough to make her come down hard in the hope that neither Ruby nor Sadie would end up repeating her own mistakes.

"You'd better get ready for school, it's your last week and in my day it was the best time. Oh, and keep a low profile tonight when the old man gets home, just in case he has any flashbacks. If he brings it up, it was me he belted okay?"

Ruby smiled and nodded her head, at times she hated her mother with a vengeance and then on days like this she loved Aida with all of her heart.

Gloria stood impatiently at the school gates puffing on a cigarette as she waited for her friend to appear and when Ruby finally arrived Gloria was desperate to find out what had happened last night.

"Fuck me, girl I thought you would never get here. So, come on then, what happened?"

"I don't want to talk about it Glor okay?"

"Well that ain't fair, I always share with you."

"As my mum always tells me, neither is a black man's arse!"

"Neither is a black man's arse what?"

"Fair."

"Oh come on Rubes!"

Sighing heavily Ruby slowly lifted up her school shirt and revealed her badly bruised ribcage.

"Oh my God! Did Joey do that to you?"

"Don't be stupid, no it was me old man, he was waiting for me when I got home."

"So you were late then, so you did it then? Oh come on Rubes, share!"

Ruby Chilvers ignored her friend and continued in through the main doors. Suddenly all eyes were upon her and as she glanced around the reception area she could see several groups of girls sniggering and pointing a finger in her direction. As she passed by she heard one of them call out 'Slag!' Heading in the direction of her form room she smiled when she spotted Joey Grant walking towards her. He was surrounded by four other boys and they were patting him on the back and treating him as if he'd just won gold at the Olympics. As the group passed by Joey wouldn't make eye contact with her and for a second Ruby didn't understand what was happening, until one of Joey's followers hung back and approached her.

"Here Ruby, fancy meeting me up Weavers Fields tonight? Joey said you're nice and tight." Suddenly the penny dropped, Joey had told everyone what had happened and the shame Ruby felt was all-consuming. Running from the building tears filled her eyes and she couldn't believe she was now being branded as the school bike. When she finally reached home she ran to her bedroom, slammed the door and threw herself down onto the bed. Her sobbing was so loud that she didn't hear her mother enter the room. Aida stood and watched her daughter for a few seconds, she had a good idea regarding what had happened and her heart broke for her eldest. Taking a seat on the bed she gently stroked her daughter's back.

"Come on now darling it can't be that bad." Ruby turned over and roughly pushed her mother's hand away. She was hurt and angry and her words came out with venom.

"What would you know about it, what could you possibly know?!!!"

Aida smiled and slowly shook her head.

"Because my girl, if what I think has happened has happened, then I went through the exact same thing. How do you suppose I ended up having you so young? The old man always blamed me for tying him down and he's punished me for it since the day we tied the bleeding knot but I never heard him complaining while he was getting his end away."

Suddenly Ruby lunged forward and threw her arms around her mother's neck as she again began to sob her heart out. Aida gave her a couple of minutes and then pulling Ruby's arms away she got to her feet.

"It's no good crying over spilt milk. I'm going to put the kettle on and then you and I are going to have a long chat. Go wash your face and then come into the kitchen."

Bending low Aida tenderly kissed the top of her daughter's head and then left the room. With her mum on her side, things suddenly didn't seem quite as bad and doing as she was told Ruby made her way to the bathroom. When she emerged a few minutes later, her eyes were still red from crying but inside, her heart was a little lighter. The tea had already been poured and

she took a seat opposite her mother and nervously waited for the questions to start.
"Now I'm not prying love but I need to ask you a few things. When did you last have your monthlies?"
"Last week, why?"
"Well, that's one good thing. Now, did a boy touch you?"
Ruby could feel her face redden and she stared down hard at her hands that were tightly clamped together in her lap.
"Ruby! Did a boy put his todger in you?"
The shame was tremendous and Ruby just couldn't share this with her mum so instead of coming clean she shook her head.
"Well thank the Lord for that. Now whatever happened you just have to try and forget about it. Ignore all those bleeding bullies, in a couple of days it will be old news and besides, you'll be left on Friday so you need to concentrate on finding a job. The old man won't support you now that you're sixteen. The fish stall down Roman Road market needs some help, it's only part-time but at least it's something. Now I've had a word and old Hilda Finnegan is expecting you to go and see her on Saturday."
Ruby nodded her head and then excusing herself made her way to her room.

The following day she attended school again and doing as Aida had told her, ignored the sneers but in all honesty, they were a lot less than yesterday. Meeting up with Gloria at lunchtime Ruby told her friend all that had happened.
"What a wanker! Don't worry mate, I told you that you can't get up the duff the first time. So you gonna go for that job?"
"I ain't really got a choice have I?"
"Suppose not but it fuckin' stinks down there. I've decided I ain't getting a job, I'm gonna do a bit of lifting with me sisters. There are plenty of places to sell the gear on and I don't have to start until the afternoon so I get to stay in bed all morning!"
Ruby just stood there with her mouth wide open, even if she had the guts she would never dare steal anything, for a start if her mum and dad found out they would kill her.

Early on Saturday morning she was up, washed, dressed and down the market by eight. She could smell the fish stall as soon as she entered the aisle, it was disgusting. Walking up to the counter she smiled meekly in Hilda's direction. The Finnegan's had kept a stall on Roman Road for three generations and as she had no children Hilda would be the last one. Wearing a plastic apron and with her silver-grey hair in a net

Hilda had a cigarette hanging from her bottom lip. Occasionally she would stop what she was doing and move away from the counter to cough. Fag ash would fall to the floor and then she would carry on working. Hygiene wasn't her top priority but the locals didn't seem to mind and fish sales were good, especially at the weekend.

"You're young Chilvers ain't you?"

"Yes Mrs Finnegan. My mum told me to come and see you about some work."

"Well don't just stand there like a bleeding spare part, come round to the side and I'll show you what's what."

Doing as she was told, within the hour Ruby had been shown how to gut a fish, restock the stall and clean away. By the end of the day, she was covered in blood and slime and stunk to high heavens but for the work Hilda had given her five pounds for her trouble.

"When you start next week it's a pound an hour and I can give you twenty hours a week. I know it's not a lot but its cash in hand so there's no tax to pay. Ruby was naive and it sounded like a fortune as she'd never even had pocket money before. Returning home she lied when she told her mother she liked it before reluctantly handing over the fiver.

"Thanks love it will help, from now on I want

ten quid a week for your keep so don't start taking sick days and don't tell the old man or he'll want the cash for beer money. Now go and have a wash before he gets in and bring me any clothes that smell and I'll rinse them out." Ruby couldn't believe that after paying her dues she would still be left with ten pounds for herself, maybe this working lark wouldn't be so bad after all.

The next month passed quickly and when there was no sign of her period Ruby began to panic. Maybe it was just all of the stress of starting work, maybe they were just late. Her low IQ and naivety saw her hatch a plan and on her next day at work, she had taken along a sanitary pad and a pair of her monthly knickers, the ones that were kept especially for her periods. Before she left for the day she smeared a little fish blood onto the pad and pushed it into the gusset of her pants. At home, she placed the pad in the bin and her underwear into the plastic laundry basket. Feeling chuffed with herself she repeated the charade for the next few days and again the following month. Aida was none the wiser and just happy that her daughter hadn't got caught out. By the third month, Ruby Chilvers knew she was in trouble. She didn't see much of Gloria nowadays so there was no one to

give her advice, she wanted to go to her mum but was petrified of the outcome. Ruby needn't have worried as with each passing month her waistline grew and she'd come home with sickness on several occasions. The smell of the fish turned her stomach and after the first couple of times, Hilda Finnegan soon twigged what had occurred. Taking Ruby by the hand she stared sympathetically into the teenager's eyes.
"I think you need to go home and have a talk to your old mum darling, don't you? This problem ain't going away and it's best to deal with it sooner rather than later, believe me I know from personal experience."
Ruby began to cry and Hilda's heart went out to her. Getting pregnant at fifteen and when abortion was still illegal, Hilda Finnegan was taken to the back streets and butchered. It had resulted in a miscarriage but also made any chance of having further children impossible. Ruby slowly nodded her head and taking off her apron began the walk home. Reaching the house she cautiously opened the front door and stepped inside just as Aida was walking along the hall.
"Not another sick day? My girl if you ain't careful old woman Finnegan will give you the sack!"
Ruby just stood there and as pools of tears

welled up in her eyes Aida had a sinking feeling in the pit of her stomach.
"On no, please tell me I'm wrong."
Ruby ran towards her mother but instead of the beating she was expecting Aida wrapped her arms around her beautiful and very scared daughter.
"Come on, come into the kitchen and we'll try and sort this mess out."
At the table, Aida took her daughter's hands into her own.
"I take it you're up the duff?"
Ruby could only nod her head as the tears flowed freely.
"And the bloke? Is he still on the scene?"
"No Mum he just used me, that's what all the trouble was about just before I left school."
"But I don't understand love, you've been having your monthly's I've seen the proof myself in the bin and when I washed your undies."
"I was so scared to tell you so I put fish blood in my knickers."
"Oh, Ruby!! You should have come to me darling and we could have sorted it sooner."
Aida could only shake her head in disbelief.
When the shock had finally gone and now with the enormity of what it would all mean, Aida told her daughter to go and have a wash and get

changed as they were going out.

At three-thirty that day Aida and Ruby made their way to the NHS doctor's surgery on Tapp Street where Aida explained that she needed to see a doctor urgently. Sadly ten minutes later when they were ushered into Doctor Doyle's room things didn't pan out how Aida had hoped. Declan Doyle had lived in England since he was a baby but he has also been raised a staunch Catholic and even though it had been legal for the last ten years, he saw abortion as a sin.
"I'm afraid I cannot allow that Mrs Chilvers. Your daughter is a healthy young woman and fit to give birth so I cannot recommend a termination."
Aida pleaded that it would ruin her child's life but Doctor Doyle wouldn't budge on his decision.
"I do have another suggestion. There is a Nazareth House in Great Yarmouth that I can refer you to. Your daughter will go there when she's around six months pregnant and stay until she gives birth. There are facilities set up for immediate adoption and then your daughter may return home and not face any shame. I'm afraid that is all I can offer you."
Aida sighed heavily and then nodded, it was

going to take a lot of work to hide the ever-increasing baby bump for the next two or three months but she would do her best.

Every day Aida would bind Ruby's stomach and send her off to work, if she was sick then she had to vomit around the back of the stall but in no way was she allowed to go home. Each weekend Aida did her best to let her daughter's tops and skirts out to allow for growth and Ruby always wore an oversized cardigan when she was at home. Luckily her father spent so much time down the Bishop Bonner that Ruby hardly saw him and when it was time to head off for Great Yarmouth, Aida told Harold that their daughter had gone to help a friend of Hilda's out for a few months. Supposedly the woman ran a bed and breakfast, the lie seemed to be accepted and if Harold had any doubts, he never aired them.

CHAPTER THREE

Apart from going to work, where Hilda kept her doing prep at the back of the van, Ruby had avoided going out in case she bumped into anyone she knew. She had been successful until a week before she was due to leave for Great Yarmouth. Aida had sent her down to the corner shop for some bread and about to go inside she stopped when she heard her name called.

"Hi Rubes, how you doing girl?"

Immediately recognising the voice, Ruby cringed. She couldn't ignore her old friend and besides, Gloria was already crossing the road to where Ruby stood. Dressed up to the nines her pal looked good and Ruby guessed she was either shoplifting like her sisters or had gone on the game like her old lady, she hoped it wasn't the latter. When the two girls were face to face Gloria looked her friend up and down and couldn't help but notice how fat Ruby had gotten.

"Fuck me Rubes you ain't half piled on a bit of timber."

Ruby felt the sting of tears and Gloria instantly felt bad for commenting.

"Oh I'm sorry Rubes. Here, you ain't up the duff are you?"

Ruby nodded as the tears began to flow freely. Gloria hugged her old friend but didn't really know what to say. Between sobs Ruby told her oldest pal all that had happened.
"I leave next week and am having it adopted."
"What about Joey?"
"What about him? He didn't want to know me after he got what he wanted. Gloria promise you won't tell anyone, even my old man doesn't know. Me and Mum have kept it a secret and that's how it has to stay. Promise me you won't breathe a word."
"I swear I won't. Oh Rubes I'm so sorry darling. You take care and maybe when you get back we can have a night out?"
Ruby smiled and nodded but as her friend crossed back over the road she knew the invitation hadn't been genuine, all she could do was pray that her Gloria would keep her word.

Finally, the day arrived and Ruby boarded a train at Liverpool Street station. Arrangements had been put into place by Doctor Doyle and she would be met at the other end by one of the nuns that helped to run the facility. Ruby was scared as it was the first time she'd ever been away from home plus she'd heard some terrifying tales of what it was like to give birth but she just had to go along with her mother's wishes. When she'd asked Aida what to expect her mother had only told her that it was the worst pain she would ever experience in her life but also the quickest to forget, it brought no comfort to Ruby, in all honesty, it scared the hell out of her even more. Yet to form any attachment with her impending child she just wanted the whole sorry mess over and done with as soon as possible.

The journey took over five hours and when she stepped onto the platform her back was aching terribly. Stretching the best she could Ruby scanned the station looking for anyone who she thought might be waiting. Spying an elderly nun staring back at her, Ruby made her way over.
"Good afternoon Sister, are you waiting for me by any chance?"
For Sister Louisa Kelly it had been almost forty years since she had taken her vows but that time hadn't made her kind and caring towards her fellow humans, it was the complete opposite. She detested the young women who had no morals and were full of sin.
"Are you the dirty girl who couldn't keep her legs shut and is now with child?"
Ruby felt her cheeks redden with shame and lowering her head she slowly nodded.

"Follow me!"
Ruby did as she was told and as Sister Louisa marched purposefully out of the station, Ruby, hauling along an oversized case, did her best to keep up. After a short drive in the sister's Morris Minor, they arrived at a large and very cold-looking Victorian house. Apart from the initial meeting, Sister Louisa was yet to speak a single word to Ruby and it made her feel awkward and even more scared. Entering through a heavy oak door, Ruby could instantly smell the linseed oil that was used to keep the parquet flooring pristine and it strangely reminded her of the assembly hall at school. Sister Louisa marched straight ahead and again Ruby did her best to keep up. Entering a second door she came face to face with another stern-looking woman who sat behind a desk but this woman was wearing plain clothes, a twinset and pearls to be exact.
"This is Mrs McParland and she runs this house. You would do best to be polite and do everything she tells you to do without question." With that Sister Louisa promptly left the room.
"Name?"
"Ruby Chilvers Mrs, me mum sent me to…"
"Shut up! You do not speak until told to, do you understand?"
Ruby stared at the floor for the second time that day, her arms were behind her back and she was

so scared that she continually wrung her hands together.

"I said! Do you understand?"

"Yes, Mrs."

"Good. Now you are here because you are just another dirty little whore who allowed a boy, probably several of them, to do what they wanted to you and the result of which is that you are about to give birth to another of the world's bastards. Luckily for it, there will be a childless family willing to take it on. You will be expected to pay for your stay here by helping with the laundry which is brought in daily from an outside hotel. You are lucky because if you lived in one of the homes in Ireland life would be a lot worse for you. Sadly in this lax country, we are not able to administer physical punishment. That said, if you break the rules you will be sent back to whatever hovel you have come from and it will be down to your parents to deal with you. Sister Louisa is waiting for you in the hall and she will take you up to the dormitory. Off you go then."

Ruby turned and left the room still wringing her hands. Shown up to the top floor which would have been the servants' quarters back in the day, she was led into a small room that contained three old iron beds. Two had items on them and the third had a bare mattress and pillow with a

folded set of sheets and a blanket on top.
"Get that bed made and I will come back for you when it's time for tea."
When the door closed Ruby placed her case onto the floor and then took a seat on the bed. Lost in thought for a few minutes she was abruptly brought back to earth when the door was flung open wide and two girls of around her age but further along in their pregnancies walked in. They immediately came over and held out their hands.
"Hello, I'm Mary Anne."
"And I'm Susan but my friends all call me Sue."
Mary Anne was from Norwich and spoke with a strong Norfolk accent that Ruby found funny but at the same time, she struggled to understand what Mary Anne was saying. Susan was from Barnet, Ruby's neck of the woods, well London at least and she immediately bonded with the girl. From her newfound friends, Ruby soon learned what the place was really like and it wasn't a place she wanted to be but she had no choice in the matter, no choice in her future or even when it came down to it, that of her own child.
"Don't look so sad girl, it ain't as bad as it sounds. The fuckin' penguins are a pain in the arse but you get used to them. Most of 'em are just frigid old bitches, they just need a good

portion that's all."

Ruby and Mary Anne burst into fits of giggles and for the first time since her arrival, Ruby had a feeling that everything was going to turn out alright. Until the very end of their pregnancies, the young girls were expected to earn their keep by cleaning the house and doing laundry. The food portions were small and bland and Ruby continually dreamed of her mum's stew and dumplings or one of her Sunday roasts. The girls had no money to buy extras so would take it in turn to steal scraps from the kitchen and they got to be good at it. As Ruby's stomach swelled she would lie in bed at night and caress her bump as she softly whispered to her baby and it had Susan and Mary Anne in fits of giggles. Where Ruby was starting to have feelings for her unborn child, the other two were totally different and couldn't wait to get the little aliens out of their bodies, something Ruby found hard to understand.

At last, the day arrived and it had started like any other had over the last three months. Ruby had washed and dressed and after breakfast, had begun her chores. That day she was to wash and polish the hall floor. About to place her mop into the bucket, she felt a whoosh as her waters broke. The girls had been given no advice

regarding what would happen when their time came and as the fluid hit the floor the other two girls helping Ruby, girls she didn't know very well, stepped back in horror. Sister Louisa who had been monitoring their work suddenly grabbed Ruby by the hand and dragged her away to a small room at the far end of the house. Tiled from floor to ceiling in stark white and with just a bed in the centre with some kind of contraption attached to it that Ruby would soon learn were stirrups, it was a cold and frightening place. Sister Louisa pushed a discoloured old towel into Ruby's hands.
"Clean yourself and then get up onto that bed."
"But Sister, what's happening?"
"You stupid girl, it's your time."
Ruby just stared at the woman and the confusion on her face was evident.
"Lord give me strength, your baby is coming."
The resident midwife Mrs Coombes was then called in and today she already had two other labours in progress so she was going to be busy and didn't have time for pleasantries. Swiftly lifting up Ruby's dress the midwife removed her underwear and then roughly strapped the feet of her third mother of the day into the stirrups. Without warning Mrs Coombes then inserted her fingers into Ruby's vagina to see how far she'd progressed. Ruby screamed out, it hurt

and she was so embarrassed that her privates were exposed for the entire world to see.

"Shut up you stupid girl, midwife is just doing her job. If you don't like it then you should have kept your legs closed and not got in the family way!"

Ruby stared at Sister Louisa and right at that moment she had never hated anyone so much.

"It's going to be a long one Sister so you might as well go and have a cuppa. I'm just going to check on the other two and see if there's been any progress and then I'll come back."

Now in the cold, stark room, Ruby began to cry, she wanted her mum but she was alone and was just going to have to deal with it. She calmed herself down by repeating over and over that it wouldn't last forever.

Twelve hours later when the contractions had at last begun to be regular and close together the midwife returned but this time it wasn't a fleeting visit. The pain was more than Ruby had ever experienced in her life and she wasn't given any help. No one told her how to breathe through the contractions, the leather straps on the stirrups were cutting into her ankles and she didn't think the pain would ever stop. Suddenly with one massive contraction, the head appeared and for a few seconds, there was nothing more.

"There will be another big one in a moment and

I want you to push with everything you have."
"I can't, I can't I'm so tired."
Sister Louisa suddenly stepped forward and slapped Ruby on the cheek.
"Shut up and do as you're told you......"
The sentence couldn't be completed as a massive agonising pain ripped through Ruby's body and she screamed out. At the same time, something was forcing her to push and soon after her baby boy had been born. The cord was cut and the baby was placed onto Ruby's chest while the midwife took care of the afterbirth. Instantly Ruby felt an overwhelming unconditional love and she kissed the top of her baby's head.
"Hello little one, I'm your mummy."
"Don't get attached to it, you won't have it for long."
Tears streamed down Ruby's face. She didn't think she would feel anything but now he was here she wanted to keep her baby.
"He is not an it, he's my little boy! Anyway, what could you possibly know about it?"
Instantly she was again struck on the cheek and as she wilfully looked at the nun, Sister Louisa's face was red with rage.
"If you know what's good for you, you will never speak to me like that again!"
"They have no manners Sister and even less morals."

The nun nodded her agreement to Mrs Coombes before disappearing from the room.
Ruby Chilvers would remain with her child for the next ten days until the baby had been registered and all of the paperwork had been put into place. While waiting, she wrote to her mother several times pleading to be able to bring her baby home but all of her letters went unanswered. Aida had been heartbroken and had sobbed as she read each word but she knew there was not a chance in hell that the old man would allow it, as far as Aida knew he wasn't even aware of the pregnancy and bringing a bastard into the house wouldn't even be a consideration as far as her husband was concerned. Registering him as Colin Joseph Chilvers, the one thing Ruby was allowed to do for her boy, she swore on oath that one day she would see him again and explain why she had to give him up, one day she would tell him how heartbroken and sorry she was.

Ten days later Ruby screamed the place down as they prised him from her arms and when he was driven away by a social worker, Ruby felt as if her heart was being ripped out. Her bag had already been packed and within the hour Sister Louisa had driven her to the station. The Sister lent over the passenger side and pushed open the door. With a nod of her head, she indicated for Ruby to get out and when the door was closed again Sister Louisa sped off without even a goodbye. It was early afternoon when Ruby let herself into the house. Placing her case onto the floor she slowly walked into the kitchen and when her mother meekly smiled at her Ruby ran into her arms sobbing.

"Oh, love I'm so, so sorry but there wasn't anythin' else we could have done. You must keep your trap shut darling because if the old man ever finds out he will kick you out. Ruby! Do you understand what I'm sayin' to you?" Between sobs, Ruby silently mouthed the word 'yes'.

"You haven't even asked me about him, Mum he is so beautiful. He has a mop of blonde hair and the......."

"Stop! It will do you no good thinking about him Ruby; you must put it all in the past for your own good. Bury it deep and never venture there again, do you hear me?"

Leaving her mother's embrace Ruby slowly made her way to her bedroom and crawled under the covers.

After returning to the fish stall, the next couple of years passed without event and Ruby was so good at the job that Hilda took her on full time.

Her sweet face and polite nature drew in the customers and none more so than the local lads who often came by after work on Fridays to get cod, jellied eels and shellfish for the weekend. One such person was Dennis Tanner a local dock worker who was a regular.

"Hey, Ruby! When are you goin' to let me take you out for a drink?"

Ruby had recently turned eighteen but Aida still watched her like a hawk, frightened that she would repeat her mistake. Dennis was several years older than Ruby but she had a soft spot for him as he was kind to her, nothing to write home about on the looks front but still he was kind.

"Tonight?"

Dennis stepped back in shock, he'd been asking her out for the last couple of months and his invitation had always been met with a blank stare.

"Really? Okay, I'll pick you up at seven then. I'll wait on the corner."

"You don't know where I live."

"Oh yes I do, I know everything about you Ruby Chilvers."

Ruby prayed that wasn't true as she watched him walk away from the stall clutching his winkles and whelks. Dennis had a spring in his step, he was a happy man now that he had a date but unbeknown to him, Ruby still had to gain her mother's permission. That didn't turn out to be as difficult as she'd been expecting. Aida knew her daughter had to have some freedom if she was ever to meet a man and settle down but that night, before Ruby left the house, she was given a strict talking too with a sharp reminder of her past. Just as before, by the time she met Dennis at the end of the road all thoughts of the lecture had left her mind. The couple strolled along in the early evening sunshine but Dennis stopped when they reached the Fox and Hounds on Globe Road. It wasn't a very big place but on Saturday nights it was filled with youngsters all eager to spend their hard-earned cash. The jukebox blared out the most popular songs and as Ruby walked inside it was Earth Wind & Fire's 'Boogie Wonderland'. Her feet began to tap and for a moment in her mind, she was back at the youth club with Gloria.

"What you having to drink darling?"

Ruby had never touched alcohol before and the only thing she could think of was that advert she'd seen on the telly for Babycham. Four drinks later and her head was swimming as she danced with a couple of friends she'd made in the toilets. Finally, the last orders were called and with his arm around her waist Dennis led her outside. The cold night air hit her like a lead balloon and Dennis had to almost carry her home. The hall light had been left on and after he opened the door for her and kissed her on the cheek he said goodnight.

The following morning with her head throbbing, she was questioned by her mother.

"So?"

"Oh Mum it was great, Dennis was a complete gent and I had my first Babycham."

"Well, as long as you behaved yourself that's good. Does he want to see you again?"

Suddenly panic set in. He hadn't mentioned a second date, what if he didn't like her, what if she had embarrassed him? She didn't have to wait too long as he appeared at the stall late on Monday afternoon just as she was closing up.

"Hi there darling, we going out again this weekend?"

"I didn't think you wanted to see me again."

"What on earth gave you that idea? Of course I do, rather hoped you'd be my girlfriend?"

There and then Ruby Chilvers fell in love, or at least at the time what she thought was. The couple went on many more dates and after being introduced to the Chilvers clan, Dennis Tanner soon became part of the family.

Six months later after a Saturday night out and when Ruby hadn't drunk too much, Dennis got

down on one knee and proposed. Instantly saying yes, the engagement was sealed by having sex under a tree in the small park opposite Bethnal Green tube station but Ruby didn't really enjoy it not like she had with Joey, there just wasn't any real chemistry or passion between them. The next morning over breakfast she raised her left hand in her mother's direction and pointed to her third finger.
"Really, Ruby?"
"Really! He popped the question last night."
Up and dancing around the room the pair were deliriously happy and even her old man seemed pleased, at last, he was getting one of the brats out of the house. The good news didn't last long as three months later when Ruby realised she was pregnant again and she hadn't heard from Dennis in over a week she started to panic. Taking a day off from work she called round to his mum's house, the least he owed her was an explanation.
"Hello Ruby love, I was waiting for you to pop in. I'm afraid I have some bad news, Dennis was arrested last week for robbery and he's up in court this Friday. He asked if you'd go and see him, he's in Pentonville. Ruby he ain't a bad lad, he just got in with the wrong crowd and made a mistake that's all."
Ruby was crying which Edna Tanner took as

devastation but in reality, they were tears of joy, he hadn't abandoned her after all. When she got home she shared the news with her mother who wasn't best please.
"Well thank the Lord you hadn't tied the knot that's all I can say."
"Well, we're still getting married when he gets released."
"Why Ruby, why would you get tied to a bleeding villain?"
"He's not a villain, he made one mistake and besides, I'm up the duff Mum and I know he will do right by me. I'm going up to the prison this afternoon."
With that Ruby walked from the kitchen and for once Aida Chilvers was lost for words but she still wished that Ruby could be more like her sister. Sadie was only three years younger but had studied and gained her exams and after leaving school she found a good job in hospitality. She was only sixteen but she worked hard and never brought any trouble to Aida's door.
The prison was a scary place and as she stepped through the main doors Ruby could hear inmates calling out from within. As this was Dennis Tanner's first offence and he was on remand and yet to go to appear in court, he was granted a special visiting order for his fiancé.

Nervously Ruby waited in line until her name was called and she was led into the visiting area and told to take a seat. A few minutes later Dennis appeared and as he sat down opposite her he still had the cheeky grin on his face that had first attracted her to him.
"Hi babe, I'm so, so sorry about all of this."
"There's nothing I can do about it Dennis but we do have a bit of a problem, I'm up the duff!"
Expecting him to be angry he just shrugged his shoulders and took her hand.
"Then I suppose I have to do right by you, just sooner than we planned. They have me bang to rights but as it's my first offence, my solicitor says I won't get much more than a year."
"So you won't be around when the baby comes and where are we going to live because my old man will definitely want us out of the house when he finds out."
Ruby started to cry and Dennis pulled a handkerchief from his pocket and handed it to her.
"Please don't Rubes, now listen to me carefully. I have my share of the proceeds from the robbery stashed away. It's six hundred give or take. I want you to rent a house and furnish it, pay a year up front and you should be okay until I get released."
Ruby's eyes were out on stalks when she heard

the amount and it didn't go unnoticed by Dennis.

"It's for our home Ruby and nothing else!"

"I know, I know but you will still marry me won't you?"

"Of course I will you soppy cow. Now give it a couple of days and when my old mum has got me letter she'll sort you out."

With that, the bell went off signalling the end of visiting time. Ruby made her way home and was full of plans and dreams but when she told Aida she was brought back down to earth with a bump.

"Well, at least it's something I suppose. When you get the cash I want you to hand it to me. I know what you're like Ruby Chilvers and it'll slip through your fingers like water."

Nodding her head Ruby agreed, her mother was right and this time it all had to be perfect, this time she was keeping her baby so getting her own home was paramount.

CHAPTER FOUR

True to his word, Dennis had written to his mother and a week later Edna Tanner cautiously handed over a small canvas pouch containing six hundred and ten pounds.

"My boy trusts you, Ruby."

"I know Mrs Tanner and don't you worry about this. I want you to know it's for a house as I'm having your grandchild."

Edna beamed from ear to ear and hugged Ruby to her.

"Oh my, well that's a turn-up for the books and a happy one at that. He's a good lad Ruby and he will look after you."

"I know he will."

By the following month, Aida had paid the deposit on a three-bedroom terrace on Herald Street. It was close to her own home and a bargain at eight pounds a week. For the first time ever, Aida had been in agreement with Dennis and insisted that Ruby paid a year's rent in advance. If anything went wrong between her and Dennis then at least Ruby and the baby would have a roof over their heads, even if it was only for a year. One hundred pounds was put aside ready for when Dennis came home to give him a bit of a head start and forty was used to buy furniture, second-hand, again at Aida's insistence. The remainder was held by Aida for when the baby arrived and Ruby could no longer work, until then she was expected to carry on at the fish stall for as long as she could.

The baby arrived that March but her delivery was so different from the last one. Midwife Pat had been paying regular visits and she had taught Ruby breathing techniques to help with the pain. Pat Hardy was a kind woman and all of her pregnant mothers adored her. She didn't judge and her only concern was that of the mothers and babies in her charge. When Ruby told her she wanted a home birth it was accepted without question which immediately relaxed the mum-to-be. The pain had started at around seven one evening and Aida ran as fast as she could to the public phone box. An excited call was made and midwife Pat arrived soon after. The pain was just as Ruby remembered but this time there were no agonising stirrups and with Aida sitting beside her holding her hand, she gave birth to another son just four hours later. Named Andrew, when he was placed into Ruby's arms she felt so much loved as she softly told him she would never leave him, this time no one was going to take her baby away. By law, the birth had to be registered within six weeks and as Dennis was still banged up, Ruby had no option but to list Andrew's surname as Chilvers. A contented child Andrew was a pleasure and with the loving guidance of Aida, Ruby took to motherhood like a duck to water.

Two days before Christmas there was a knock at the front door early in the morning and when Ruby opened up to say she was shocked was an understatement. Standing on the step and looking thin and gaunt, Dennis Tanner smiled lovingly.
"Hello darling how you doing?"
Ruby flung herself into his arms and smothered him with kisses.
"Oh, Dennis I've missed you so much."
"Easy girl! Now where's the little fella?"
Walking Dennis through to the front room he glanced all around at what was now his home. She had made it nice, there was a fire roaring in the grate and a Christmas tree in the corner with tinsel and sugar mice hanging from the branches. Spying an old pram near the kitchen door he walked over and stared down at his son.
"He's a bruiser Rubes and no mistake."
Taking her by the hand Dennis led Ruby upstairs to the bedroom. Expecting or at least hoping for some passion she was sorely disappointed as he pushed her down onto the

bed. There was no foreplay, no tenderness and it hurt like hell as he entered her. Ruby cried out but he ignored her pleas for him to stop. The baby began to cry when he heard the commotion but still Dennis continued. Finally, when he was spent he allowed Ruby to go and see to Andy.
"Go and make the kid shut up, that fuckin' noise is doing me head in."
Doing as she was told Ruby slowly descended the stairs. This wasn't how she remembered her Dennis, prison had changed him and not for the better.
Over the next few days, things seemed to go from bad to worse. Dennis had a massive fallout with Aida and told her never to darken his doorstep again. Ruby was in floods of tears daily because of it but it made no difference.
"Please Den! My mum helps me no end with Andy and I don't know what I'll do without her."
"Not a chance! I ain't having that old cow, coming round to my gaff and sticking her fuckin' oar into my business. If you want to see the bitch you'll have to take the brat and your scrawny arse around to her house. Now get me a cuppa."
Ruby dutifully did as she was told, her mum would just have to understand that things had to change. When Dennis got his old job back on the Docks it was a relief, at least she didn't have

him in the house all day pawing at her and forcing her to have sex but within a month Ruby was pregnant again. Going against her mother's advice she went ahead with the pregnancy. It wasn't easy, although very loving, Andy was a needy child and continually clung onto her skirt hem. Ruby was worried about what would happen to him when her time came but surprisingly Dennis said the boy could go and stay with Aida. Dennis Tanner was already bored, he had no time for the child and spent every night down the pub, it was as if history was repeating itself but there was nothing Ruby or her mother could do about it.

At the end of October that year Ruby again went into labour and giving birth to a daughter who she named Shirley, was the hardest labour to date. After staying in the hospital for five days with not one visit from Dennis, she was finally allowed home that weekend. Aida was waiting at the house with Andy and Ruby couldn't believe how well her son looked. His crawling had come on in leaps and bounds, he'd put on weight and was laughing and giggling but that would soon stop as soon as things got back to normal.
"I best get off now Ruby before that fuckin' arsehole comes home from work."

"Oh please stay a bit longer Mum; I don't think I can cope with the two of them on my own."
Aida held her daughter by the shoulders.
"You can and you will just like I had to do. You know where I am if you need me darling now go and be a mum to those two little ones."
Walking towards the front door Aida stepped back when it suddenly opened and Dennis Tanner walked in.
"What the fuck are you doing in my house?!"
"I'm now leaving; I just brought your son home."
"Well, no need to stay any longer then is there?"
"You really are a piece of fuckin' work Dennis Tanner."
Aida barged past and slammed the door as she went. The noise woke the baby and as soon as Andy set eyes on his father he began to cry as well.
"Put that kid down and get up those stairs."
"Don't you want to say hello to your daughter? And besides, I'm still bleeding Dennis!"
"Makes no odds to me."
Doing as she was told Ruby placed Shirley into the pram and lifting Andy, put him in the playpen. Both children were screaming the house down and her heart went out to them but there was nothing she could do. Ruby didn't want to antagonise her husband, Dennis was yet

to start beating her but she wouldn't have to wait too long for it to begin. Ruby had registered Shirley as a Tanner but as for marriage she flatly refused. Her life was so unhappy and in her mind, if things ever got too bad then she could simply walk away, though how she would hope to do that with no money and two children in tow was a different matter altogether.

The years passed by and during the day when there was just the three of them, the house was happy and filled with laughter. Aida, who adored her grandchildren would visit daily but she always made sure she was gone long before Dennis came home from work. With military precision, as soon as he walked into the house there was silence. He ruled with an iron rod and they all, including Ruby, knew not to speak unless he spoke to them. The evening meal had to be eaten in complete silence and the children, even at such a young age, didn't dare refuse to eat anything they didn't like or they would be in for a beating. When the table was cleared and Dennis had drunk his cuppa he would head for a wash and then without a word, would disappear slamming the front door behind him. Then and only then, could Ruby relax and resume the job of being the loving mother, that she was when he was at work.

Time went by quickly and two years later Harold Chilvers passed away in his sleep. No tears were shed by Ruby for her father as she knew that her mother would finally have some peace in her life and could hopefully start to live a little. The years sped by and before Ruby knew it Andy was about to celebrate his sixteenth birthday and the impending celebration brought back memories of Colin. Ruby wondered where he was, and what he was doing, was he happy? Her husband and children didn't even know he existed, it was better to keep that part of her past locked away in her heart or at least that was what her mother had told her and now so many years had gone by that it would be impossible to tell them that they had an older brother. Andy hated his father with a vengeance, hated hearing the bastard paw at his mother every night and beat her when she refused so he'd made a vow to himself that he would work and scheme and save until he had enough money to get a place for them and that didn't include his bastard of a father. Shirley was coming up to her fifteenth birthday, she was a bright girl but very withdrawn and it constantly worried her brother. He watched her like a hawk at school and boys knew to stay well clear or they would receive a thrashing from her brother who had already made a name for himself as a bit of a hard nut. At Andy's birthday tea, he was surprised to see his Nan there, not to mention the fact that his father was delaying his nightly pub visit and was sitting at the table with the rest of them, though no conversation passed between Dennis and Aida.

"Well boy, you're a man now and I've got you a job down the docks with me. You start on Monday."

Ruby closed her eyes for a moment as she knew the fireworks were about to start.

"Docks!? I ain't working down no docks and especially with you."

Dennis Tanner was on his feet in seconds and slammed his fists down onto the table making them all, including Aida, jump out of their skins. For a moment Ruby thought Dennis was going to thump his son but he didn't.

"Yes, you fuckin' will! You can start bringing money into this house, you've ponced off me long enough. Be ready Monday morning or bleeding well find somewhere else to live."

About to argue back Andy was stopped when he felt his mother's hand on his and looking in the direction of his grandmother he saw her wink. Dennis looked at each of them in turn daring

any of them to speak but when no words were forthcoming he turned and walked out.
"Right, my little darling! Now we can enjoy your birthday."
Aida rubbed the hair on his head and smiled.
"I wish Sadie could have come today Mum."
Ruby's sister had studied hard and unlike Ruby, she hadn't shown any interest in boys. Ten years earlier she had moved to Brighton as the assistant manager at the prestigious Grand Hotel. Now the manager she hardly ever came back to London and apart from a few odd visits over the years for her mother's birthday, had never returned to Bethnal Green to live. Her marriage had been a small affair or so she had told her family. In reality, it was on a grand scale as her fiancé came from money but none of Sadie's family had been invited.
"I know love but your sister has her own life and I've accepted that it doesn't include us. We should be grateful that she escaped and left this bloody place. I did get a letter from her last month, said her boys were doing well in school and Charles had just been promoted at work so they were about to move to a new house."
"She's doing good then? I'm pleased for her."
"Me too, I just wish I got to see her kids but we can't have it all can we? Now let's get tucked into that cake, me stomach thinks me throats

been cut!"
Even Shirley giggled at that remark and it made Andy smile to see, she was a real loner who always stayed close to their mum and it bothered him. She should be out with friends enjoying herself, the only problem was his sister didn't seem to have any friends. Shirley didn't get any aggravation at school because of who her brother was but nor was she welcomed with open arms by any of the other girls and he somehow felt responsible for that.

By his twentieth birthday and still working at the docks, Andy had saved up a small fortune from illegal trades and it allowed him to purchase, with the aid of a small mortgage, a house on Chudleigh Street in Stepney. Spending every free spare moment he decorated and furnished the house until he was happy that it was time to share the news, news that the three of them, even his gran if she wanted, could at last be a proper family. Initially Ruby had been reluctant but once she saw the place she was over the moon. Aida decided to stay in her own home for as long as she could but come the day that she needed a little more help then she would gladly join them.
"We need to make a plan Mum, you have to pack up what you want to take but hide it from

that old bastard. Shirley, you can do the same. I've got a mate with a van and tomorrow night when he's gone down the pub we're leaving for good!"

The following afternoon Ruby and Shirley were on tenterhooks but also extremely excited and when Dennis came home from work and Ruby placed his dinner in front of him she smiled which made him frown.

"What's so fuckin' funny you leery cow?"

"Nothing Dennis, just pleased to see you that's all."

Shirley was sitting on the old sofa and she had to stifle a giggle when she heard the conversation. It was so tempting to laugh out loud so getting up she sought refuge in her room until it was time to leave. Finally at just before seven Dennis went out and Andy, who was at the end of the road sitting in his mate's van, gave it a few minutes just in case the old bastard had a change of heart, it was highly unlikely but you never knew. Luckily he didn't and by the time Dennis Tanner entered his local the van had been packed and they were on their way to a new free life. When the Old George called last orders and when Dennis had staggered home all was deathly quiet in the house as he placed his key into the lock. Imagining that they were already in bed he went through to the front room and the mess on the table had him irate in seconds. Dirty crockery and cutlery from dinner still sat on the table, the chairs were still pulled out and soiled pots and pans with remnants of encrusted food filled the kitchen sink.

"Ruby! Ruby!!!! You lazy fuckin' bitch, get your arse down here now!!"

When there was no movement of any kind Dennis stomped up to the bedroom but all that greeted him was an unmade bed and the wardrobe doors wide open showing nothing inside. Suddenly he began to panic and stormed through to Shirley's room and then Andy's, he was greeted with the same scenario. Mumbling under his breath that the ungrateful cunts would be back as they couldn't manage without him, Dennis went to bed. By tomorrow they would be back with their tails between their legs begging for his forgiveness, he was sure of it. The following evening he didn't go to the pub and just sat in his armchair waiting. By day five and when there was still no sign of them he was enraged and marching round to Aida's house he banged on the door with so much force she thought it would cave in.

"Where are they you old cow!? I know they're in there!!!"

Aida opened up but not before she had grabbed a carving knife from the kitchen drawer.

"They are not here Dennis, they've moved away and it serves you bleeding well right. You've given my girl a life of hell and now you're on your own sunshine!"
"Why you……"
Aida waved the knife in front of her and Dennis took a step back.
"I wouldn't if I were you. You are nothing but a fuckin' bully and you've got what was coming to you. It was the worst day's work she ever did meeting you and my Ruby deserves so much more from a man! Now fuck off before I call the Old Bill."
With that Aida slammed the door, she was shaking and sweating in fear but she also felt exhilarated. Dennis Tanner could only stand there for a few seconds with his mouth open in shock. Well if that's the way they wanted it then so be it, he didn't need them around his neck bleeding him dry and now he would never take them back. Walking off down the street he continually muttered under his breath, 'Fuck 'em, fuck the lot of 'em.'.

CHAPTER FIVE

By 2004 Andy had been working at the docks for eight years, Dennis was also still employed by the dock board but not once did a word pass between father and son. No one knew exactly why the two men were at war but it was an unspoken rule that you didn't poke your nose into a man's business, especially when it was in connection with a family member but some had it on good authority that Dennis' wife had left him. Dock work was hard graft and Andy hated it but he didn't complain and had managed to stash away a shed load of cash by stealing whatever he could and selling it on. It had started with food parcels and small electrical items but he quickly moved on to higher end products such as whisky and cigars. For a fee, the captains on the ships would give him the nod when anything expensive was in the cargo. He also made as many contacts in the illegal world as possible and he would visit the pubs known to be frequented by villain's with gifts, informing them that he could lay his hands on almost anything. Andy had a plan for his future and the word Docks wasn't in it. It soon became well known that if you wanted something out of the ordinary then Andy Chilvers was the one to go to and after supplying Harry Richardson with a box of King of Denmark cigars, his name was soon regularly mentioned within the circles of many of the criminal firms. Harry Richardson was climbing the villainy ladder, he was also about to propose to his girlfriend so it was important to impress her father, a wealthy city financier. A box of ten of the cigars, known to be the fourth most expensive in the world due to each one being decorated with gold foil, studded with Swarovski crystals and featuring a band with the buyer's name on would have set Harry back well over thirty grand but Andy had supplied at half that price. He didn't usually give such a handsome discount but well aware that Harry could come in useful in the future, he made an exception. The box had been stolen in Sweden and after the name band had been changed, they were then brought into the docks by one of the ship's crew. Harry had been elated and a friendship was instantly formed between the two men that would last for many years.

A random check one cold Monday afternoon by a security officer saw Andy lose his job on the spot when he was caught with two bottles of high-end single malt scotch stuffed into his coat pockets. It might have been small compared to some of the things he robbed but contraband was contraband and stealing wasn't tolerated in any way shape or form by the company. Instead of arguing and trying to proclaim his innocence Andy just shrugged his shoulders and walked away. The dock board was always reluctant to prosecute due to bad press, so apart from losing his job nothing else was done and he had a notion he'd been grassed up by his old man but for now he would let it go. In any case, it was the kick up the backside he needed and within a couple of weeks he had set up his own firm of villains, men who would rob their own grandmothers if it would bring in a few quid and they were exactly the sort of blokes that Andy needed on his side. A small warehouse was leased on the Kierbeck Business complex on the north Woolwich Road. The buildings surrounding the unit were mostly offices but as he only received deliveries at night it was an ideal spot. Situated close to the Thames but more importantly near to London City airport, it was perfect for the more high-value and unusual items that Andy was asked to obtain from time to time. After a few palms had been greased, pilots of private jets were able to smuggle cargo out of the country without too much trouble. From the off business was very profitable and Andy soon had a long list of clients and an even bigger bank account but he knew he was sailing close to the wind where the Old Bill was concerned. He needed to appear legal, so he decided to diversify and began to buy up derelict properties at knockdown prices in and around London. With the help of commercial mortgages courtesy of a bent bank manager Harry had introduced him to, the business grew rapidly. Numerous accounts at builders merchants were opened in the name of AC Construction and vast numbers of building materials were purchased. False paperwork had been provided using a long firm Andy had set up but the materials never made it on site and instead were moved to the warehouse where they were sold on. A short holiday was taken to the Cayman Islands and after several bank accounts were opened, one in his name and the others in his mother's name but with him as signatory, everything was almost in place. A couple of trips back and forth courtesy of his contact's private jets and the illegal money he had earnt was soon banked without leaving a paper trail. Within a couple of months of purchase, the properties were then placed back up for sale at below the market value for just enough to clear the mortgages and then snatched up by foreign buyers with fictitious documents. Payment was via the Cayman accounts and hay presto the money was now back in the United Kingdom but more Importantly, it now appeared clean and the cycle would then begin all over again. When the accounts for materials hadn't been settled after three or four months, debt collection agencies were sent to the addresses but it was a lost cause when they were informed that the properties had been sold and the new owners knew nothing about any unpaid bills. Not one stolen item brought in by Andy's men was taken directly to the warehouse; instead meets were set up all over London. The items were inspected and then placed into the fleet of four white vans that Andy had purchased. Only a handful of trusted men knew the exact location of the warehouse, the thieves Andy dealt with had no scruples and if they could steal from others then it was a foregone conclusion that they would steal from him if given the chance. Rob Winter, Sandy O, Joe Redmond and Mike Long were the trusted men. Andy also paid a team of three, Shaun Milligan, John Smithson and Gary Graver, to act as security around the clock. Working shifts, they made sure that the place was never left unattended and Andy also had the latest in closed circuit cameras and alarms fitted. If someone managed to break in then they had to get past whichever guard was on duty with the added fact that the most valuable items, which at times included antiques and works of art, were locked in a large reinforced room that only Andy had the key to.

By the time he reached thirty, Andy Chilvers had left the family home and moved into a large modern apartment in Ferdinand Magellan court, Newham. High class, the apartment had a concierge, pool and Gym. Andy was over the moon on the day he got the keys but the same couldn't be said for the reaction he received back at Chudleigh Street. Ruby hadn't been pleased with the news, she liked her kids at home with her as it made her feel safe but for Andy, the move would make his commute closer to the warehouse and besides, if trouble should ever come knocking then his mother and Shirley were well out of it. Recently Hilda's health had been in decline so he suggested that his grandmother move into the house which she accepted and it also gave his mother someone else to fuss over. Aware that Ruby was, for want of a better word, slow, he often wondered where his brains came from as it definitely wasn't from his mother or his father. Maybe it was from Hilda, his Nan was an astute old bird and you couldn't, even in her advanced years, pull the wool over her eyes about anything. Visiting at least once a week to make sure that the three women in his life were

okay, it soon turned into every Sunday when the family would share an enormous roast and talk about what they all had done that week, and obviously, Andy was always economical with the truth but only to protect those he loved.
"So Son, what's been happening in your world this week?"
"Not a lot Mum, just a bit of trading and meetings, nothing exciting sadly."
Suddenly Shirley spoke and they all looked at her bewildered as she never really said much apart from yes and no.
"Andy, when can I come and see your flat?"
"One day sweetheart, I'm just a bit busy at the minute."
Shirley lowered her head and it hurt him to think that he'd disappointed his sister as she never asked for anything. To him her life was boring and at twenty-eight she hadn't even been on a date.
"Okay, darling I'll pick you up one afternoon next week and take you over."
His sister beamed from ear to ear and they all began to tuck into the food, Ruby might not have been very bright but she sure as hell could cook. Three days later and just as he said Andy collected his sister and drove her over to Newham. Andy's flat was furnished well and everything from the furniture to the linens was

expensive. Not that he did much entertaining, especially with the fairer sex. Chinese whispers had started long ago that maybe he was queer but nothing could have been further from the truth. It wasn't that he was picky; he just wanted to get it right if he ever met someone that he really liked but to date that hadn't happened. Of all the men in his employ, Andy was closest to Rob Winter. The two had been in school together and if he was ever to trust someone it would have been Rob but the problem was Andy didn't trust anyone. His mantra was 'If you didn't trust then you couldn't be let down'. It had been that way for his entire life and up until now had seemed to work well. Life was good, business was extremely good and Andy Chilvers was a happy man.

"So? What do you think Sis?"

"Oh, Andy it's fantastic and so modern." Shirley ran the palm of her hand over the sumptuous silk cushions and then wandered through to the bedrooms and kitchen.

"I want to get a place like this one day but not until Mum and Nan have gone. I could never leave them; they're too old to be on their own."

Andy smiled and nodded his head but he knew it was all a fantasy, Shirley wouldn't be able to cope alone but he wasn't about to burst the little dream she had. Driving her back to Bethnal

Green they talked more than they had in years and it warmed him to think that maybe his sister was at last coming out of her shell but as soon as they walked back into the house she once again retreated into the safety of the bubble she had built around her. He'd never been able to understand why she was like this as Ruby had been the perfect mother to both of them. Possibly she was damaged from the time she'd lived with the old man. Suddenly a thought flashed through his mind, a thought so heinous that he immediately forced it to disappear. Around the same time, Andy crossed paths with Konstantin Ivanov, a high-ranking member of the notorious Russian Mafia, known locally in his homeland as the Babanin & Sons. The family business portrayed a legitimate front so long as you didn't look too hard. Andy had been invited for an evening out by Bobby Richmond, well known in the West End as a club and bar owner come armed robber and definitely someone you didn't mess with. Bobby's head office was situated in a club he owned named the Pink Flamingo on Wardour Street in Soho. He had taken a shine to Andy several months earlier when he needed a favour in locating an item and Andy had come up trumps without much difficulty. Bobby had been overjoyed and now the two men were firm friends and would socialise together at least once a week.

One Friday evening and with little notice, Bobby had called his friend and told him that he was entertaining some business clients later that night and he would really appreciate Andy's presence. It was an offer he couldn't refuse and not because of fear, there could be new contacts in the offing and Andy Chilvers never passed up on a business opportunity. Entering the club at just after nine that night he was immediately guided to the roped-off VIP area. The Pink Flamingo was buzzing with city types wanting to spend their easily earned fat bonuses but no amount of money would ever enable them access to this area no matter how much they pleaded or how much cash they waived in Bobby's direction. Andy made his way up to the bar where Bobby Richmond and two others were drinking and laughing at some joke they had just shared.
"Andy!! How the fuck are you my old mucker?" Bobby vigorously shook his friend's hand and then turned to the man standing on his right.
"Konstantin, this is the guy I was telling you about. There ain't anything Mr Fixer here can't make happen or not yet at least. Andy, say hi to Konstantin Ivanov."
Andy stared up at the thick-set man who stood

head and shoulders above him. With a shaven head and large neck tattoo, Konstantin was the epitome of a Russian and a bad one at that. Holding out his hand, Andy was surprised by the gentleness of the shake as he'd been expecting his own hand to be crushed.
"Pleased to meet you, Mr Ivanov."
"Please no formalities, call me Konstantin."
For the second time in as many minutes, Andy was again surprised. He'd expected a strong Russian accent but apart from just a hint of a twang, the man spoke perfect English. The look of surprise was evident on Andy's face and Konstantin smiled.
"I have Russian blood my friend but I was educated here in London. Now then, Bobby has nothing but praise for you and holds you in very high esteem."
"Well, that's good to hear. Are you buying then Bob or what?"
The men laughed which relaxed the meeting and the drinks soon began to flow. The other man in the group was never introduced and it didn't take much to work out that he was Konstantin's bodyguard and that he was armed. That fact unnerved Andy for a short while, he may have been a villain but guns, all except those his security men carried at the warehouse, were definitely off the menu. Andy hated them and

preferred to be looked upon as a businessman rather than a gun-carrying gangster. Bobby was called away for a while as there was a problem in the entrance foyer so Andy and Konstantin began chatting one to one. They soon found out they had a lot in common, both enjoyed the finer things in life and both had a passion for Arsenal football club.

"Would you like to join me tomorrow at the match? I have a box at my disposal and would love it if you could come."

"No need to ask twice pal!"

"Good, good. I will have my driver collect you at two."

"You want me to write my address down?"

Konstantin laughed; for once Andy was acting a little naive.

"No need I already have it. I make a purpose of finding out about anyone I will be spending time with. In my line of work, you have to be careful."

Andy was just about to ask his newfound friend what that line of work was when Bobby reappeared and the real partying began. When the Russian went to the toilet, Bobby leaned in close.

"So, what do you think?"

"About what?"

"About Konstantin you thick cunt!"

"Yeah, seems like a nice sort. He's invited me to the match tomorrow."

"Fuck me! I've been waiting weeks to be asked; he has a private box you know and is on first names with most of the players. I went to a party at his house a couple of months ago and Van Persie and Clichy were there, even Wenger popped in for an hour."

"No way!"

"I fuckin' kid you not! Stick with me my son and you're going up in the world but by all accounts with that invite you're doing okay on your own."

The two began to laugh and as Konstantin and his man returned Bobby waved his hand for another bottle of Louis Roederer to be brought over. With a price tag of two hundred and sixty-five pounds a bottle Andy knew that Bobby was out to impress and he was in no doubt that some serious business was going to be up for discussion as soon as he left for the night. Unaware that he would be the topic of conversation, Andy enjoyed the men's company for the next two hours and when he could feel the champagne beginning to take hold he said his goodbyes and called it a night.

CHAPTER SIX

Andy had been up with the larks, he was really looking forward to the match but even more than that he was looking forward to getting to know a possible new client. At two on the dot Konstantin's driver pressed the intercom and Andy made his way downstairs. The navy blue Range Rover with rear blacked-out windows was brand new and as the driver held the door open for Andy he felt a bit embarrassed. He was also a little surprised that the Russian wasn't inside but with the plush cream leather seats that were heated, he sat back to enjoy the ride.
"Where's Konstantin?"
Surprisingly the driver was English and he looked at Andy through the rear view mirror as he spoke.
"Mr Ivanov is already at the ground Sir as he has some business to take care of before kick-off."
Expecting to be dropped outside one of the main pedestrian entrances Andy was surprised when the barrier lifted and the vehicle drove straight into the ground and stopped outside the VIP section.
"If you'd like to follow me Sir I will show you up to Mr Ivanov's box."
Andy had been in hospitality boxes before but

nothing like this, his shoes seemed to sink into the golden carpet as he climbed the stairs. Stepping into the double box he glanced all around. The black leather furniture had been polished within an inch of its life so that it gleamed under the lights and fine works of art hung from the walls. Andy had been in the game long enough to know that they were not copies and must be worth tens of thousands of pounds and that was a conservative estimate. Walking up to the massive window that overlooked the pitch he couldn't believe how amazing the view was.

"Best Box in the ground Sir. Mr Ivanov will join you shortly. May I get you something to drink while you wait?"

Andy scanned the drinks trolley that along with an array of the finest cut glass crystal also contained every type of alcohol you could possibly imagine. Andy puffed out his cheeks as he scanned what was on offer.

"In that case, I'll have a scotch please, on the rocks."

As he sipped his drink and looked down onto the pitch he knew this was the kind of lifestyle he wanted for himself, he was already doing well and had plenty of cash but nothing in this league. The afternoon was a great success and the two men hit it off well, a lot of laughter and conversations were shared with the help of copious amounts of alcohol and the icing on the cake was Arsenal beating Tottenham 3:1. When Konstantin and his driver dropped Andy back at his flat the two arranged to meet for a drink the following Monday lunchtime.

Arriving at his mother's house for lunch the next day Andy was still buzzing from yesterday and he couldn't wait to share news about his new pal with his family. When he walked into the front room Ruby and Aida were already sitting at the table waiting but there was no sign of Shirley.
"Alright, you two?"
Ruby looked up into her son's face and there were pools of tears in her eyes.
"Whatever's the matter Mum?"
"It's your sister. Got in with some bleeding bloke and he's started knocking her about."
"What!? When did this start and why didn't you tell me about this before, where is she?"
Andy Chilvers could feel his blood start to boil as he stared at his mother waiting for an answer.
"I didn't know son, she's been keeping it a secret. Told us she had a new friend and I thought it was a girl, I mean your sister has never shown the slightest interest in men. She's upstairs, and hasn't been out of her room since yesterday."

For once Aida was silent, she didn't know what to say and she was scared her grandson would do something stupid and get himself into trouble.

"Nan?"

"I really don't know boy, I mean if you go in all guns blazing then she's likely to dig her heels in regarding this man and I use the term loosely as in my book any bloke that lays his hands on a woman ain't no man at all. I think the women in this family are fuckin' cursed when it comes to the opposite sex, present company not included in that of course."

Andy turned, walked from the front room and made his way upstairs. Standing outside his sister's room he sighed heavily before gently tapping on the door and then walking in.

Shirley was sitting up in bed playing on her laptop, she was dressed but her hair was a tangled mess and it was evident she'd been crying. As she turned her face upwards he saw the fat lip and black eye.

"For fucks sake babe, who did that to you?"

"It's not what you think Andy, honestly it ain't. I can get a bit lippy at times and I pissed Wayne off when he thought I was flirting with his mate but I wasn't. He was sorry after and swore he'd never do it again."

Andy took a seat on the bed beside Shirley and

taking hold of her hand smiled tenderly but he was clenching his teeth in anger.

"My darling you are never lippy and even if you were, no one has the right to lay their fuckin' hands on you. Now what's his last name?"

"Why? What are you going to do to him?"

Andy knew that if he said 'I'm going to beat the fuckin' shit out of him!' she would stay tight-lipped. Knowing he couldn't actually do anything himself or she would never forgive him Andy thought of asking Konstantin for help, he had his own blokes but he needed distance from whoever was going to help him out and in the East End there were always whispers, whispers that he couldn't afford for his sister to hear.

"I promise you babe I won't lay a hand on him I just want to have a little chat, I promise."

Shirley eyed her brother suspiciously but as she studied his face and he smiled, she knew she could trust him. Her brother had always looked out for her; he was a good man and as far as she knew, had never told her a lie.

"His last name is Andino and his mum and dad run the Athens cafe on Bethnal Green Road."

"He's a fuckin' Greek!?"

Again Shirley eyed her brother with suspicion.

"Yes but he was born here and he's so handsome Andy, I was shocked that he would even look at

someone like me."
"Someone like you? Why babe? You're beautiful but I know Greeks can be fuckin' hotheads and very jealous. I just need to have a chat and tell him you would never betray him. Now come on let's go and have dinner, Mum's worked hard and I'm fuckin' starving."
Taking her hand they both went downstairs and the two women at the table smiled with relief. Andy looked in his grandmother's direction and winked. Aida slowly nodded her head, she knew her grandson would never let this go without some payback but Andy was a smart cookie and she was sure he would handle things in the right way.
"Come on you two, tuck in before it goes cold."
The subject wasn't mentioned again but Ruby and Aida both knew that trouble was brewing.

On Monday and as agreed, Andy walked into the Crown & Two Chairman on Dean Street at one o'clock. Konstantin spent most of his time in Soho, particularly in the Chairman as it was known, as he had a seventy-five per cent share in the place. That was initially how he had first come into contact with Bobby Richmond. Bobby's club was on Wardour Street which ran parallel to Dean and all pub and club owners checked out any competition. The two men had

instantly hit it off but Bobby hadn't made as good an impression on the Russian as Andy Chilvers had. Konstantin had quickly found out everything he needed to know about his new friend both business-wise and personally, in their line of work you never took anyone at face value, if you did then you were an idiot and liable to experience trouble of some sort or another. Standing at the bar Konstantin smiled broadly when Andy entered.
"Welcome my friend. Scotch?"
"Thanks but I think I'd better stick to larger."
"Had a heavy night?"
"No nothing like that. I just need to keep a clear head."
The men took a seat at a table in the rear and for a few moments, Konstantin studied his friend.
"You seem troubled?"
"Oh just family stuff, you know how it is, just when things are going well…."
"Can I help in any way?"
Andy was silent for a few seconds as he stared into the man's eyes and thought of what to say.
"It's my baby sister, got in with some Greek cunt and he's knocked her about a bit. Shirley's a good kid and doesn't deserve that but if I do anything personally then she'll know and never forgive me. My family mean everything to me, Konstantin."

"Just as it should be my friend, why don't you let me handle the problem for you?"

Again Andy was silent, this was what he wanted to hear but he didn't want it to seem as if he was jumping straight in and taking liberties with his newfound friendship.

"I have to go and talk to the bloke because that's what I told Shirley I'd do but I promised not to lay a hand on him."

"Then go and have your talk and tomorrow I will take care of the rest. Be with your sister tomorrow afternoon so that when she gets the news she will know that it wasn't you."

"Thank you, Konstantin, how can I repay you?"

The Russian patted the back of his friend's hands and something about his next sentence didn't sit well with Andy.

"There will come a time when I need your help and then we will be even."

The two men ate a light lunch before leaving separately and Andy headed over to the Athens cafe on Bethnal Green Road. The place was old-school Greek with checked plastic tablecloths, dark wooden beams and lots of shouting coming from the kitchen. A couple of old men sat in a corner drinking coffee and playing Tavli, Greece's national board game but apart from that the place was empty. Andy sat down and waited for someone to serve him. It didn't take

long before a bloke in his early thirties walked up; his expression was sour as if he'd rather be doing anything than serving customers.
"What can I get you?"
"I would like a quick word with Wayne if he's about."
"Who wants to know?"
With those words, Andy realised who he had come to see was now standing right in front of him.
"I ain't here for any trouble. I just want a chat, I'm Shirley's brother."
Wayne took a step backwards in fear.
"Look pal, if I'd come here for aggro you'd be on your fuckin' back by now. Sit!"
Wayne did as he'd been told but the way he continually moved about in his seat told Andy that the cunt was nervous.
"You laid your hands on my sister!"
"It was a stupid argument that got out of hand that's all. We've sorted it and I promise I won't ever touch her again okay?"
The bloke was so cocky and it took all of Andy's resolve not to punch his lights out there and then. Glad that he had shared his woes with Konstantin, it didn't stop Andy from feeling disappointed that he wouldn't get to see the payback.
"I'll take you at your word but if you go back on

it then you will pay the fuckin' consequences.
Do you understand me?"
Wayne vigorously nodded his head and
standing up Andy then walked out of the café.

The following day and just as Konstantin had
advised, Andy walked into his mother's house at
a little before two that afternoon. The three
women were all seated in the front room
watching some old black-and-white movie and
Ruby smiled when she saw who their visitor
was.
"Hello there, boy, what a pleasure to see you
mid-week."
"Had a bit of business around Roman Road and
I couldn't be this close without popping in to see
me three favourite girls. So, is there any tea
going?"
Instantly Ruby was on her feet, she loved caring
for her family and none more so than her son.
"Coming right up. Mum? Shirley?"
They nodded their heads in unison, switched off
the television and walked over to the table. A
few minutes later and cups, a steaming hot
teapot and a plate of Jammie Dodgers were
placed down on the wooden surface. Ruby
talked nonstop and what she was uttering was
stupid nonsense which was unusual but when
Andy glanced at his grandmother's face she just

looked down and slowly shook her head. Andy planned to ask Aida what was going on before he left but the thought left his mind when Shirley's mobile burst into life and after listening for a few seconds she began to cry.
"What is it babe, what's wrong?"
"It's Wayne, someone has just hurt him and he's in the hospital. Oh, Andy, who would do such a thing?"
"I don't know babe but get your coat and I'll take you down there."
It was a seven-minute trip to The Royal London Hospital on Whitechapel Road and the only conversation that passed between brother and sister was when Shirley suddenly turned and stared at Andy.
"It wasn't you was it?"
"Wasn't me what?"
"Wasn't you who hurt my Wayne?"
"For fucks sake Shirl I've been with you for the past half hour so unless I can perform bleedin' miracles then no and I resent you even asking me. I visited Wayne yesterday and he swore he would never lay a finger on you again and that was good enough for me!"
"I'm sorry Andy, forgive me I'm just upset that's all."
When they entered the accident and emergency they were shown through to a small side room

where Wayne Andino lay in a bed unconscious with tubes coming out of his nose and mouth. His mother was wailing loudly and when she tried to climb onto the bed with her son, she had to be pulled off by her husband. Andy felt not one ounce of remorse even if it did cross his mind that Konstantin or the men he had used to carry out the attack, might have just overstepped the line a tad. A few seconds later and a doctor entered. He informed the Andino's that Wayne would need surgery on his broken ankle but he was certain that their son would make a full recovery, although it would take several months of physiotherapy. As Andy placed his arm around his sister's shoulder in a fake show of concern, Shirley sighed heavily with relief.
"I'm going to get back to mum's darling, you coming or do you want me to fetch you later?"
Shirley had no intention of leaving her boyfriend until he'd had his operation so Andy made his way back to the car with a slight spring in his step.
Letting himself back into the house he was met by Aida in the hallway.
"Everything okay boy?"
"The cunt got what he deserved."
"I thought that was the case, come on and I'll put the kettle on."
As Aida turned to walk away she felt her

grandson's hand on her arm and turned back to face him, well aware of what he was about to ask.

"What was all that about with Mum earlier?"

"I'm not really sure darling but she's been acting strange over the last few weeks. Most of the time she seems normal or at least hides it well but sometimes it's like she's losing the plot. Yesterday I went into the kitchen and caught her about to put the plastic kettle onto the gas hob. Lord above knows what would have happened if she'd succeeded. She tried to cover it up by saying that her mind was thinking about something else but I could see she was embarrassed."

"You think she needs to visit the docs?"

Aida sighed.

"Leave it for a bit and let me watch her sweetheart, I need to be a hundred per cent before we go down that route. It runs in the family you know."

"What does?"

"Dementia or Alzheimer's as they call it now. Your granny, my mum, had it. She died the year before you were born and I can remember her telling me that my Nan went a bit daft in the head as she got older. There was no label back then and people would say that the old ones were just a bit senile. Senile my arse, thankfully

I must have been lucky as it seems to have skipped a generation. I pray to God I'm wrong love, because if it is then we're all in for a fuckin' rough ride."

"Please don't worry Nan, we don't know anything yet."

Entering the front room with broad grins on their faces they both acted as if all was well with the world but inside Andy could feel a knot forming in the pit of his stomach.

CHAPTER SEVEN

Over the ensuing months, Andy and Konstantin's friendship grew. Andy really liked the Russian and many nights were spent at either Bobby Richmond's club the Pink Flamingo or Konstantin's pub the Crown & Two Chairmen. The two men would meet up at least once a week and when Konstantin had a new girl on his arm there would be dinners where a friend of the new girl would come along to make up a foursome. The women were mostly Eastern European and did nothing for Andy sexually or intellectually. He wasn't attracted to the heavy makeup and garish clothing and they mostly seemed like airheads with little to say but he would never insult his host and despite the failed attempts to pair him off he usually had a good time. Business was growing by the week, the properties were coming in thick and fast and he had more new clients wanting knock-off stuff than he could handle. Around the same time, Andy would be shown what Konstantin Ivanov and his men were really capable of and it scared the hell out of him. It happened one Saturday lunchtime when the two were sharing a drink in the pub. Suddenly the door burst open and two of Konstantin's men came in almost dragging a man who had been brutally beaten. Walking straight past their boss with their victim groaning in pain, they disappeared through a door at the rear of the bar.

"Fuckin' hell Konstantin, what on earth is going on?"

One look at his friend's shocked expression and the Russian laughed as if he'd just been told a joke.

"Come with me, Andy."

Doing as he was asked Andy placed his drink onto the bar and followed. The back room was accessed through a long dimly lit hallway and one of the heavies was standing guard outside a door at the end of the corridor. Opening up for his boss, Andy and Konstantin walked inside. Seated on a chair in the middle of the room was the beaten man who was now handcuffed and with his head hung low, blood and spittle dripped from his bottom lip. The second heavy was menacingly leaning over him and Andy had a bad feeling in his gut but there was nothing he could do. This was wrong in every way and his brain was telling him that the poor sod in the chair, wasn't walking out of here, at least no alive. One of the men punched the victim so hard in the face that the man's head flew backwards and as if in slow motion, blood spurted from his nose and sprayed the air.

"I'm out of here!"
"Andy, stay where you are! I want you to see what happens when someone betrays me."
"Konstantin I really don't think I ……"
Andy was silenced when his friend walked around so that he was facing the seated man. Smiling he pulled out a handgun with a silencer connected and as if it was an everyday occurrence, he grinned in Andy's direction, aimed and then shot the victim straight between the eyes. The power of the bullet again forced the man's head backwards and for a few seconds, Andy was fixated on the small hole in the victim's forehead. Initially, there was no blood which surprised him but then a trickle began and Andy suddenly felt sick to the stomach.
"Right, let's get back to our drinks as I assume you have many questions, my friend. Dimitri, call the cleaner!"
Not needing an explanation for Konstantin's last sentence, Andy was out of the door in seconds. Back in the bar he took a seat on one of the stools but he was visibly shaken and when a neat whiskey was placed in front of him he downed it in one.
"Why, why the fuck did you do that and why in hell's name did you show me?!!!"
Konstantin took a swig of his own drink, all the

while studying his friend's face for any sign of further emotion or lack of loyalty.

"We have become close no?"

"Well yes but…."

"It wasn't a question Andy. I'm not sure if you realise what my line of work entails and as such I needed to show you. I enforce punishment on anyone that crosses me or my bosses back in Russia. I have it on good authority that the cunt back there was about to spill his guts to the Old Bill. No beating would ever be enough to stop someone like that from grassing so there is only one avenue that can be taken."

"I understand that but what have I got to do with any of this?"

Konstantin looked around the bar to make sure he wasn't being overheard.

"You know how I helped you out with that little problem a while ago?"

Thinking back, Andy now wished he had never asked for the favour but could only nod his head. After what he'd just seen he was dreading what he would be asked to do but with that thought, he knew better than to show his cards.

"I, my firm back home, have a slight problem. As you must be aware our business is not exactly legal."

Again Andy nodded his head but he could feel this conversation was serious and it was a conversation he really didn't want to be having. "We need our cash cleaned and you have the perfect business to do that for us."

"And what if I don't want to, what if I refuse?"

"Well, firstly I did you a favour and said I may call on you to do the same in return and also and more importantly, my bosses back home would not be happy and I really don't need to spell out what that could mean for you."

There and then Andy knew he had been played, Konstantin had him over a fucking barrel and there wasn't a thing he could do about it, not if he wanted to carry on breathing. He moved his head to show agreement and then smiled, all the time his mind was silently screaming 'You cunt! You cunt!'

"Of course and we're friends so I won't let you down. What exactly will it entail?"

"We have a vast amount of funds offshore and we need it cleaned so that it can be reused in this country. We will invest in your property company over a period of time; it will be small amounts to begin with, so as not to raise suspicion. You will purchase as many properties as possible and my company will provide you with a Russian workforce to renovate the buildings. For this service, you will pay highly inflated wages to us. Those buildings will then be marketed and on completion of the sale, the funds will be paid straight into your Cayman Island company accounts, a company we are now partners in and will remain there for future investment. The remainder will go back into your British company. Only the wage payments will be paid to us, which will allow us to withdraw some of our newly cleaned money for running our operations here in the city and there is no need for concern, the bank manager works for my bosses, well he's on the payroll at least."

Andy had to admit that it was a good plan but he couldn't help thinking that he had drawn the short straw and there was nothing he could do about it.

"So when do you want to start?"

"Over the next few months, the money will be slowly placed into your business accounts and as soon as enough capital has been amassed it will be time for you to begin."

"So, how much are we talking about Konstantin?"

"I estimated between forty and fifty mill in the first year and then we can see how it goes."

Andy tried not to look shocked but he didn't do a very good job of it and Konstantin laughed out loud.

"I could see you weren't happy and was thinking is it worth all the trouble? You're a bright man and can work out the maths for yourself. In the next few years, you will make millions my friend."

Offering his hand the two men shook on the deal and the meeting then came to an end. On the drive back to the warehouse Andy mulled over all that had been discussed, yes he would be rich but at what cost? He also knew he was between a rock and a hard place and now couldn't get out of it. Konstantin had planned this from the very beginning, he knew all about Andy's business, his bank accounts, even details on his family and everything and everyone would be at risk if he had a change of heart.

A few days later Andy was at the warehouse on a Sunday morning. He often went in on a Sunday before going to his family for lunch. The place, apart from the security guard, was quiet and it allowed him time to think and carry out his paperwork in peace. Tapping into his computer he checked on the Cayman accounts, it was something he did regularly. There were four in total, his personal account which was as it should be and three further accounts in Ruby's name that were for business use. On paper, he had fictitious foreign investment companies who were willing to back him. When the first account came onto the screen his jaw dropped.

Three million had been deposited with a further million in each of the other two. Raising his hand he wiped his brow, it was clammy and now the nerves started to set in. What if it didn't all go as planned? For God's sake, this was Russian mafia money that he was now in charge of. Backing up his computer and then closing it down he leaned back in his chair and just stared into space. He needed help, phoning Shirley he asked her to delay lunch by an hour and then he set off for Soho. It was noon and the Pink Flamingo was closed but making his way around to the back he climbed the metal fire escape staircase and rapped hard on the steel door. Bobby Richmond kept a small flat on the top floor and there were only a select few who were aware of its existence and his wife Wendy wasn't one of them. Andy seemed to wait for what felt like an age but finally, the door swung open and a bleary-eyed Bobby screwed his eyes shut at the glaring morning sun.
"Hello Pal, what you doing about so early?"
"It's almost fuckin' noon Bob and I need your advice urgently."
"Come on in and put the kettle on while I get rid of last night's little hottie. Fuck me she was a real goer, I'm knackered and my ball sack feels like it's been put through the wringer."
With his open dressing gown swinging from

side to side and showing of his semi-erect manhood without a care, Bobby disappeared down the hallway. Andy walked into the open-plan lounge/kitchen and immediately noticed the remnants of last night's party paraphernalia. An empty bottle of gin was on the sofa, several empty cans of larger were on the glass coffee table along with a rolled up twenty-pound note and a small amount of coke that they obviously hadn't needed. Bobby Richmond was in his mid-fifties, overweight and drank like a fish, Andy sighed and shook his head, his friend would end up killing himself if he carried on like this. Fifteen minutes later and Bobby reappeared, showered, dressed and with a spring in his step.
"So what's on your mind mate?"
"I've got myself backed into a corner and I don't know what the fuck to do to get out of it?"
Bobby picked up his coffee and walking over to the sofa, pushed the empty bottle onto the floor before he sat down. He really liked Andy Chilvers, he was a straight-up guy, well as straight as any villain could be and it was evident that his friend was really troubled about something.
"Take a seat and tell Doctor Richmond all about it."
Usually, Bobby's silly jokes made Andy laugh

but not today.

"It's Konstantin."

"Why doesn't that surprise me?"

"He helped me out a few weeks back when some ponce beat up my sister. Now he's calling in the favour and the payment he wants is fuckin' huge compared to what he did for me."

"I'm sorry Pal, I should have warned you what a cunt he is before I introduced him. Is it money laundering by any chance?"

Andy looked shocked, was his business common knowledge?

"How do you know?"

"I know, because he tried it on with me! It got a bit fuckin' scary for a while, he said he wanted to invest in the club and filter the cash through the books."

"So how did you stop it from happening or did he change his mind?"

"The Russians don't change their minds on many things but I used my nous, told him I was under investigation from the Inland Revenue so it would be risky but I was willing to help or at least he thought I was. If there's one thing they shy away from its having their business looked into by anyone and luckily for me the subject never got mentioned again."

"So are you under investigation then?"

Bobby Richmond began to laugh as he slowly

shook his head.

"No you soppy twat but it got that Russian cunt off of my back."

"I'm sorry I shared any of your information with the Russian Andy but after that first night in the club when we'd had such a fuckin' blinding time, he came to see me the next day. Said he really liked you and then we had a few drinks and you know me after a few scotches, loose lips and all that. Not for a single fuckin' minute did I think he was pumping me for info so he could stitch you up!"

"I know you didn't mean anything Bob and it's okay but how do I get out of it?"

Bobby Richmond sat back on the sofa and didn't speak for a couple of minutes. Instead, he took a swig of his coffee before lighting up the last Benson he had and then throwing the empty packet onto the coffee table. Suddenly there was a large cloud of billowing smoke in the room as Bobby drew on his cigarette several times in quick succession. He then began to cough, wet racking coughs that lasted for several seconds and his face took on a scarlet tinge. Andy wrinkled his nose in distaste, he hated the smell of cigarettes, always had and no one in his family had ever had the filthy habit. Bobby pulled an imaginary strand of tobacco from his mouth, a habit he'd gained when he was in

prison and only smoked roll-ups.
"You okay?"
Bobby mouthed the word 'yes' as he continued to cough and when he was finally able to compose himself he answered Andy's earlier question.
"Out of it? You can't get out of it mate, not unless you want to fuckin' disappear and even then your family wouldn't be safe. Believe me when I say that those cunts will stop at nothing and would continue to run your business even if you were dead. Don't think of trying to use the same excuse that I did as they will know in a heartbeat that you are lying to them."
"So I'm fucked then?"
Taking another puff, Bobby was quiet again as he thought and suddenly he smiled in his friend's direction.
"Go along with it for a while but in the meantime make plans. Get new identities for yourself and your family and don't share the information with anyone. Find somewhere abroad, somewhere remote and buy a gaff. When you've finally had enough and are ready to leave, transfer the money into other accounts that the Russians don't know about and won't be able to trace. How to do that will be up to you to find out. As for passports and any other documents you might need I might know a

geezer who can sort that."

"I don't know how to thank you, Bob?"

"No thanks needed Pal, I think the world of you and I also hate the fuckin' Russians so it will be a pleasure."

Andy got up to leave and as he headed towards the door he stopped and turned when Bobby spoke again.

"If you decide to go down that route mate, not a word and I do mean not a fuckin' word to anyone. Konstantin has ears everywhere and if he gets even a fuckin' hint of your plans you'll be toast."

Andy stared at his friend for a few seconds and then left via the fire escape. He couldn't say he actually felt better but at least there was a way out if he needed it. He already knew he wouldn't seek out Bobby's help regarding identification and passports for the family, the man had already shafted him once whether he meant to or not. Harry Richardson had always said he'd help Andy and as no one knew of their association then it would be far safer.

Convincing the women in his life to up sticks and settle in a foreign country would be a different matter altogether but he supposed there was no point in worrying about that at the moment. Up until now, his life had been good but now someone was trying to control him, no not trying, actually controlling him and there wasn't a damn thing he could do about it if he wanted to stay alive.

CHAPTER EIGHT

On Monday morning, Debbie Montgomery kissed her husband on the cheek as he set off for work and then making herself a coffee she sat down at her computer. The Montgomery's were affluent, clean living and both had good jobs. Colin worked at the local branch of Barclays in Cambridge as the manager and Debbie worked from home for the NHS. The couple had been married for close to twenty years but sadly had never been able to conceive a child of their own. For some strange reason, Colin had always been dead against adoption which was a bone of contention in their marriage. He only revealed the reason one night after a few too many glasses of red when the couple had begun to argue about the topic. Explaining that he had been adopted and even though he loved his adoptive parents dearly, he didn't want to do the same to another child.
"I can't believe we've been married all this time and I didn't know. Why did you never tell me Colin?"
"I don't know, I suppose I'm ashamed. Who am I Deb's, where do I come from? Sometimes I really don't know who I am."
"Oh don't be so silly darling of course you do,

you're Colin Montgomery and my husband who I actually love very much."

"I know you do but it isn't really me is it? I mean I know where I was born but apart from that the only thing I was allowed to keep was my Christian name, everything else was hidden from me and I was never told why. It's played on my mind for most of my adult life and even if I didn't share that with you it's still caused me a great deal of pain."

"So why didn't you ask Lydia?"

"I tried to once, a long time ago but you know mother, if she doesn't want to discuss something then she just keeps changing the subject. I suppose my father would have shared any information but by the time I was ready to ask him about it he was already too ill. I know the Law has changed and I have a right to view my adoption report but something deep inside keeps stopping me."

"Why don't you try again with your mum?"

Just like the wind, Colin's mood changed in a split second.

"For God's sake Deb! Just let it go will you."

Knowing the question was rhetorical Debbie had to let the matter drop, if only for that night. The next day any conversation between the couple was limited, Colin knew he had spoken sharply to his wife and deep down it bothered him.

Debbie set about her housework and after a few hours the couple were back on friendly terms but now ever since that argument she'd been like a dog with a bone and without Colin's knowledge, had set time aside a couple of hours a week trying to search out any information she could. To date, she hadn't had any success but that didn't mean she was about to give up, quite the opposite in fact. Colin could have siblings, maybe even nieces and nephews and if Debbie couldn't be a mother herself then she would gladly settle for being an aunt. Opening up a Facebook account was relatively easy but even though she could find her way around the NHS software, it was a slightly different matter with social media. The settings were a nightmare, if she made everything friends only then the word would never spread but by going public with her posts she could attract all manner of weirdos. Deciding it was the only way she set about asking people to contact her if they or anyone they knew had ever lived in the Great Yarmouth area and had a baby boy adopted circa 1977/78. It would be like looking for a needle in a haystack hoping for someone that might remember Colin's mother but what other choice did she have? She knew he had a right to apply for his file but the authorities would never allow her access without Colin's permission and there was no way he would agree to it. So Facebook it had to be and it was a long shot at best but that was all she had, the fact that he'd been born in the seaside town at the long-closed home for young mothers and that his mother's Christian name was Ruby. A few people on Facebook replied but it never came to anything until she suddenly received a private message from a woman named Susan Mills who had been at the home in the very late seventies and had known a girl by the name of Ruby Chilvers. Susan couldn't provide much more information only that the woman was from Bethnal Green in London and had given birth to a son named Colin who had been put up for adoption. Debbie thanked the woman, it had to be her husband but regarding locating the woman, well it wasn't much but it was at least something to start with.

In the East End things were running smoothly for Andy though he now wished he'd never got mixed up with the Russian. Profits were off the scale and business was good but that couldn't be said regarding things with his family. Aida had taken herself to bed and refused to see a doctor and Ruby seemed to be getting further and further away from reality. Andy hadn't been home to see his family for a couple of weeks, work had taken him over to the Caymans and the properties were so busy that he constantly needed to be on site. In reality, he was scared, scared of what was going to happen but he finally decided that he really needed to spend some time with his mum and sister. Making arrangements with Shirley, he told his sister he would be over for lunch the following Sunday. On that day, the state of what was going on finally hit home. As soon as he arrived for the meal he noticed that the house was grubby and no delicious aromas were coming from the kitchen. Shirley was doing the best she could but the strain was noticeable on her face and when the lunch was served up and Ruby walked in carrying a dish of supposedly boiled potatoes that hadn't been anywhere near a saucepan, he sighed heavily and slowly shook his head. His sister saw his reaction and raised her eyebrows and just shrugged her shoulders.

"Shirley, let's go for a walk after lunch babe." He could see the tears in her eyes and his heart felt broken. They both knew what was happening and now it was just finding a way to deal with it, if that was at all possible. With the dishes cleared away and when Shirley had fed her grandmother a sandwich, much to Aida's disgust, the siblings went for their walk.

"Why didn't you tell me things had gotten this

fuckin' bad Shirl!?"

"Oh I don't know, you're busy and I was coping but it's getting' harder and harder. I only ever get to see Wayne at night and by then I'm tired all the time as Mum constantly wants attention. If I try to tell her something, like about the vegetables today, well she gets so pissed off with me that it's easier just to keep my trap shut."

"We need to take her to the doc's darling, when we know for sure then I'll sort something out okay?"

Shirley nodded her head, she loved her brother dearly and he was always as good as his word.

"So how are things going with the Greek?"

"I wish you wouldn't call him that. His name is Wayne as you very well know so please don't call him the Greek again Andy and for your information, it's going very well thank you. It's just a shame we can't spend more time together."

Since the beating he'd received at the hands of Konstantin's men, Wayne Andino seemed to be behaving himself. He no longer hurt Shirley physically but Andy was totally unaware of the emotional abuse she received daily either in person or on the phone. Tired of working at his family's café he had recently started an evening technology course at the Mulberry College over on Ben Jonson Road in Stepney. He had taken to the course like a duck to water and things between the couple had improved slightly as he tried to teach Shirley everything he was learning. Visiting the house three nights a week when his class was over and when Ruby and Edna were tucked up for the night he showed Shirley how to properly use social media. Last Christmas Andy had bought his sister her first laptop as a surprise and now for the first time, she was really enjoying using it.

A few weeks into his course Wayne turned up at the house in an excited state. He couldn't get through the door fast enough and was talking ten to the dozen as he barged past her and went straight into the front room.
"You're never gonna believe this Shirl, I was at my class and just logged onto Facebook and…."
"Wayne! Slow down a bit will you; I can't understand a word you are saying."
Normally her words and tone would have been like a red rag to a bull but he was too excited to bring her back down to earth with his usual cruel comments. Taking a seat on the sofa he placed his laptop onto the coffee table and switched it on. Logging onto his profile he scanned down the posts until he found what he was looking for.
"Take a look at this!"

Shirley scanned the words but didn't understand what she was reading.

'Searching for a Ruby Chilvers, who resided in Bethnal Green in London around 1977. Ruby gave birth to a baby boy, who was put up for adoption. Anyone who has information please direct message me. Debbie Montgomery'

Not as slow as Ruby, Shirley still wasn't the brightest bulb in the box and when she looked from the screen to her boyfriend, Wayne frowned at her lack of enthusiasm.

"What?"

"Fuck me Shirl; you are a proper thick cunt at times. It's your mum the woman is talking about."

"Don't be daft, my mum never had a baby and gave it away."

"And just how many Ruby Chilvers do you know that lived in Bethnal Green at the right time? Just because she never told you don't mean it didn't happen!"

Shirley thought for a few moments before she spoke. This was bad news and worse still if it was the truth. It was no good asking her mother as Ruby was in her own little world most of the time and Andy would hit the roof if he found out about any of this.

"Okay, I'll have a word with me Nan but if I was you Wayne I would leave it alone because if

Andy gets wind of it he will fuckin' lose the plot!"

Suddenly images of the beating he had received flashed through his mind. He had always known that it had come from Andy Chilvers no matter how many times Shirley had denied it.

"Okay, but ask your Nan and I think it would be a good idea for you to open up a Facebook account so you can follow the post. No one will know who you are as your surname is different. This has really intrigued me Shirl so I expect you to do as I say."

Rather than receive another spiteful tongue lashing, she nodded her head in agreement but she needed to wait a while. There was an appointment booked for the following morning at the doctor's and it was going to be hard enough for her and Andy to get Ruby to attend without any further aggravation.

Her brother arrived at ten the next day and Shirley was already stressed when he walked in.

"Morning Sis, everything okay?"

"No, it bloody well isn't Andy! It's been a bleeding nightmare trying to get her ready and Nan hasn't stopped demanding my attention since she woke up this morning. She's banged on the floor so much that I have a headache now."

Andy bent over and kissed his sister on the

forehead.

"You sort Mum out and I'll go and see to Nan." Before walking into Aida's bedroom Andy knocked and then popped his head around the door.

"Are you decent in there Duchess? Only I don't want to catch you in the altogether."

Aida Chilvers chuckled as she tried to prop herself up in bed.

"Now what's all this I hear about you not playing ball this morning? It's not like you to be naughty and you know Shirley has to get me mum ready to go to the quacks."

"I'm scared Andy."

"What on earth, are you scared of Duchess?"

Aida was quiet for a moment almost as if she was somewhere back in time and the pain etched on her face told Andy it wasn't somewhere she wanted to be.

"Nan?"

"You know I told you that both of my parents had dementia. They call it that Alzheimer's nowadays you know but back then they didn't know too much about it. Anyway, they both had to go into a home, my old mum especially as she got so violent that we couldn't handle her. I think it might have skipped a generation, I mean I might be a difficult old cow at times but I still have all my faculties. What I've seen of late, how my Ruby is behaving, well I don't need no doctor to tell me she has it."

Aida was starting to repeat things herself but he knew with his nan it was just old age so he didn't pull her up on it. Andy sat down on the side of the bed for a moment and then took hold of her hand in his.

"Darling don't jump the gun but if that's what this is then so be it. We will look after her I promise and there won't be any going into a home for mum. Now stop worrying, concentrate on yourself and start behaving. Promise me you'll give Shirley a break, she's doing the best that she can."

"Andy! We're ready!"

Aida nodded her head as she wiped away the tears.

"I have to go now but I promise as soon as we know anything I'll come and tell you, sweetheart."

Today was a good day for Ruby Chilvers, she was lucid and chatting with her daughter like there was nothing wrong with her.

"Where are we off to?"

As Andy secured the seatbelt around his mother's waist he kissed her tenderly on the cheek.

"We just need to get you checked out at the surgery Mum."

"Is it because of my memory?"
Andy could feel his heart breaking, she knew there was something wrong but there was little he could do to placate her. Glancing over the seat to where Shirley sat he smiled and winked. "That's right mum but it's just a check-up darling so nothing for you to worry about." Arriving at the Albion Health Centre on Whitechapel Road, Andy entered first followed a couple of minutes later by Ruby and Shirley. It had all been planned in advance and as the two women walked inside Andy was nowhere to be seen as he was already sitting in a side room with Doctor Khan. He explained how his mother was on a day-to-day basis and that they were all concerned. Andy shared the most recent information he had received from his Nan and also told Doctor Khan that today was a good day and to most people his mother seemed perfectly normal.
"It's usually a slow decline Mr Chilvers but there are several simple tests that I can carry out that will tell me what I need to know. I will need to see your mother alone but I will invite you and your sister to join us after the examination." Reluctantly Ruby followed the doctor but continued to glance over her shoulder towards her two children as she walked.
"What did he say, Andy?"

"Not a lot, he has to do a few tests and then we'll see."

It didn't take more than ten minutes before Doctor Khan opened his door and asked them to come in and take a seat. He smiled as they sat down but to Andy the smile was fake and he guessed they were in for bad news.

"Right! Your mum has done everything I have asked of her and sadly your suspicions were right. There is no real medication available, well non that makes much of a difference. Good care, brain stimulation and spending time talking with her is all I can recommend at the moment, it will go some way to helping slow down the speed at which the decline will occur. I really am very sorry."

Shirley began to cry but stopped when her brother squeezed her leg. Ruby just stared around the room in a daze as if she was on another planet and was completely oblivious to what the doctor was saying. Back home on Chudleigh Street, the three entered the house and the mood was sombre. Shirley walked into the kitchen to make tea while Andy went upstairs to break the news to his grandmother. Tentatively knocking on the door he walked in and Aida was leaning forward in anticipation, her eyes wide open, desperate for the news to be good. When her grandson slowly shook his

head Aida's hand flew up to her mouth.
"My poor, poor girl! You know she's had a bleeding shit life, Andy?"
He didn't reply, didn't need to as he was well aware of what his mother had endured.
"Her dad treated her like dirt, then there was your fuckin' father, the poor little cow never stood a chance not since all that heartbreak when she was seventeen."
"What happened when my mum was seventeen Nan?"
Suddenly Aida realised what she'd just said and it wasn't her secret to tell, she'd made a promise years earlier to never mention the baby and now she just might have let the proverbial cat out of the bag.
"Oh I don't know, I'm getting confused that's all, happens when you get to my bleeding age."
Andy eyed his grandmother suspiciously but for now he didn't have the time or inclination to question her further. It was time to sort his mum and Shirley out, from now on things were going to get very difficult and so very sad. The thought pained him but there was absolutely nothing he could do about it.

CHAPTER NINE

When Wayne arrived the next evening he was eager to find out if the gossip was true.
Cornering Shirley in the kitchen, in hushed tones he asked what Aida had said.
"I ain't had time to ask her yet."
Turning his back, Wayne's next words were sharp in tone and she cowered slightly.
"Fuck me Shirl, I ask you to do one thing for me and you can't do it. I don't know why I waste my time coming here."
Shirley walked around so that she was facing him and just as he'd hoped, he saw the look of desperation and fear in her eyes. She was lonely and so as not to be alone, would do anything to stop him leaving, anything so that she wasn't on her own.
"Please don't say that sweetheart, you know I think the world of you and I couldn't cope without you in my life. I'll go and talk to her now okay? Best you wait in here as mums not in bed yet and I don't want her kicking off if she sees you, she might be fine but it depends on what mood she's in."
Slowly climbing the stairs she tapped on her grandmother's bedroom door and then walked inside. Shirley wasn't looking forward to the Conversation as her Nan could turn on a six-

Pence from being sweetness and light to the devil incarnate when she was put out.

"Hello my little darling, what can I do for you?"

Shirley sat down on the edge of the bed and then took her Nan's hands in her own.

"What do you know or understand about Facebook Nan?"

Aida frowned, what a stupid bloody question to ask.

"I do know, I suppose it's a load of idiots on those computer things just talking to each other about a load of old rubbish. Why?"

"Well, someone is looking for a Ruby Chilvers and says she had a baby and that she had it adopted."

The look of horror on Aida's face was obvious for anyone to see and Shirley's palm flew up to her mouth.

"Oh, my God! So it's true then?"

Aida took a moment to gather her thoughts and think about how she could get out of answering but she quickly realised that she couldn't. The secret, a secret kept hidden in the dark for so many years and now it was going to be out in the open. The one thing to console her was the fact that this Facebook thing was nothing to do with her so she was blameless

"Sweetheart it was a long, long time ago and best not to go opening up old wounds don't you think?"

It wasn't really a question it was rhetorical but Shirley wasn't bright enough to understand that.

"A bit bleeding late for that Nan, someone's looking for her and not talking about it ain't going to stop them knocking on the door any time soon now is it? I think you need to tell me everything Nan so that I'm prepared."

Slowly Aida revealed all and Shirley couldn't believe what she was hearing. When her grandmother had finally finished talking, they were both in tears. Shirley wasn't angry with her mother but at the same time, she was hurt that she had a sibling somewhere out there and she'd been denied the chance to get to know them.

"So you see my little darlin', your old mum really has been through the wringer. You going to tell Andy?"

Shirley thought for a moment, she hated lying but then not saying anything wasn't exactly as lie was it.

"Not for now Nan, I think it's best if we just wait and see what happens don't you?"

Making her way downstairs to the kitchen all she could do when she saw Wayne was to nod and then she broke down in floods of tears. Wayne held her close but he didn't really feel any empathy, all he wanted to do was stir the

pot and see what came out.
"We need to contact the person who's looking for your mum and do it as soon as possible before she finds this house. It will be easier that way and less stressful on your Mum and Nan."
Shirley kissed him tenderly on the lips, to her he was a good man and for that she was grateful.
"As soon as I've got Mum into bed we can get started but I really don't know what Andy's going to say about all of this Wayne. I've talked it over with Nan and decided not to tell him, that's unless things progress. He'll only create a stink and I just can't deal with any more stress."
As Shirley walked from the room Wayne Andino sniggered, this was going to be fun and finally, he would get one over on that cunt Andy. An hour later and the couple, at last, took seats at the dining table.
"Did you open an account like I said?"
Shirley shook her head, she'd been so busy and if she was totally honest, didn't have a clue what to do. Wayne frowned and she could see he wasn't happy but for once he didn't berate her. Instead, he opened up his laptop and logged into his own account. Scrolling down the posts he finally located what he was looking for.
"Here it is! Oh, it's from a woman so she must be your sister. How does that make you feel Shirl?"

"It can't be my sister as Nan said the baby was a boy."
"Maybe the old girl got it wrong. So, come on, how do you feel?"
"Well, I'm nervous I suppose but a little bit excited, I always wanted a sister. So, what do we do next?"
"I'll message her but I won't give too much away though."
Debbie Montgomery was just about to turn in for the night. Colin was already snoring his head off in the next room so she knew she wouldn't be able to sleep. About to log out she was shocked when she saw a message sign ping up in the corner of the screen. It had to be concerning Colin as she didn't use social media for anything else. Cautiously she clicked on the logo and couldn't believe what she began to read. The account was in the name of someone called Wayne but the message was coming from a woman.
'Hello, my name is Shirley Tanner and Ruby Chilvers is my mother. From the questions you have been asking it looks like we could be sisters?'
Shirley was about to have a real go at Wayne, he said he wouldn't give too much away but he'd lied. Angry and scared she was just about to voice her upset when his message was

answered.

'Hello Shirley, my name is Debbie and I am looking for my husband's family so unfortunately you possibly have a brother, not a sister. Colin doesn't know I'm searching for his mother so maybe it would be better if I came to see you before I let him in on things?'

Wayne was about to reply when Shirley grabbed his arm.

"Don't you dare!"

"If we don't arrange a meeting Shirl she will find your mum eventually, it's better if we sort this out, that way we can stay on top of things and if she ain't all that then we can simply say your old lady has snuffed it. What do you say?"

Shirley took a moment to think and then slowly nodded her agreement. It was further agreed that Debbie would travel to London the following Wednesday and would meet Shirley in Weavers Fields Park. Over the years swings, slides and benches had been installed and the area turned into a proper park. Shirley didn't know of her mother's history with the place and Debbie certainly wasn't aware that her husband had been conceived there late one night many years ago. Wayne was insistent that he would also be in attendance but for the first time ever, Shirley put her foot down. This was private family business and she was going alone. He

tried to change her mind several times but she wouldn't budge and eventually, he gave in and called it a night but on the understanding that she told him every last detail when she got back. Andy was calling in at the house almost every day but it was getting more and more difficult as the amount of work from Konstantin seemed to grow by the week. Ruby was demanding and Shirley looked worn out most of the time. Remembering what the doctor had told them he talked to his sister about mental stimulation.
"So, what do you suggest big brother as I don't think I can cope for much longer. Nan is going downhill fast and seems to be competing for my attention and as soon as I try and sort her out, Mum is calling for me. Honest to God, I feel as if they are tearing me in two."
"Look babe; try to get her on the internet."
Shirley just stared open-mouthed at her brother. While she loved her family dearly, he didn't have a clue what was going on in the house.
"You are fuckin' kidding me!?"
"Let her loose with a laptop, what harm can it do and like the doc said, she needs mental stimulation."
"I don't think that's a good idea."
"Why no, what harm could it do?"
"Well, for a start she wouldn't know how to use one."

"So? Even if tapping the keys is all she can manage, it will at least occupy her."

Shirley had backed herself into a corner, she couldn't tell him about Debbie Montgomery so she had no option but to agree.

"Okay but on your head be it. I'll get Wayne to sort it out but she'll probably only fuck it up."

"She will have one by the end of the day I promise, so need to involve the Greek."

Shirley's eyes narrowed and he knew he had spoken out of turn.

"Nothing too complicated Andy as it will only confuse her even more. See if they have one for a child."

Andy laughed out loud but he could see her reasoning. Kissing his sister on the forehead he set off for the High Street to go laptop shopping. Now sitting alone in the kitchen, the more she mulled over the idea the more Shirley thought it was at least worth giving it a try. She decided to get Wayne to open a Facebook account for her mum when he next came over after his class. If it brought her a bit of respite from her mother's incessant chatter then it would be worth it and possibly some of Ruby's old friends could be on there but she prayed if Debbie saw the account she wouldn't contact Ruby, at least not until after the two women had met at the park. A little over an hour later and her brother returned.

"What you got there Son?"
"Don't be a nosey parker Mum; it's nothing to do with you."
Andy placed the newly acquired computer onto the top of the kitchen unit knowing Ruby wouldn't be able to reach it. If he'd explained what it was for she would have hounded Shirley to set it up and he was sure that it wasn't something his sister would be able to do or if she could it would have been made all the more difficult with their mother looking over her shoulder and asking question after question.

The following Wednesday Shirley had asked the neighbour, Mrs Armitage, to sit with Ruby while Shirley went to the dentist. She hadn't bothered to ask her brother as he would want to know all the ins and outs and would probably sort out transport for her. It had been easier to tell a fib than to go into details, she hated lying to Andy but justified it to herself that for once it was the best thing to do under the circumstances. After promising Mary Armitage that she wouldn't be any longer than a couple of hours, Shirley nervously made her way to Weavers Fields. It was five to two and taking a seat on one of the benches she continually looked in all directions. Suddenly a woman approached, dressed in expensive clothes she made Shirley, in her jeans,

hoodie and trainers feel like a poor relation but when Debbie spoke her voice was soft and kind and Shirley knew that this was a woman she wanted to get to know.
"Hi, I'm Debbie; do you happen to be Shirley?"
Shirley nodded and readily accepted the coffee that Debbie handed her. There was a Costa close by and on the off chance she had purchased the two drinks as a kind of icebreaker, it seemed to be working.
"The last thing I want to do is to cause any trouble for your family Shirley but my husband is suffering. He told me that he doesn't know who he is like he's never truly belonged."
"Did he grow up in a kid's home?"
Debbie laughed; nothing could be further from the truth.
"No, he was adopted and was an only child. He didn't want for anything as his parents were very comfortably off financially but his mother, Lydia, she's a very difficult woman and that's putting it nicely."
Shirley laughed out loud when she heard this, difficult; she hadn't met Ruby or Aida yet.
"Anyway, he asked his mother about his real parents but she wouldn't tell him. By law, he now has a right to find out but I think he's scared. Unbeknown to him I took the bull by the horns so to speak and decided to do it for him.

So what can you tell me about any of this Shirley?"

"It's not good I'm afraid. My mum got pregnant when she was sixteen and back then you didn't keep a baby that was born out of wedlock or so me Nan told me. Everything I'm telling you has come second-hand from her."

Debbie hated interrupting but placed her hand on Shirley's arm for a second.

"You're telling me that your mum doesn't know we've been in contact?"

"No, but I'll explain about that in a minute. Anyway, the boy in question didn't even know me mum was up the duff."

The phrase made Debbie want to laugh, her own accent was almost perfect due to the private elocution lessons she had taken as a child but what she was hearing now was a typical cockney accent and she marvelled at the use, now and then, of the word me instead of my. For a second she wondered if that was how Colin's mother spoke and if she did how he would react to it. As much as it pained her to admit it, her husband was a snob and looked down on anyone that didn't speak perfectly.

"Mum was forced to have the baby adopted but me Nan says she never stopped thinking about him. She then met me dad and they had my brother Andy and then me. Denis Tanner was a complete bastard to us and me mum but thankfully he popped his clogs a few years back. Andy bought us the house and me Nan moved in when she couldn't cope alone. Now I get to the difficult part."

Debbie studied the young woman's face and could see that she was struggling to find the words she needed.

"Take your time sweetheart."

"My mum has Alzheimer's."

Suddenly Debbie felt as if she'd been kicked in the stomach. To get this far, to actually find Colin's biological family and for his mother not to even remember his existence was heartbreaking.

"How bad is she Shirley?"

"She has good days and bad. Sometimes it's as if she's normal and then others where she just has a meltdown and thinks I'm trying to do her in. Me Nan says she still talks about the baby but she's never mentioned him to me or my brother."

Debbie felt relief and she knew the feeling was selfish but if Ruby had good days then she would be able to meet Colin and hopefully tell him that she had always loved him.

"So what do we do now?"

"Well, I have to go home and talk to Colin. It won't be easy and I know he will feel that I've betrayed him by going behind his back but hopefully, once he's calmed down he will want to meet your mum. Will you tell her?"

"I don't think that's a good idea. Even if she ain't away with the fairies, if I tell her and he don't want to see her that would only upset her and I would rather slit me bleeding wrists than do that and besides, I ain't told Andy yet and for a fact I know he won't be happy about all of this."

"I understand completely Shirley, let's keep in touch via Facebook and see how it goes shall we?"

The two women stood up from the bench and when Shirley awkwardly flung her arms around the woman Debbie was shocked, to say the least. "You take care darlin' and I think I'm gonna like having a half-sister-in-law."

With that they parted and walked away in different directions, they were each deep in thought regarding the volcano that was about to erupt for both of them. Hopefully, the fallout wouldn't be too bad but Shirley knew her brother could go off like a bottle of pop if he didn't like something and Debbie knew that if she couldn't work her magic, Colin would refuse all contact and give her the silent treatment for weeks, it was something he had become fond of doing lately.

CHAPTER TEN

Andy continued to run his original business out of the warehouse and while it was still very profitable, he'd been forced to take his eye slightly off of the ball as Konstantin wanted him to be more involved with the houses and when Konstantin said jump if you knew what was good for you, you asked how high. Daily, Andy wished he'd never gotten involved with the Russians but there was no going back now, thankfully his second in command Rob Winter had taken over most of the warehouse and sourcing work but Andy had only given him a free hand up to a thousand pounds, any purchases over that and Rob had to run it past his boss first. He was a loyal bloke and while he might skim a few products off of the top if it was something he really fancied, he never took liberties and it was only if they had several of a particular item that he would indulge himself and Rob saw it as a perk of the job. Andy was aware of Rob's somewhat light fingers but he also knew that it was never things that were expensive and besides, everyone had to have a sweetener in their work, it kept them keen. The property side of things was booming and they now had fifteen addresses on their books, all in different stages of completion. The Polish and Lithuanian workers were good but as Andy couldn't understand the lingo, it could make things difficult at times.

Six months in and the problems had soon started to show. Recently it appeared that they were going through far more materials than usual. Andy had checked and rechecked to make sure he wasn't mistaken but when the sums still didn't add up, he decided to tackle the problem himself. Andy arrived at the biggest site early one Monday morning. The house was a large six-bed detached on Marlborough Place in St Johns Wood and it would hopefully command a sale value of around fifteen million. Purchased in a derelict state for five million with projected renovation costs estimated at three to four million there should be a good profit but somehow those projected costs had soared beyond belief and the profit forecast was now looking highly unlikely. Andy was on the ball and knew material prices had been hiked up by the suppliers but still, the vast amounts they were spending couldn't be explained. Walking into the main reception area that was being used as a temporary tea room, Andy nodded to the workmen and then asked Luka Emsky, the project manager, if they could have a word

outside in private. Luka was Russian by birth but had been in London for years and even though there was a slight accent his command of the Queens English couldn't be faulted. Standing over six feet tall and built like the proverbial brick shit house, to say that Andy was a tad intimidated by the man was an understatement. Although Luka's work couldn't be faulted, Andy had an inkling that he'd been taken on purely to keep an eye on everything and everyone and that included Andy.
"What's up Boss?"
"Well, you and the men are all doing a fantastic job Luka but we seem to be overspending and I can't work out where the costs are coming from or where they have been spent."
Luka stepped forward and only stopped when he was close to Andy, so close that Andy could feel the man's breath on his face.
"You calling me a thief Boss?"
"No, no not at all but I have to be accountable for what's being spent and the amount of materials purchased for this job in the last month is ridiculous and if I'm honest Luka, I can't see where they have been used and there is very little material wise that's laying around. Perhaps you can show me?"
Luka took a step back from Andy and placed his

massive hand on his boss's shoulder.

"You worry too much Boss. Everything is good, the job is on target and my men work hard."

Andy was nervous and his eyes darted around the room but stopped when he noticed something odd.

"I don't doubt that but you still haven't answered my question Luka and what's in all those boxes?"

Andy was referring to a wooden pallet containing a single level of small cardboard boxes with Chinese or some other oriental wording printed on the sides. Pushing Luka's arm away Andy walked over to the pallet and about to place his hand down he didn't even reach the surface before Luka grabbed him by the shoulder. Looking up he instantly noticed the menacing look on Luka Emsky's face and immediately he could feel the tension in the air. By no means a coward, he also wasn't a fool and knew he was vastly outnumbered should the rest of the workforce decide to stand up for their foreman.

"That is none of your business!"

Placing his palms up in submission Andy just shrugged his shoulders.

"Okay! Okay, have it your own way but don't say you haven't been fuckin' warned! I am accountable for this project and if it goes tits up there's no way I'm taking the flack because you couldn't get a handle on the spending. And, for your information, anything on this site is my business!"

Walking swiftly from the house he could feel several pairs of eyes boring into the back of his head and Andy only relaxed when he was once again in the safety of his car. When his phone began to ring he was glad of the distraction that was until he heard his sister sobbing on the other end.

"Whatever's the matter Shirl?"

"Oh Andy you have to get over here, Mums going nuts and I can't calm her down."

Racing back to the family home he was met with chaos as he entered. Ruby was having a meltdown in the front room and nothing Shirley was attempting would calm her. Aida was banging on the bedroom floor and calling out and to Andy it was nothing short of a madhouse.

"Oh thank God you're here! She's been like this for the past hour."

Ruby was pacing up and down, crying and pulling at her clothes. Backwards and forwards across the front room floor she seemed to get more and more agitated with every step she took. Andy made his way over to his mother and taking her hands, looked deeply into her eyes as he spoke in a soft gentle tone.

"Now what's all this about sweetheart, why are you getting' so upset?"
As soon as Ruby heard her son's voice she immediately simmered down.
"I can't remember, I can't remember anything Son and it's driving me round the bleeding bend. One minute I feel alright and the next I don't know me own bleeding name."
As if a miracle had just occurred Ruby Chilvers was now back to her old self but the time lapse between being lost in her dementia and returning to normality was getting shorter every week.
"I know darling but you ain't well and our Shirley is doing her best to care for you and Nan as well. Shirl put the kettle on, will you? Now sit down Mum, I'll just go and check on me Nan and then I'll be straight back."
Ruby grabbed his hands and stared up into his handsome hazel eyes.
"You're a good boy Andy and I love you very much."
"I know you do and I love you too sweetheart."
Giving her his warmest smile he walked into the hall, climbed the stairs and sighing heavily entered his grandmother's bedroom. Aida was sitting propped up in the bed and the look on her face was one of pure rage.
"Oh so someone's finally bleeding come to see

what I want then, I could have been lying here dead for all you lot knew."

He didn't have time for this and as his Nan had most of her faculties she was just playing up and it had to stop.

"Well if you had been then there wouldn't be a problem would there."

Hilda gasped at his words, never had her grandson spoken to her that way before.

"Look Nan there's no point in having a face like a smacked arse, this ain't fuckin' on! Me Mum has just had a meltdown and Shirley couldn't leave her to come and see to you! Now, if it's all getting too much, would you rather go into a care home? If that's what you want I can arrange it because our Shirl can't take much more. Between you and me mother, you're tearing her in two. If you keep pushing and she cracks, then where would you be?"

He knew the mention of a care home would put a halt to her bad behaviour, at least for a while.

"No! Please don't do that Andy, I'm sorry, really I am. I just get lonely stuck up here all day on me jack jones."

"Okay then but you have to play the game Nan and right now how things are with me Mum, she has to take priority. You could always go down and help Shirl you know, would you like me to get a stair lift fitted to make things easier for you?"

"Oh, that would be lovely boy."

Aida thinly smiled and nodded her head and it made him feel so mean but there was no other option. Kissing Aida on the forehead he told her Shirley would be up as soon as she could and then he returned to his sister in the kitchen. Shirley looked drained and he could clearly see her eyes were red from crying.

"I don't know how much longer I can do this Andy. She isn't sleeping, if I get a straight three hours a night I'm bleeding lucky before she has me up and out of bed."

"I'm going to get Nan a stair lift so she's got no excuse not to come down. As far as Mum's concerned, why don't you let me get you some help?"

"You mean have a stranger in the house? I don't think Mum would like that. They would be looking around and saying I ain't doing things proper or the gaff ain't clean enough."

"No, they wouldn't and darling it ain't all about mum, your needs have to come into it. Now I ain't talking about twenty-four-hour care but why don't I contact one of those agencies and get someone in say, a couple of times a week to give you a break? You could go shopping or for a walk?"

Shirley nodded and Andy hugged her before

taking a cup of tea through to his mother.
"Here you go, darling. Now how have you been getting on with the laptop I got you?"
Ruby smiled and for the next five minutes told her son all about the new friends she had on Facebook. His mother talked nonstop and he realised it was good for her to have an interest, it wouldn't stop the decline but if it delayed it just a bit it would be worth it. Within a couple of days it had been arranged for a stair lift to be fitted and by the end of that week help had also been hired. With Sue Pritchard now calling on Wednesday and Friday afternoons things quickly began to ease up. Ruby took to the young woman who was always polite and friendly and Shirley began to enjoy her time off even if it was limited. What none of them realised was the fact that Sue Pritchard was totally lazy and as soon as Shirley left the house she sat Ruby at the table with the laptop and then plonked herself down to watch television all afternoon. Aida hadn't taken to the woman so even though she now had a stair lift she chose to stay in her room when the help was in. She had tried to tell Shirley what the carer was like but referring to Sue as 'that fat lazy slob' did nothing to get her granddaughter on side. The only respite Shirley had was on the days when Sue Pritchard came to the house or when her

mother was playing about on the laptop. Shirley had got Wayne to sign Ruby up to Facebook and it seemed to occupy and ease the symptoms of her dementia but what Shirley didn't do was to regularly check what Ruby was up to and who she was talking to. Her mother had over a thousand friends and she posted every few hours. It was almost obsessive and a lot of her typing was just letters banged out on the keyboard and made no sense at all but it kept her happy and she ignored the trolls who berated her for her insane posts but sometimes, when her brain wasn't foggy and she was able to type with clarity her posts made sense. Occasionally she would receive a kindly word or just a like from someone with pity but then she would plague the person who had responded until they had no option but to block her. Keeping her mind active seemed to be helping Ruby and even if Shirley knew it wouldn't last for long it was worth it. Regarding Sue, if Aida was trying to put a spanner in the works and upset the applecart, she could think again.

Two weeks later and it was coming up to the property review date. Every few months Andy was required to report to Konstantin with the books and profit sheets and he hated it. Their friendship had declined over the last couple of

months and he'd soon realised that he had been used, pure and simple. Walking into the Chairman, the bartender pointed to the end of the bar where Konstantin sat reading a Russian newspaper while drinking from a small expresso cup. As Andy approached Konstantin looked up and pointing to his cup, smiled at his visitor.
"Drink?"
"No thanks pal I can't stand the stuff, wouldn't mind a nice cup of Rosie though?"
Konstantin nodded to the barman who looked Russian but had in fact been born and bred in Barnet.
"So how is it going? Is this a swift visit or do we need to go into the backroom so you can spread your papers out?"
"We have a big problem and I think that would be a good idea, Konstantin."
Konstantin slowly closed and then opened his eye before silently getting to his feet and walking towards the back room. Andy followed closely behind and he wasn't looking forward to the ensuing conversation that he was in no doubt would cause voices to be raised. When they were inside and the door had been firmly closed, Konstantin spoke.
"So, what's happened?"
"We're spending far more than was planned and there's no reason for it. I tried to ask Luka but

he just got arsey and, to be honest, he got a bit threatening. Now I ain't talking about a few grand here Konstantin, it's over thirty. Then there are the boxes."

"What fucking boxes?"

"A pallet with a load of what looks like shoe boxes with Asian writing on them."

"Oh, those boxes!"

"You know about it!? What the fuck is going on?"

"Calm down my friend, take a seat and I'll explain everything."

Andy was angry but he knew better than to show his feelings, Konstantin was alright so long as you didn't piss him off and Andy had seen the consequences of what would happen if you did, thankfully he had only been a spectator at the time but the victim was made to violently suffer before being killed. Waiting until the tea had been brought through; Konstantin then circled the room as he spoke.

"My business partners back home found out that one of the major building suppliers here in the UK, purchase some of their kitchen brands from overseas, especially from China and especially white goods. We have been placing large orders with this company and before the cargo sets sail for England, the mechanics are removed and the items are packed out with heroin and cocaine.

When the delivery arrives the boxes are taken out and the white goods are dumped. So far we've been extremely lucky but should that luck run out then we will deny any knowledge. The Chinks are slippery bastards at the best of times and as far as Customs are concerned, they could be sending the class A over here themselves. But I'm not one to count my chickens as the saying goes and that's why Luka didn't want you touching the cargo and leaving any prints."
"Fucking drugs! I never signed up for that mate."
"Maybe not but you're in it now and there's no going back my friend."
"So going over budget isn't a worry to you then?"
"Of course not, and as you've already said, we could in all probability make a small loss on that particular property but the gains, albeit illegal, are far, far greater. Don't concern yourself with losing out on your sale percentage, you will be well compensated. Now if there isn't anything else, I would like to get back to my paper."
Konstantin smiled but it wasn't genuine and Andy gathered up his paperwork without speaking another word. As he walked through the bar towards the main doors he could see that the Russian was already engrossed in his newspaper. He didn't know if it was intentional

but he had been made to feel completely humiliated. He was now part of a drug smuggling ring and he hadn't even been consulted. Konstantin was sly and Andy accepted that the Russian would sell Andy out with no hesitation if things went wrong. Once again there was nothing he could do but go along with things until he could make his escape and that escape had to come soon before things fell apart and he lost everything.

CHAPTER ELEVEN
LAGOS, NIGERIA

Obi Adamu took a seat at the table and wondered what the day would bring; he wasn't looking forward to standing on the corner and just hoping that today he would get picked for a day's work. Money coming in had been slim over the last month and he didn't know how much longer they could continue. His wife Chioma, affectionately called Chi-Chi by her friends and family, was always after money and Obi would swear his wife was able to spend in her sleep. On the day they married, Obi had promised her a home and fine clothes but when he wasn't able to make those items materialise and when Chi-Chi was forever complaining, he knew they had to search out their fortune elsewhere. Originally from the small town of Jimeta which was close to the Cameroon border, the couple decided to head to Lagos in search of a better life. With a distance of over eight hundred miles and with no buses running they had to wait until they could get a lift, at least for some of the way. Luckily a friend of Chi-Chie's family, Abiola, was a lorry driver and was about to make a trip to Enugu. He offered the couple free passage but informed them the trip was long and that it wouldn't be comfortable. The couple were desperate and just as they had been told, the trip took over thirteen hours and they were stuck in the back of the lorry in the searing heat. Abiola did stop a couple of times to eat and rest but that was the only time Obi and Chi-Chi were able to get out into the fresh air. Plastic pots had been provided so that they could at least go to the toilet but Chi-Chi felt humiliated as she relieved herself in front of her husband. When the rear door opened for the final time she cried with happiness even though she knew they would have to find transport for the remainder of the journey. Fortunately, there was now a bus route and as Chi-Chi took her seat, she sighed with relief. When they at last arrived, neither of them had expected Lagos City to be so big or so busy, with a population of just under twenty-six million it made Obi think of an ant colony. It was hot and humid and Obi's shirt was wet to the touch within a few minutes. In reality, the climate was on par with Jimeta but body heat from so many people made it feel even hotter. A room was booked in the budget Oak Hotel and as soon as they opened the door Obi saw Chi-Chi's face drop. The furnishings were old and battered and the room hadn't seen a lick of paint in years. The air conditioning buzzed so loudly it could only be used for a few minutes at a time, that's if you wanted any peace. At a cost of five thousand, Nigerian Naira per night, about five pounds sterling, the couple only had enough money to last them for ten days. It was Obi's entire life savings and when it was gone the couple would be destitute. With Chi-Chi refusing to look for work, stating that she was now a wife and hopefully, soon she would be a mother, that's if her husband pulled his socks up, it was down to Obi to provide for them both.

The day after they had arrived, he set off early and headed for the financial district but with just a basic education, he was laughed out of every business he enquired at. By the third day, he was full of utter despair and disappointment, not only with not finding a job but with how his marriage was panning out as well. In the late afternoon sun, he took a seat on a bench, placed his head in his hands and tried to think of something he could do, anything that would stop them from having to return to Jimeta and the shame that it would bring.
"Excuse me Sir but are you okay?"
Looking up Obi's eyes met the face of a kind-looking man about the same age as himself. The man held out his hand and shook Obi's warmly.
"I'm Babak Madueke but my friends call me Baba. You look as if you have the weight of the world on your shoulders, my friend?"

"You are correct but I don't seem to be able to do anything about it."

"Why don't you tell me, a problem shared can often be solved?"

Obi didn't need to be asked twice, he doubted the man could help but just to unburden his load would help. Obi told about his lack of education, his lazy ungrateful wife and how they had moved to Lagos in search of work but that he hadn't realised it would be so difficult.

"I see, well I might just be able to help you."

In the grand scheme of things, Babak Madueke wasn't a bad person and surviving in this country was challenging, so it went without saying that a man will do anything to feed his family and that's how it had begun for Babak, in the beginning at least. It turned out he was a tech wizard and had started a scamming network two years earlier. Now the rewards enabled him to live the high life and he wasn't about to quit for anything. Always on the lookout for new employees, he saw something in Obi, maybe it was just the desperation but even that would always force a man to work hard and that was the kind of people Babak needed. Obi suddenly sat up straight and listened intently to every word.

"I want to pay for you to attend Lagos City Polytechnic to study IT for six months. I will provide adequate housing for you and your wife and a good salary while you are training. When you complete the course, all I ask is that you work for me for a minimum of three years. After that time you may remain in my employ or leave."

Obi couldn't believe what he was hearing and vigorously nodded his head.

"Oh thank you, Sir, thank you."

"Wait! There is a catch as with all attractive things in life. My company scams rich Westerners out of their savings. Now I know this is probably not the sort of work you are comfortable with but it is very profitable and why should they have all that there is to offer in this world when in this country we struggle just for food and shelter? These people have bulging bank accounts but are still greedy for more so if they lose a small percentage, who is it really harming?"

The shock on Obi's face was evident and about to refuse the offer he suddenly stopped himself. Why should others always have wealth? His mother had raised him to be kind and giving but living on the high moral ground had got him absolutely nowhere, well now it was his turn to have a good life.

"I understand and I can live with that if it means giving my wife everything that her heart desires."

Racing home to Chi-Chi he couldn't wait to share his news though the exact details of what he would be doing he kept to himself. By the end of the week, the couple picked up the keys to their new apartment on Toyin Street. Listed as a luxurious self-contained one-bed apartment, once again Obi saw his wife's crestfallen face as they stepped inside. It was just one room with a small toilet and shower cubicle in nothing more than a cupboard in the corner and the kitchen was basic and situated in a lean-to on the side of the building. The one saving grace was the fact that it had been recently decorated and Baba had promised them a delivery of good quality furniture which would arrive the following day. Obi took his wife in his arms and stared into her enormous eyes, eyes he had fallen instantly in love with on their first meeting.

"I know this isn't what you dreamed of Chi but it's certainly better than the hotel and as soon as I qualify and start earning some real money I promise I will find us somewhere you can be proud of."

Chi-Chi roughly pushed his arms away and as she walked from the apartment she screamed at him.

"Promises, promises!! That's all you ever give me Obi."

Just as they'd been told, the furniture arrived on time and it was good quality with only a few marks of wear which slightly lifted Chi-Chi's mood. By the end of the next day the small space resembled a home and for the first time since leaving Jimeta Chi-Chi was able to cook in her very own kitchen.

Two days later Obi started at the polytechnic and to say he threw himself into his studies was an understatement. He excelled in every aspect, so much so that he actually completed the course two weeks early, much to Babak's delight.

Babak Madueke ran his small BM tech company from a modern office in the Central Business District of Lagos. He paid his staff well and paid his taxes on time, leaving no reason for the government to investigate him. In total he employed eighteen staff, ten, what he liked to refer to as scouts, staff who scoured the internet for any leads that could result in a lucrative scam. Those leads were then handed over to a higher level and the lengthy work could begin. It could take weeks, even months for a plan to reach fruition but when it did it was usually vast, at least by Nigerian standards. Babak wanted Obi at the higher level, he was adept and quick to learn and Babak knew that after some intense training, he would be a valuable member of staff but more importantly, earn Babak lots of money. It was a long game but his newest employee had a kind manner and would be good at cultivating relationships with prospective victims. For his first couple of cases, Obi was given small investment opportunity scams and after all of them had been successful he was handed a file and given twenty-four hours to read and memorise the information. He decided to take the papers home with him and spend the evening making notes and writing down possible role-play scenarios. Chi-Chi had cooked dinner but wasn't interested in talking to him; she had recently become fixated on the re-runs of the Nigerian soap 'Tinsel' and was glued to the television at every given opportunity. After eating his food Obi took the folder outside and began to read but by the time he finished, he was morally torn in two. Someone was searching for a woman and Babak's scouts had managed to track this person down. The poor woman had been forced to give away her child, what right did he have to cause her even more pain by raking up the past? On the other hand, he needed to provide and if he refused, Babak might well fire him. With a heavy heart, he knew what he had to do and closing the file he went inside, dreading what the next day would bring.

It had been a good morning all in all, Ruby's memory loss had only bothered her for a small amount of time so she had behaved and given Shirley some peace for once. When she had finished her lunch and while Shirley was washing the dishes Ruby got herself comfortable at the table and opened up her laptop. Recognising the Logo Ruby clicked and as she read the message her hand flew up to her mouth and then she slammed the lid shut. Her eyes darted in all directions, she couldn't believe what she had just read and gradually raising the lid again she slowly took in each word.
'Hello, my name is Colin and I am trying to find my mummy and I think that might be you?"
Ruby felt the tears as they began to well up in her eyes and she studied the profile picture of the man messaging her. His beautiful white skin and amazing head of blonde hair reminded her of Joey and suddenly she was back in Weavers field on the night that at the time, had been so special but had quickly turned into a nightmare. Unbeknown to Obi, the women in the office couldn't have chosen a better profile picture. Personally he didn't like it but if it did the job then who was he to complain. With one finger Ruby began to slowly tap in a message. Her spelling was poor but if you took your time then her words were just about readable.

'Is that you Colin? Oh Colin I've waited for such a long time."

Bingo! Obi had made contact and even at this early stage, he could tell that his victim was vulnerable which again caused him uneasiness but as Babak passed Obi's desk and slapped his employee on the back, Obi knew he had no option but to begin the chase. The researchers had done a good job after spotting Debbie Montgomery's plea on social media and after delving further had been able to locate Ruby Chilvers.

"Yes Mummy it is me your son and I've waited such a long time too."

"Where are you Colin, when can we meet?"

"Soon I promise, I just have a few loose ends to tie up and then I will travel to England."

Ruby's brow furrowed, she was confused, how was her baby in a different country? There was a pause and Obi wondered if he'd lost her. Babak had instructed them to never reveal their whereabouts and to use a fictitious country but in this case, maybe it was a bit too much.

"Oh of course mummy I realise you're unaware that I live in Holland. The couple who adopted me took me there when I was still a baby but I have been desperate to find you."

Ruby relaxed but how dare they have taken her child all the way to Holland. Well, when he returned she was going to make sure he stayed. Obi kept the rest of the conversation short, it was better to leave them hanging so after making the excuse that he had to go back to work he told Ruby that he would be in contact very soon. Disappointed, she closed the laptop and then stared at Shirley who was engrossed in some silly afternoon TV programme. She so badly wanted to share her news but even the dementia didn't stop her from remembering that none of them, except for Aida, knew of Colin's existence.

In Lagos Obi closed his computer and sat back in his chair, it had been a successful afternoon's work. This was his third case and after the other two had paid out well, Babak had been pleased with the results. Of course, the peopled he scammed kept trying to contact him and Obi would continue with the fake relationship right up until the moment the cash had run out or they realised they were being scammed. Heartlessly he would then block the person, never to be bothered by them again. Only once during this current assignment would he feel any real guilt and would wake up in the middle of the night covered in sweat but when Babak, strangely before he had even completed his assignment, handed him a very generous bonus, the guilt would immediately evaporate. Life for

Obi Adamu and his wife Chi-Chi was good and now he was going to be able to afford all of the beautiful things he had promised her on their wedding day.

CHAPTER TWELVE

It had been two weeks since Debbie Montgomery had met up with Shirley. Since then the women had kept in constant contact via social media but Debbie was yet to reveal anything to her husband and deep down Shirley wondered if she ever would. With Mother's Day fast approaching Debbie realised that there was no better time to come clean so she put her plan into action. No matter how busy their lives were, the couple had always kept Friday nights just for them, now referred to as a date night and would go out for a nice meal or to the theatre. Debbie booked a table at Midsummer House; it was one of their favourite restaurants, expensive but special to them both. The couple only lived a ten-minute stroll away but more importantly, for Colin at least, it was Michelin starred. Debbie loved her husband dearly but he could be the proverbial snob at times which she didn't find particularly endearing. That night she prepared a nice meal and just as they had finished she broached the subject of their approaching date night.
"I've booked Midsummer House for Friday evening darling."
The look of excitement on her face was evident and he didn't have the heart to disappoint her

but for the first time, he had been about to cancel their special night. Colin had recently begun an affair with his newly appointed secretary Tracey Baxter and had made plans to whisk her away for a dirty weekend. Now that Midsummer had been booked, a place that was difficult to get a reservation for at the best of times, he would have to put up with Tracey's miserable face at work for the next week.

"How on earth did you manage that?"

"I phoned on the off chance and fortunately for us, they had just had a cancellation. How lucky was that and I know you love it there."

"Yes, I do darling and thank you."

Inside Colin was seething but Debbie would never know that. He was fond of his wife but the marriage hadn't turned out as he'd expected and he hated the boredom of it all. With Tracey it was exciting, the sex was off the wall and for the first time in ages he felt alive. Friday came around all too quickly and to begin with, the evening was a success. The restaurant was full but then that was nothing unusual. The couple, being regulars, were looked after well and Colin enjoyed the food so much that he almost forgot that he should have been shafting his secretary. Tracey was so tight and he couldn't get enough of her but never mind, his wife would have to satisfy him just for tonight. Debbie leaned across

the table and tenderly took her husband's hand.
"I need to talk to you about something Colin."
His eyes suddenly narrowed with panic and also suspicion.
"You're not pregnant are you?!"
That would have been Colin's worst nightmare and in any case, he didn't envisage spending the rest of his life with Debbie, something he'd realised a few months into their marriage. She was sweet enough and quite easy on the eye but he hankered after more excitement and that journey didn't include his wife. Debbie laughed out loud; sometimes he really did come out with the strangest of things.
"No silly of course not. I've managed to locate your mum."
Immediately he pulled his hand away and his brow furrowed.
"What!? Why, why on earth would you do that?!!!!"
Getting to his feet, Colin threw his napkin onto the table and glared at her.
"You had no right, no right at all Deborah!"
Storming from the dining room, Debbie, red-faced with embarrassment, was left to settle the bill. The other diners were staring and even the waiter that had served them felt sorry for the poor woman. With her shoulders back and with as much dignity as she could muster she walked

from the room and out of Midsummer House. Colin was nowhere to be seen so not only had he embarrassed her, he had left her to walk home alone across the park in the dark. Sighing heavily she nervously set off but she hadn't got more than a hundred yards when she heard someone running up behind her. Turning on her heels as fast as she could, Debbie was relieved to see it was her husband.

"Thank God it's you, I was getting a little uptight, and you never know who's about in this park after dark."

"I'm so sorry Debs I never should have reacted that way; it was just a bit of a shock that's all. Come on, let's go home and you can tell me everything you've found out."

Debbie looked at him amazed, he'd changed from a monster into the man she loved and she was completely confused. Unbeknown to her he wasn't being nice, he'd had time to weigh up the situation and he definitely couldn't afford a divorce at this time in his life.

"Okay, but why you behaved as you just did, I have no idea. You know I would never do anything to hurt you so why you acted like that I just don't understand?"

"I'm sorry alright? This is a big deal for me Deb and I'm just not sure that I'm ready."

"Well if you're not ready now then you never

will be. Time is so important and it could be running out darling."
The couple talked long into the night as Debbie revealed all about Ruby and Shirley but she left out the bit about Ruby's dementia. Debbie thought that just might be too much at the moment and by the time she'd finished Colin had somewhat reluctantly agreed to a meeting.
"What if it all goes wrong Deb's?"
"Then at least you tried, imagine if something happened to your mum, you would always wonder what if I'd met her, what would it have been like?"

The next day after Colin left for work, Debbie opened up her laptop. She couldn't wait to tell Shirley and just hoped her half-sister-in-law was online. Thankfully Ruby was still asleep and Shirley was able to use her own computer without interruption. Recently Ruby had been glued to her own screen every waking moment and continually disturbed her daughter when she was online. When she saw the message pop up, Shirley couldn't believe what she was reading.
'Hi Hun, I told Colin last night and he wants to arrange a meeting.'
Shirley took a moment to think things through, she was being underhand by not telling Andy

but she was only too aware of what he would be like if she revealed all that had happened. Finally, she replied but her message had her worrying from the moment she pressed send.

Andy was becoming more and more concerned about Konstantin's dealings and after mulling things over for the whole day, he decided to seek out further advice from Bobby Richmond.. A little before nine that night Andy headed over to the Pink Flamingo. As usual, Bobby was holding court and it was something Andy loved about the man. Bobby was known for his hospitality, he was also very funny and people gathered around him like flies on shit. Spying his friend, Bobby made his excuses and shook off the two buxom blondes that were hanging onto his every word and walked over to where Andy stood watching the ridiculous shenanigans of his friend.

"Well, you're a turn-up for the books, ain't seen you in ages!"

"Been busy Bob but by God I need your advice now."

Bobby could see the fear etched on Andy's face but he didn't mention it. Winking, he placed his arm around his friend's shoulder.

"Say no more, come on up to the flat and tell me all about what's worrying you."

When drinks had been poured, the two men took a seat on the dilapidated old sofa that had seen more action than a soldier on the front line. Andy revealed what he had found out regarding the drug importing and when he'd finished Bobby just sat there open-mouthed.

"Fuck me that's heavy stuff. Is the Russian aware that you know?"

"It was him who told me after I started asking too many questions. Money laundering is one thing but importing fucking drugs!? How the fuck do I get out of this crazy shit Bob? If it goes tits up, the only one the Old Bill will be interested in is me; it's my name on all the order forms even if I don't know what's going on most of the time."

"For once I'm lost Pal, I do know that a good shag will help you figure things out, at least it always helps me. How long since you've emptied your sack?"

This was the last thing he wanted to hear from Bobby but Andy just smiled and shrugged his shoulders.

"Come on then, let's go get you sorted. There's a nice little piece downstairs that will suit you just fine. I've been trying to fuck her for the last couple of months but she ain't having any of it. You on the other hand are just her sort. You can bring her up here if you like?"

Andy looked around the room and his expression spoke volumes.

"Don't worry; I put clean sheets on the bed this morning so it must be your lucky day after all."

Making their way back down to the club, Bobby guided his friend over to the bar where several women, all stunning to look at, were enjoying cocktails and eyeing up the talent.

"Anastasia, this is my good friend Andy."

The woman smiled and Andy was instantly smitten. With long legs and a body fit for any model, Anastasia Petrov was every man's dream. Her accent was impeccable so Andy had no idea that she was Russian as Bobby hadn't revealed her surname. He also conveniently forgot to mention that she knew Konstantin and was even on the man's payroll. The two danced for a while and when Andy invited her up to the flat she readily accepted. Within seconds of closing the door, the two were greedily exploring each other's bodies. Anastasia, known to most as just Anna, had removed her figure-hugging dress with one swift pull and Andy's toned upper body was already bare.

Passionately kissing, they almost fell through into the bedroom and Andy was pleased that Bobby had been true to his word and the room was clean. Pushing him down onto the bed, Anna moved down his torso and unbuckled his trousers, then released his rock-hard penis with expertise. Next, she took his entire length into her mouth. Andy groaned in pleasure as she slowly slipped his manhood in and out while caressing his shaft with her tongue. Just as he was about to climax she moved her body on top of his and took his long shaft of meat inside of her. Riding him like a bronco, it wasn't long before they both climaxed. With laboured breath and glistening with sweat, the couple lay side by side on the bed. Neither spoke for a while, the moment was too good to spoil with chatter but a few minutes later Andy was good to go again. The sex continued into the early hours and by the time they were finally exhausted, Bobby had been right, Andy felt more relaxed than he had in quite some time. Turning on her side so that she was facing him, Anna smiled.

"So Andy, what is it that you do?"

"Do?"

"You know, for work?"

"A bit of this and a bit of that."

Andy laughed and then placing his hand onto her arm, revealed that he was in construction along with a business partner and that most of their work consisted of renovating large London properties.

"But what is it you actually do?"

"Well, a bloke called Konstantin provides the cash and I run the whole shebang but to be honest I want out. It wasn't what I signed up for and that Russian cunt is taking the piss. So, what do you…."

He didn't continue when he felt the muscles in her arm tighten in fear.

"Do you know him? Konstantin Ivanov?"

Anna didn't reply to the question, the only words she uttered were 'I have to go' and then grabbing her dress she scrambled off of the bed and disappeared from the room. Andy was confused and after slowly dressing, he checked that she wasn't in the bathroom and then made his way back down to the club. The Pink Flamingo was about to close up for the night and spying Bobby at the bar, he walked over and tapped on the man's shoulder.

"Oi, Oi! Filled your boots then I see?"

Andy was in no mood to make jokes and with a serious look on his face he spoke in a hushed tone.

"What do you know about her Bob?"

"Anna? Why?"

"Well, when I mentioned Konstantin she clammed up and scarpered as quick as a flash."

"Oh fuck me, you mentioned him! I didn't think you were going to talk to the slag, just fuck her! She works for him and don't ask me what she

does because I ain't got the foggiest. Oh mate, what on earth did you tell her?"
"Nothing really, she was gone as soon as I mentioned his name."
"Well thank fuck for that. You'll just have to wait it out and see if she tells him."
"Ain't anything to tell, unless she expands and tells him more than I shared, you know what birds are like. Look, thanks for tonight but I'd better get off now."
Andy then raised his eyebrows and sighed, which thankfully went unheard with the dying noise in the club. Saying his goodbyes he made his way to the rear of the Pink Flamingo where he'd parked up. Alone inside his car, he didn't start the engine for a while as he ran over everything in his mind. He hadn't said anything wrong, or at least he didn't think he had so hopefully he wouldn't be in any danger but he'd wanted help and had hoped that tonight he would find a solution to his problems, instead, he'd possibly created even more. There was nothing for it, he would go home, take a shower, try and get some sleep and then tomorrow he would visit the Russian to find out if anything, had been relayed back.

CHAPTER THIRTEEN

Ruby Chilvers had now been messaging the stranger on Facebook for over a week and she still couldn't quite believe that her Colin had actually gotten in touch. Sitting and waiting for him to come on line was always nerve-wracking as she knew she wouldn't be able to cope if they lost contact again. Shirley studied her mum and when she saw Ruby just staring at the computer screen she thought it was Ruby's dementia and that her mother was on another planet somewhere. Finally, the message icon popped up and once more mother and son were reunited. Obi told her all about his wife and daughter who he called Susan and how happy he was. He decided to invent a fictitious pregnancy for his daughter, hoping that the woman wouldn't be able to resist her first great-grandchild.

'So Mummy, do I have brothers and sisters?'
'Yes my darling, you have a brother called Andy and a sister called Shirley.'
'Do they have children? Do I have any nieces and nephews?'
'No sweetheart so yours will be my first great-grandchild and I haven't even met my granddaughter yet. When can we meet Colin, I'm so desperate to see you and your family."

Colin or Obi, was fishing, trying to find out about other relatives and any possible complications they could create.

'I desire to see you too Mummy but I have a few financial problems and I cannot come to England until I am able to sort them out.'

Ruby didn't question his strange command of the English language as all she could think of was holding him in her arms again. It had been so many years, years that had felt like an eternity.

'I'll help you, sweetheart.'

'Oh thank you but I don't think you can, I have to pay twenty thousand euros this month alone.'

Ruby thought for a moment, she didn't know how much money she actually had anymore, Shirley took care of her pension so what was in the bank she really didn't know. Each message took several minutes for Obi to receive and the woman's spelling wasn't very good. Ruby had never been academically adept but the dementia was slowly robbing her of the little she had learned way back in her school days.

'Let me see how much money I have and we can chat again tomorrow.'

After sharing typed kisses, the chat ended and Ruby switched off the laptop and made her way as quietly as she could up the stairs. As she tiptoed passed Aida's bedroom she could see

Shirley helping her grandmother to wash and the two were arguing but that wasn't anything new. Creeping further along the landing she was able to get into her own room without being seen or heard and she was as excited as a little child, sadly another symptom of her worsening Alzheimer's. With the door pushed shut but not quite closed, Ruby slowly pulled out a large metal box from under her bed. All of the family's important documents were kept there, birth certificates, pension and bank documents, anything that Andy might need if he had a problem to sort out for his family. Opening the lid she lifted out her bank books but there was little more than five hundred pounds in total. Spying papers addressed to her from a bank in the Cayman Islands she took her time and read as much as she was able. Ruby didn't understand it but she did know what the box at the bottom of the page showing the figure five and lots of zeros meant. Pulling out more letters, four more to be exact she read all the figures and knew she was rich beyond her wildest dreams. Ruby didn't know how she had accumulated so much wealth or why her children had never told her about the money but she didn't care, it was in her name and that meant she would be able to help her boy. Folding the letters neatly, she tucked them into the front pocket of her apron, an apron that she still insisted on wearing everyday even though she didn't cook or clean anymore. Giggling like a child she tapped the fabric, pushed the box back under the bed and made her way back downstairs without being seen or heard.

Up with the larks, Ruby refused breakfast and just sat staring at the computer screen. Shirley could only sigh in frustration but if her mother was happy then so be it, at least it gave her more time to concentrate on her Nan and Aida was becoming more cantankerous by the day. She was however concerned at her mum's lack of appetite and decided to monitor the situation, if she refused her lunch then Shirley decided she would call the doctor's surgery. Just before noon, Ruby saw the first message appear on the screen and she beamed from ear to ear as she clapped her hands together.
'Hello mummy, how are you today?'
'I'm fine Colin thank you sweetheart and I've found a way to help you out of the muddle that you are in. I appear to have far more money than I realised, lots and lots of money actually.'
Ruby proceeded to tell her long-lost son all about the bank accounts she had found and when Obi saw the figures typed on the screen he couldn't believe what he was reading. Hardly

able to contain his excitement he called out loudly to Babak.

"Boss! Boss you have to come and see this!"

Sitting at his desk but with the door fully open, Babak stopped what he was doing and stared over at his employee. When he saw the wide grin on Obi's face he was more than a little intrigued. It had to be something good as Obi would never shout at him; he was usually such a quiet polite man. Strolling out into the communal office he headed over to Obi's desk.

"What's wrong?"

"Look! Look at this!"

For a few seconds, Babak studied the screen then turned to face his employee.

"Surely that can't be right?"

"I don't know, she does seem a bit simple but I would like to continue just in case. It could be too big of an opportunity to let go without delving further."

Babak patted his employee on the shoulder and nodded his head.

"I agree, keep me updated Obi, this could be our biggest deal to date."

Obi returned to the chat and thanked Ruby very much. He then told her that he had to go to work but he would be back in touch later in the day. With a broad smile, Ruby closed the laptop just as Shirley entered the room.

"What are you grinning about Mum?"
"None of your business, you are far too nosey at times my girl. I might be getting old but I do still have a right to my privacy."
"Okay, okay, keep your knickers on. Now, are you going to have a bit of lunch?"
Ruby nodded her head and Shirley sighed with relief, a call to the Doc wouldn't be necessary after all.

The meeting between Colin, Ruby and Shirley had been set for Friday morning. Shirley had chosen it as she knew it was Andy's busiest day at work so there was less chance of him dropping by the house. She had asked Debbie and Colin to come to Chudleigh Street so that Ruby would be in the comfort of her own home, there was less chance of her having a meltdown if she was in familiar surroundings. Shirley was yet to break the news and she wasn't sure how her mum would react. By the time Friday came Obi had already scammed one of the accounts to the tune of five million. Ruby had handed over the account number and password; she also told him that there was plenty more if he needed it. Obi had decided to leave it for a few days until he made another move but the two still chatted daily online. He wanted to keep her sweet and continually told her how he longed to see her and that he wished she had been the one to raise him. As Ruby read the words her heart melted and she would have given him anything within her power. Closing the laptop she jumped when Shirley leaned over her shoulder and began to speak.

"Mum, we have some visitors coming today."

"Don't do that! You scared me half to death and besides, you know I don't like strangers in the house Shirley. Anyway, I'm busy today so you will just have to tell them to go away."

"And why exactly are you going to be busy today?"

Ruby was getting angry with the questions so she just blurted out 'I have to talk to my son'.

"You mean Andy?"

"No I don't, I mean Colin."

She waited for the barrage of questions but strangely they didn't come.

"I know all about him and he's coming to the house Mum; he's coming to see you."

Jumping up from the table Ruby began to dance around the room as she sang her words.

"He's coming, he's really coming, my baby's coming to see me!"

Shirley smiled, she ignored her mother's earlier comment about talking to Colin as it was probably just the dementia, it couldn't be anything but that.

"So are you going to have a wash and put a clean dress on? You don't want him to see you looking scruffy do you?"

In the past Ruby had always been so well turned out, not one to wear makeup, she had still taken pride in her clothes but since her illness had progressed, it took enormous effort on Shirley's part just to get her mother to clean her teeth. Her clothes always had the remnants of the previous day's food down the front and sometimes she would refuse to change them for several days.

"I'm never scruffy but I will make an extra effort today for my boy."

Ruby then made her way upstairs as fast as she could. Shirley slowly shook her head, just to see her mother willing to wash and change was a relief. Usually it turned into a war of words and at times Ruby had even struck her daughter when Shirley pushed too hard. Less than ten minutes later her mother entered the front room wearing her best dress. Shirley had to force herself to stifle the laugh that was desperate to escape her mouth; Ruby was wearing bright pink lipstick and electric blue eyeshadow. To say anything would hurt Ruby and Shirley would rather die than do that. Debbie had been warned about the Alzheimer's and Shirley just hoped she had shared that with her husband or it was going to be one hell of a shock.

On the morning of the visit Debbie was up at seven, she had planned the trip with military precision but getting Colin out of bed was another matter altogether.
"Darling if you don't get your act together we will be late; it's at least an hour's journey you know."
"I'm not going."
Debbie momentarily stopped applying her lipstick and turned to face her husband who had rolled over in the bed and then proceeded to pull the duvet up so high that she couldn't see his face.
"I beg your pardon?"
There was a muffled 'you heard me' and Debbie marched over to the bed and yanked the duvet to the floor. Her husband slept naked and he wasn't best pleased to have his lower body exposed even if it was to his wife.
"What the hell are you talking about Colin?!"
"I said, I am not going! What part of that sentence, do you not understand?!"
Taking a seat on the side of the bed Debbie took his hand in hers and tenderly smiled.
"It's just nerves love and no one can blame you. I mean it isn't every day you get to meet your mother after so many years but we really can't

let them down at this late hour."
"She is not my mother, she just gave birth to me that is all."
Debbie Montgomery spent the next hour trying to talk her husband into attending the meeting but he wasn't having any of it and finally, she was forced to accept his decision.
"For the last time Deb I'm not going! Do yourself a favour and just leave it will you."
They should have been on the road over an hour ago and now with or without him she was going to be late which was rude and cruel considering how ill her mother-in-law was, the poor woman must have been so confused when Shirley broke the news, that's if she could even remember having a child and giving it away in the first place. Tapping a quick message to Shirley via her phone, she told the woman that she would be at least an hour late but she didn't let on that she was going to be arriving alone.
"Well I'm still going Colin, they are expecting us and it would be bad-manners to just not turn up."
"Please yourself. Say high to Mumsie for me."
His sarcasm was cutting but as she glanced over her shoulder he had pulled the bedcovers up and over his head again. Debbie grabbed her car keys and slammed the front door as she left but Colin was already on the phone to his secretary

Tracey and was too engrossed in his text to notice that his wife had gone. Within ten minutes of Debbie leaving, Tracey's car pulled into the drive. It was the first time she had been to his home and to say she was impressed was an understatement. The property was on a lovely road, a very expensive road and it was large and furnished beautifully, even if that was down to the current Mrs Montgomery. If Tracey played her cards right, it could one day all be hers, she just had to get rid of his wife first. Opening her coat to reveal nothing but a pair of black lace panties, Colin's eyes were instantly out on stalks as he answered the front door. "Hello, handsome."

"Get up those stairs Miss Baxter I need you to do a spot of dictation."

Tracey giggled and as she passed him at the bottom of the stairs he smacked her backside and licked his lips in anticipation.

Debbie pulled up at Chudleigh Street exactly one hour later than planned and as she locked the car she could feel the onset of nerves. Tapping on the door she waited for it to be answered and as she did she smoothed down her long dark hair and wiped the corners of her mouth in case her lipstick had bled into the crevices. When Shirley opened up she didn't meet Debbie's gaze and looked passed her sister-in-law, desperate to get a glimpse of her half-brother. Not seeing anyone she looked at Debbie quizzically.

"I know this isn't what we planned Shirley but he's changed his mind and there was absolutely nothing I could do to make him come. I'm so sorry, it's cruel and he's wrong in his decision." Even though she tried her best to hide it, the disappointment on Shirley's face was evident.

"My boyfriend Wayne started all of this and now I really wish he hadn't. Would you still like to meet Mum?"

Debbie moved forward and tenderly took hold of her half-sister-in-laws hand.

"Of course I would and thank you."

Walking into the front room, Shirley instantly saw Ruby sitting and staring at a blank computer screen again. Debbie didn't say anything for a few moments, the resemblance between the woman and her husband was remarkable. Maybe once she had been introduced Ruby would allow her to take a picture on her phone. If Colin saw how alike they looked he might have a change of heart.

"Mum, this is Debbie and she's Colin's wife."

Ruby studied the stranger standing in her front room and then smiled.

"Pleased to meet you, where's my boy?"

Taking a few steps forward Debbie smiled.
"I'm so sorry but in the end, he couldn't make it, work stuff."
"Oh I understand, he told me he was very busy but it doesn't matter as he will message me later."
Debbie and Shirley could only stare at each other completely perplexed. Shirley then made them all tea along with a plate of expensive biscuits that she'd bought especially. There was general chitchat but when Ruby asked about her granddaughter Debbie didn't know what the woman was talking about or how to answer. Not wanting to upset Ruby she just said 'She's fine thank you'. A short while later and after she'd managed to take a photograph, Debbie realised it was time to be on her way before any more ridiculous questions were asked so Shirley walked her to the door.
"I'm sorry about that but it's the dementia, she really thinks she's a Nan to some non-existent child but I can't hurt her by telling her it's all in her head,"
"Of course, you can't sweetheart and what are a few little white lies if it makes an old woman happy."
The question was rhetorical and even Shirley knew not to answer. The two women hugged and swore to meet again soon before Debbie got

into her car and drove off. She contemplated going up west to do a spot of retail therapy but then thought better of it. Colin had taken the day off of work and it would be nice to go home early and surprise him.

CHAPTER FOURTEEN

Unaware of what was happening at his family home; Andy had been paying his weekly visit to each of the sites. It was just before four on Friday which meant payday; none of the foreign workers would accept a cheque, so it required him to hand deliver the cash. The end of the week always made Andy nervous, carrying a briefcase, almost full of cash, meant he was a perfect target for thieves. It would only take loose lips from one of the men for a planned robbery to take place and he was sure Konstantin would never accept he'd been mugged of the payroll without being in on it. So afraid that the situation could easily happen, Andy had recently begun to take his old employee Rob Winter along. There was safety in numbers and besides, Rob had nothing to do with this side of the business so he didn't ask too many awkward questions. In all honesty, Rob wasn't bothered why he was being taken along, a change of scenery once a week wasn't to be sniffed at so he had no complaints. Arriving at the house on Marlborough Place in St Johns Wood and the last destination of the day, Andy told Rob to stay in the car. Luka Emsky enjoyed putting fear into people, it was a joke to him,

especially when it involved Andy and Andy didn't want to put Rob in that situation.
"Boss."
"Afternoon Luka, is everything going to plan?"
"Sure is."
Making his way inside Andy, along with Luka, walked from room to room handing out the wages. When there was only Luka and himself left he handed over the Russian's pay, nodded his goodbye and was about to leave when Luka grabbed him by the arm making Andy spin around in fear.
"Boss wants to see you."
There was no need to mention Konstantin by name and instantly the order, because that's exactly what it was, instilled panic in Andy.
"When?"
"As soon as I pass on the message, so I would say within the next half an hour."
The distance between Marlborough Place and Dean Street was just shy of four miles but the journey would take at least thirty minutes, possibly longer as it was Friday and everyone in the city would be rushing to get home for the weekend. Returning to the car Andy handed Rob a hundred and told him to get a cab. Rob looked at the money and then smiled, first pub on the way would do nicely and a hundred would pay for a lot of drinks. As if Andy had

read his mind he raised his voice slightly.
"And I want the change!"
Rob sighed, nodded and then headed off down the road, whatever his boss was mixed up with he was clad that it didn't include him. Just as Andy had anticipated, the traffic was horrendous and he didn't walk into the Crown & Two Chairman until well after five. As usual, Konstantin was sitting at the bar drinking coffee only this time he wasn't alone. On a stool beside him sat Anastasia Petrov and she stared hard at the visitor as he approached.
"Konstantin. Anna."
Konstantin had been waiting to see if Andy acted like he had never met the woman which would have got the meeting off to a very bad start. Andy had gambled on the fact that she had told the Russian everything that had happened on the night they spent together so he was going to be upfront and act as if it was nothing of consequence.
"Luka said you wanted to see me?"
"Let's go through to the back. Anna, bring us some drinks."
The beauty didn't speak and instead made her way around to the back of the bar. The two men walked along the rear hallway and Andy could feel there was tension though he didn't know why until Konstantin spoke.

"Was she a good fuck?"
"In all honesty, I'd had a skinful and can't remember. Look, if she's your woman then I'm heartfelt sorry Konstantin I never…….."
Konstantin held up his hand and stopped Andy midsentence.
"No, she is not though I have fucked her several times. She may well be beautiful Andy but sluts like that are ten a penny and can never be trusted. I need you to pack a bag and your passport and meet me back here at seven tonight."
"Why?"
"We have to take a little trip; my bosses wish to meet you. It will only be for two nights and our flight leaves Heathrow at nine. Are you okay with that?"
Andy knew it wasn't really a question; he had no choice in the matter. Feeling a knot tighten in the pit of his stomach, the thought crossed his mind if he would be returning from Russia in one piece.
"Yes, of course, Konstantin. Do you know what it's about?"
Just then the door opened and Anna walked in carrying a tray containing two glasses and a bottle of Vodka. Placing them down onto the table she turned and walked back out again without saying a word. Anna didn't

acknowledge Andy in any way and he found it strange considering how intimate they had been.
"They don't confide in me I'm afraid but I'm sure all is well."
Pouring them both a drink Konstantin raised his glass in the air as he said 'Nah zda-rouh-yeh!' Andy replied with 'Cheers' though inside he didn't feel he had much to be cheery about. Declining the offer of a refill, Andy left the pub and made his way home, he had wanted to pop into his mums to check everything was okay but now there just wouldn't be time. Tapping his phone he called his sister and when Shirley saw who the call was from she swallowed hard. Lying to her brother didn't sit well but she couldn't share anything with him just yet.
"Hi Andy, how's things?"
"All good thanks sweetheart, I was going to pop in but I have to go on a business trip tonight so I won't get there until sometime on Sunday. Mum okay?"
Shirley took a moment before she answered and looking over to where Ruby sat engrossed in her laptop she smiled.
"She's fine brother. So, where are you off to?"
He didn't want to tell her the truth so instead he told her he was going to Spain.
"Nice for some I must say."
He knew she was joking but at the same time it

was sad that his sister had never been out of the country, never been out of London in fact or laid on a beach or swam in the ocean and it was all down to him and his need for her to take care of Ruby.
"I promise I will take you away soon darling. I'm going to sort out some care for Mum and then whisk you off to somewhere hot for a week. I have to go now sweetheart as I need to pack. You take care and I'll see you the day after tomorrow. Andy ended the call and just hoped he would get to see his family again but it was by no means a certainty.

As Andy had been making the wage payments, Debbie Montgomery had pulled into her drive. She frowned when she saw the strange car parked in front of the garage, maybe it was one of Colin's clients as it wasn't unusual for him to see clients at home. Being as quiet as she could so as not to disturb them she let herself inside. Closing the door without a sound, she suddenly heard giggles coming from upstairs. Her chest tightened, she wasn't ignorant and knew there was only one explanation. Debbie didn't want to go up there but something deep inside forced her to climb the stairs. Her heart was beating double time and her feet felt like led and climbing each stair took strength. Slowly turning the handle on the bedroom door she suddenly flung it wide open only to see some strange woman riding her husband like a bucking bronco. They were so deep in the throes of passion that they hadn't heard her enter and walking over to the bed she stared down at her husband who was experiencing so much pleasure that he had his eyes tightly closed. Suddenly Tracey Baxter glanced sideways and when she glimpsed Debbie she shrieked out forcing Colin to open his eyes. He didn't say a word and just stared at his wife open-mouthed. Debbie felt as if she was about to vomit, the pain she was feeling was worse than anything she had ever felt physically. Running into the en-suite she just made it in time to the toilet basin and then hurled up the entire contents of her stomach. Tears streamed down her face and she could hear them racing around in the next room as they tried to get dressed. When the front door at last slammed and a car engine could be heard starting up she finally entered the bedroom and expecting Colin to have gone she was surprised to find him sitting on the edge of the bed with his head in his hands. Debbie walked from the room without speaking a word and when he realised that his tears were not working Colin called after her.

"Deb! Debbie please, it's not what it looks like."

"No of course it wasn't Colin."
Strangely, his sad voice as he tried to make something up made her smile. Down in the kitchen she made herself a coffee and sat at the breakfast bar knowing that he would appear any moment to plead his case. Right on cue, five minutes later he walked in and looked as sheepish as a little boy who had been caught out smoking or some other such childish prank.
"Can we talk?"
"I'm not stopping you but there isn't anything you can say that will make things better."
Colin saw something in his wife's eyes that he had never seen before, a cold hardness, almost as if she was numb to any feelings she might have had for him.
"It's only happened the once I promise."
Debbie laughed out loud in a sarcastic manner and he didn't like it, she was making him feel like a liar, which is exactly what he was.
"If you think I believe that you are an idiot. You had me Colin, I adored you. I never refused you intimacy and yet you bring that whore, because that's exactly what she is, into our home and you have the audacity to fuck her in our bed! Do you actually believe that she would be interested in you if you weren't a bank manager and live in a lavish house? Well, she can have you because I will never forgive you. The most important

things in our marriage, for me at least, were trust, loyalty and above all else monogamy. I want a divorce and don't try and talk me out of it as it would be futile."

"What about my job? What about my promotion and my career?!"

"What about them?"

"If the head honcho finds out I will be overlooked for any promotions, fuck, I could even lose my job. Damien Preston the CEO is all about family values and he would find some way to get rid of me."

"Probably and I can see why you are so worried, shame you care more about your job than you do for me. So, I have a deal for you. I will keep my mouth shut and you can carry on seeing your little trollop but I want you out of this house. I will attend any social engagements you need me to until the divorce comes through. You will not contest it and will allow me to file for adultery."

"That's a bit…."

"I haven't finished yet Colin. You will give me half of your investments and don't try to be sneaky as I know exactly what you have. You will also give me half of our savings and I get to keep this place as I can't afford to buy another and I don't see why I should lose my home when you have caused all of this. My parent's holiday home is not up for discussion either and it will remain solely in my name. If you don't agree to my terms then I will fight you in court and believe me, it will get very messy. It's a one-time offer, non-negotiable and will cease to be on the table in the next thirty minutes. So, what's it to be?"

Colin Montgomery didn't speak for several seconds as he mulled over the offer. It wasn't what he wanted but on the plus side he could soon earn more to make up for his losses and at the end of the day he would get to be with Tracey every night.

"Deal, when do you want me to leave?"

"Now and you are not to come back for anything! At least not without asking my permission first."

Colin left the room and a few seconds later she heard him stomping around in their bedroom. A few minutes after that, she heard him descend the stairs and walk out of her life forever.

Taking a bottle of white wine from the fridge, Debbie grabbed a glass and made her way into the front room. Glancing all around at the stunning furnishings her eyes stopped at the beautiful French clock they had purchased in Paris on their honeymoon. Then there were the expensive pictures that hung on the walls, all bought on various trips they had taken together.

In the past, the items had been her pride and joy as they held such sweet memories but now she couldn't bear to look at them anymore. Tomorrow they would be up for sale and Debbie didn't care what she got for them. Colin had driven straight to Tracey's flat. Situated in a converted Victorian house it wasn't what he expected and definitely not what he was used to. Loud music could be heard coming from the top floor and as he made his way to her first-floor apartment he could hear shouting and screaming from the flat below. He knocked on the door and then sighed heavily as he waited for her to answer. To say she was shocked was an understatement when she saw who was standing there.

"Colin! What on earth are you doing here?"

"I've left my wife, it was a choice between you and her and when it came down to it, there was no choice darling."

It was a complete lie but it had the desired effect as Tracey wrapped her arms tightly around his neck. Holding onto him she sexily kissed his neck as she imagined all the things she could buy when she eventually became the next Mrs Montgomery.

"Deb has agreed to a divorce and to keep her mouth shut until it's finalised. You have to do the same Tracey, as far as the big boss knows, all

is fine in the Montgomery household."
"So I don't get to move into the big house?"
"No, part of the agreement is that Debbie gets to keep it."
"The greedy bitch!"
"Tracey! Please don't talk about Debbie like that, she's the innocent party in all of this. I no longer love my wife but I do have a deep respect for her."
Tracey Baxter didn't like what she was hearing but if it meant having all the luxuries she desired then she was happy to oblige, after all, she wouldn't be married to him forever. As cunning as Colin was, Tracey Baxter was ten times worse and had planned this from the moment she had started working at the Bank. Admittedly it had all happened a lot faster than she had expected but on the bright side, within the next five years, she could be married and heading for divorce. The only downside was the fact that Stevie, her long-time boyfriend, wouldn't be able to come to the flat for a while.

CHAPTER FIFTEEN

As Debbie Montgomery's life was falling apart, Andy had packed and was on his way to the Crown & Two Chairman. Pulling up next to Konstantin's Range Rover in one of only two parking spots at the rear of the pub he grabbed his overnight case, locked the car and slowly shook his head at this absurd situation as he went inside. The place was buzzing with the weekend crowd who had finished work for the week and had money to burn. Unlike in the daylight hours, there were two burly doormen now on duty, Russian of course. Konstantin was seated in his usual place and as Andy made his way through the hordes of drinkers he could feel his heart beating wildly in his chest. This was all so wrong; why the fuck had he got mixed up with these people in the first place. On the drive over he had mulled over everything in his mind but couldn't for the life of him reach a conclusion as to why they wanted to see him on their home turf. The only saving grace, as far as he could see it, was the fact that he held all of their money and no matter how corrupt and brutal these people were there was no way, without him, that they could get their hands on any of it. The place was so rammed that he was

almost level with Konstantin before the man saw him. Glancing at his diamond-encrusted Rolex, Konstantin smiled.
"Dead on time as usual, shall we go?"
Knowing it wasn't a question, Andy didn't bother to reply.

Flight BA0194 from Heathrow to Moscow left on time and Andy was impressed by the service he received. The first-class seats were leather, roomy and extremely comfortable and when dinner was served on china plates he smiled to himself, this wasn't what he was used to, even his trips to the Cayman island paled into insignificance compared to this. The journey would take three hours and forty-five minutes but there was little conversation between himself and Konstantin, which concerned Andy. In the past they had talked freely about all manner of things but now there was only an awkward silence. Resting his head he tried to get some sleep but his mind was racing with a hundred different scenarios making it virtually impossible. When the plane landed at Domodedovo airport it was eleven local time and Andy was tired beyond belief. Thankfully there was no queuing and the two were swiftly escorted through departures to a waiting limousine.

"Fuck me; I've never gotten through an airport that quickly before."

"Amazing what can happen when you're connected, my friend."

It was the first time Konstantin had used the word friend in a long time and Andy wasn't sure if it was just a turn of phrase or if he did mean it, somehow he didn't think so. The journey continued for another wearing hour and a half but finally, they came to a stop outside the Carlton Hotel in the centre of Moscow. Striding into the foyer, Konstantin booked them both in as Andy took in the opulence of the place. The Hotel was decadent and over the top and naturally, there was a lot of gold leaf everywhere but it had been done very tastefully. The Russians certainly liked their bling but he supposed it was the result of so many years of poverty and oppression. Within a matter of minutes they were shown up to their rooms and Andy was first to enter but as he went to close the door he heard Konstantin's voice.

"Andy, do not leave the hotel under any circumstances; I will let you know when the bosses want to see us."

Hearing the door click shut Andy sighed heavily, he didn't want to be here, didn't want to be a part of some mafia network and just longed to be back at his warehouse trading in dodgy gear and happy with his lot. This world was beyond him and even though he liked the vast amounts of cash he'd been receiving, he would trade it all in a second if things could just go back to how they were. The bedroom was as classy as the rest of the hotel and Andy could see that no expense had been spared, surely if they were about to top him they wouldn't have laid out a bucket load of cash on this place. Staring out of the window he took in the view and Red Square looked amazing even at night. It was now past two am and yawning widely he knew he had to get some sleep. Kicking off his shoes he lay down on the bed and didn't know anything more until he woke a seven the next morning. Breakfast had been pre-ordered by Konstantin and was served via room service. The food was traditional and not really to Andy's taste, he was starving and could eat a horse and chase the jokey as Ruby always said but when he lifted off the silver plate covers he was disappointed. There was some type of porridge, doughnuts, Russian black bread, apple cake, some kind of stuffed buns called Piroshky, potato pancakes and Russian tea which Andy found revolting. Eating a couple of the doughnuts because he was ravenous all he could think of was one of Mable's full English fry-ups at the café on Newham High Street. By midday he was bored senseless, there were no British channels on the television and any films on offer had been dubbed in Russian with no subtitles. Lunch was served at one pm and was as dismal as breakfast, for a five star hotel Andy was far from impressed with the food. Luckily he fell asleep again and only woke when he heard Konstantin knocking on the door. Opening up he glared at the Russian.

"Thank fuck for that I'm bored shitless and what's with all this strange grub? I'm fucking Hank Marvin."

Konstantin ignored the rhyming slang and the rude question and walking straight past Andy, he entered the bedroom.

"Right, we have been summoned to Aurora's tonight at eight."

"Aurora's, what's that?"

"It's a club and where my firm operates from, their office if you like. I just want to give you a few tips on behaviour. Dress smartly, be polite and most importantly of all, don't speak until they speak to you which they may or may not do."

Andy sighed and rolled his eyes, this was a total nightmare.

"For fucks sake Andy, if you do any of that tonight it won't go down well. A car will be collecting us at seven forty-five so be ready

because they don't tolerate lateness."
It was now just before five so deciding to take a leisurely bath to kill some time, Andy walked towards the bathroom ignoring Konstantin. Thankfully a few seconds later he heard the bedroom door close.

Ready and waiting Andy sat on the end of the bed when the knock came at the door. The two men made their way down the foyer where a burly, Stoney-faced man was waiting for them. The drive to Aurora Men's Club took just over ten minutes and the journey was taken in complete silence. Something had changed between them but Andy didn't have a clue what or why, maybe Konstantin was as scared as he was. The club was loud and filled with cigar and cigarette smoke, something Andy wasn't used to since the ban had come into force back home. As they made their way down the grand staircase Andy held onto the highly polished chrome rail and wondered how many men before him had come down these stairs to meet their fate. Drum and bass music loudly bleared out making it impossible to think straight let alone hear anything being said to him. Konstantin led the way through the crowds and passed the bevvy of beauties dancing naked on the stage. When they reached the members area

Konstantin stopped at the plush velvet central booth where three men sat. All were well into their sixties and dressed in outdated seventies suits with open-necked shirts revealing oversized gold crosses. Andy swallowed hard, he had never seen men who looked so menacing and he could feel the bitter acid as it began to fill his cheeks. About to take a seat he was stopped when Konstantin grabbed his arm and whispered in his ear.

"We do not sit until we are invited."

The three men, in turn, spoke to Konstantin but Andy hadn't got a clue what was being said and in all honesty he didn't care, all he wanted was to get the hell out of here and onto the first plane home. Images of the airport left his thoughts when one of the men, who introduced himself as Lev Baranov, spoke to him. Andy stammered slightly as he answered.

"So Mr Chilvers, what do you think of our beautiful motherland?"

"V, v, very nice thank you."

The man laughed as he drew on a massive cigar but it wasn't genuine laughter and it unnerved Andy. Realising this must be the big boss he again swallowed hard when he noticed the man nod his head, which was an indication to Konstantin for something or other to happen. Whispering in Andy's ear Konstantin told him it was time to go but when they reached the stairs, instead of going up Konstantin led him to the other side where another flight went down to only God knew where. Andy puffed out his cheeks; with the heavy aroma of the cigars he was starting to feel physically sick. Well, this was it, this was where it would all end and he hadn't got the first idea why. On the lower floor, they walked along a corridor, equally as ornate as the rest of the club. Reaching a set of heavy wooden double doors, Konstantin pushed them both open together to reveal what Andy could only describe as a dungeon. The walls were built in raw stone as if the room had been carved into the side of a rock face. Four men, all as big as the doormen up in the club, stood staring at the far end wall and as Andy and Konstantin walked over, Andy recoiled at the sight in disgust. Hanging from chains on the wall were a man and a woman. Both were naked, bloodied and beaten and he could instantly tell that the woman was already dead. Her stomach had been sliced open and her entrails hung down to her ankles. The guts were still steaming so Andy knew it had only just happened and he wondered if this horrific act had been carried out as a show just for him or if he was indeed next on the list. The hanging man was pitifully screaming out in Russian but his cries were in vain, his aggressors showed no pity and the drum and bass music from the club above could be heard pounding a beat so loud that it made it impossible for his cries to be heard by anyone upstairs.

"Fuck me, Konstantin! What the hell is going on?"

The Russian turned and Andy couldn't believe he was actually grinning as if he was taking pleasure at the sickening scene in front of them.

"These two traitors worked for my bosses. They stole from us and then decided to leave so don't feel pity for them. Stupid idiots, to think they could get away with it and us not to find out. This is what happens to anyone who tries to leave our network Andy and my bosses wanted you to witness their punishment first-hand."

Suddenly it all became clear, Anna had indeed opened her mouth and that's why he was being taught a lesson and the reason Konstantin had cooled towards him. The chained man was still pleading for his life and his eyes kept darting sideways towards the dead woman, a woman he had loved and who he'd had to watch die in the most brutal way, right in front of his eyes. Suddenly one of the men stepped forward and drew a razor-sharp knife deeply down the thigh of his captor. Blood spurted out and the man screamed in agony.

"Fuck this for a game of soldiers, I'm outta here!"
Andy strode off towards the doors and he could hear Konstantin laughing out loud as he walked out but before they closed behind him, the screaming suddenly stopped. Up in the club, he just waited by the stairs, he didn't have a clue where the hotel was or how to get transport. Luckily a few minutes later Konstantin walked up the stairs.
"Did you kill him?"
Konstantin's eyes narrowed as he spoke and the look sent a shiver down Andy's spine.
"Not personally. Now give me a moment, I won't be long."
Making his way over to his bosses he must have given them a report and then after saying his goodbyes Konstantin returned to Andy. The driver was waiting outside in the car and the return journey was again taken in silence. Andy stared out of the window, in shock at what he'd just been witness to. He had always been able to take care of himself if it came to a fight but what these men did was on a different level altogether. Back in his hotel room, he laid on the bed for a while. Their return flight wasn't until eleven the following morning so Andy reluctantly undressed and tried to get some sleep. As he relived all that he'd seen a single

tear ran down the side of his face. Those poor people, no one deserved that! Animals were the only description he could come up with for the Russians but even that was an insult to animals, maybe monsters was a better description.

The next morning he received the same shit breakfast via room service and again all that he could stomach was a couple of small doughnuts. The two men didn't speak on the way to the airport and only passed the odd yes or no during the flight. Customs was relatively swift and traffic was light so with the time difference they reached Soho at just after two. When Konstantin's Range Rover pulled up at the rear of the Crown & Two Chairman, Andy was all set to get straight into his car but was stopped by the Russians words.
"Come inside, we need to talk in private."
The pub was full of Sunday lunchtime drinkers so they didn't bother entering through the bar and instead walked straight to the office via the rear door. Andy was desperate to get back to the peace of his flat so he hoped he wasn't going to be forced into too much conversation.
"I assume you are still reeling from all that you saw?"
Andy could only stare at the Russian and no words passed his lips.

"You should be more careful who you confide in my friend. The whore you fucked is loyal to me and my bosses and told me straight away that you are unhappy and that you want out. Obviously, I was duty bound to inform Moscow and last night was to show you what will happen if you ever contemplate leaving us. You have to understand Andy, when you join a business such as ours you become family, a family that you can never leave."

"Pity you didn't fucking tell me that when you conned me into all of this."

Konstantin frowned and slowly shook his head as he spoke.

"I didn't con you into anything my friend, retribution and greed was your mistress and you would have agreed to anything she asked."

"Maybe but you didn't tell me exactly who was involved and why."

"Are you really that naive? Did you honestly think that a group of businessmen would invest millions into your tin pot company without conditions? Go home, rest and think about this conversation. I will not raise the subject again and I hope we can continue doing business as before. The decision is yours Andy but if you chose to leave then rest assured they will hunt you down and you will not live long enough to enjoy your freedom and the same will go for your mother, sister and grandmother."

Andy was filled with fury and right at that moment he knew he could have ripped out the man's throat just for mentioning his loved ones but he didn't and instead, he turned and left the office without a goodbye. He had just been threatened and there was no way to retaliate. As he climbed into his car he decided now more than ever he had to find a way to escape. It would be far more difficult than he'd first thought but nothing was impossible and deep down he was prepared to take the risk but the one thing that bothered him was Ruby and Shirley, his Nan as well, how would they cope with being taken off to some far-flung place with no option? In the grand scheme of things, it was better than dying and at least there would be a mountain of cash to help ease the transition. Deciding to go straight over to Stepney and the house on Chudleigh Street, Andy pulled out onto the main road. He was desperate to see his family and make sure they were happy and well, if only for the time being.

CHAPTER SIXTEEN

Before he'd even put his key in the lock Andy could hear horrendous screaming and shouting coming from inside the house. As he entered the front room he couldn't believe what greeted him, his Nan sitting at the table with her head in her hands and surrounded by the dirty plates and cutlery from lunch. Ruby was pacing up and down waving her hands in the air and Shirley was following her doing all she could think of to placate their mum but nothing was working.
"Come on Mum please don't be like that. Whatever's got you so wound up, please tell me and maybe I can help."
"You can't, you can't, you don't know him." Ruby was now constantly wringing her hands together as she paced back and forth.
"He said he would message me today and he hasn't and he said he would."
"Who said they would message you, darling?" Suddenly Ruby lashed out and caught Shirley on the side of the face. Her daughter winced and pulled away so that she was out of her mother's reach. Suddenly everyone stopped when a voice boomed out.
"What the fuck is going on in here!!!? I could hear you out on the street! Mum? Shirl?"

Shirley ran over to her brother and flinging her arms around his neck she began to sob uncontrollably.

"I can't go on Andy, I can't do this anymore. Look at this."

Pulling up the sleeve of her jumper she revealed an arm covered in purple bruises and Andy could tell that they were fresh. He also didn't need to ask who had inflicted them as he whispered in her ear.

"Do you still have any of those sedatives the quack gave you?"

Shirley nodded her head.

"Go and fetch a couple make mum a cuppa and then dissolve them."

Walking over to Ruby Andy took her hands in his and she stared up into his face but her eyes were like glass and dead as if nothing was going on inside of her head.

"Come and sit on the sofa Mum and tell me all about it, maybe I can sort it out."

Ruby smiled and for a fleeting moment she was back in the real world. Doing as he'd asked she sat down.

You're a good boy Andy and mummy loves you very much.

"So come on then Mum, let me know what's got you so upset."

For a few seconds, she looked at him and was

desperately trying to remember what it was and suddenly it all flowed back, her motherly instinct was far stronger than dementia, at least it was at the moment.

"My son said he'd message me but he hasn't and I'm worried someone has hurt him, you see he owes people a lot of money. I gave him some but maybe it isn't enough, maybe they have got to him."

Andy didn't have a clue what her ramblings were about but he decided to play along, he would do anything so long as it calmed her down.

"I see, so would you like me to look into it for you Mum?"

"Would you, would you do that for me, darling?"

"Of course, I would. Look here's our Shirley with a nice cup of tea."

As she glanced up to take the cup, Ruby noticed her daughter's tear-stained face.

"Andy, why has our Shirley been crying? What's wrong Shirl, why have you got a red mark on your cheek darling."

"Don't you worry about that for now, just drink your tea and have a rest and I promise I'll get to the bottom of all of this Mum."

Taking a seat at the table with Shirley and his Nan, Andy waited for the drugs to take effect and it wasn't long before Ruby's head was resting on a cushion and she was snoring softly.

"So, would either of you like to tell me what the hell has been going on here?"

"Don't look at me; I'm in me room most of the time. But I will say it's like a bleeding looney bin at times."

Aida then stared at Shirley as if the young woman would have all of the answers but she just shrugged her shoulders.

"All I can say is that she spends hours in front of that bloody laptop just staring at the screen but please don't take it away Andy. It gives me a bit of piece and you've now witnessed what she can get like. I think it's time we thought of a care home."

"No!!!!"

They both stopped dead in their tracks at Aida's outburst.

"You are not putting my girl in the nuthouse. I've seen what they are like and it was going into one of them that killed my old mum."

"Nan, it's not like that anymore. Look, what if we promised to show you any place we find before we do anything? Deal?"

Aida took a few moments to mull over what had been suggested. She didn't like it but through pursed lips she nodded her agreement.

"Deal but it had better be like fuckin'

Buckingham Palace or my Ruby stays here!"
Andy heavily sighed, what a load of shit to deal with and he already had enough on his plate.
"I think we're jumping the gun a bit. Shirley go and get mums laptop would you."
Switching the machine on, Andy, with Shirley's help, logged on to Facebook. When Wayne had initially set up the account Shirley was adamant that she wanted the password. As it was her mother never logged out but just in case, Shirley would able to reconnect Ruby with her newfound friends. Scanning through the posts there was nothing out of the ordinary though Andy did take offence at some of the posts that the trolls had written; people could be so cruel and were real scumbags at times. Next, he went down the messages and there was correspondence with only one person, someone by the name of Colin. Along with her brother Shirley read each message and her eyes were wide open when she saw what her mother's long-lost son had supposedly written.
"What the fuck is all that about?"
Shirley didn't reply and as Andy continued to read he suddenly had a sinking feeling in the pit of his stomach. The penultimate message had been when the bloke was thanking Ruby for the money but saying that it wasn't enough and then the last message from Ruby was just a list of

numbers.

"What on earth are those Andy?"

He didn't answer and in seconds he was out of his chair and running up the stairs as fast as his legs would carry him. Dropping onto the floor with a thud in his mother's bedroom, he peered under the bed and sighed with relief when he saw that the box was still where he'd put it. Sliding it out he lifted the lid but apart from his mother's old bank passbooks, it was empty. Frantically searching the room he emptied drawers and side tables, he even pulled the mattress off of the base but he still couldn't find what he was looking for. Now he was sweating and coming back down the stairs he rushed over to the dining table.

"Where are the papers?"

"What papers?"

"A while back I put a box under mum's bed for safekeeping. It had paperwork for my business and money that I'm looking after for some associates, fuckin' nasty associates if I'm truthful. The box is almost empty Shirl and I'm in deep fuckin' shit."

Shirley Tanner glanced over at her mother and suddenly noticed something sticking out of her apron pocket. Walking over she gently lifted the papers out and returned to the table.

"Are these what you're looking for?"

Andy opened them up and nodded his head. Logging onto the Cayman accounts he wearily typed them in one at a time. As each filled the screen revealing zero balances he could feel the nausea beginning to rise from the pit of his stomach.
"Fuck no! Fuck, fuck fuck!!!"
"You okay Andy only you ain't half gone a funny colour."
"Am I acting as if I'm fuckin' okay!!?"
Shirley's bottom lip began to quiver and he knew he had spoken out of turn; none of this was her fault.
"I'm sorry darling but no I'm not Shirl; I'm in trouble, deep, deep trouble. I think we all are!"
"What's mum gone and done, is it anything we can put right?"
Andy rested his forearms on the table and massaged his forehead with his fingers trying to work out what to do.
"No sweetheart, there isn't. It's gone and I will be held accountable I'm afraid."
"So what you going to do?"
"The only thing I can do is go and admit to what's happened and hope the men I mentioned can come up with a plan that doesn't include topping me."
Shirley sat bolt upright in her chair.
"They wouldn't really do that would they,

Andy?"

Even though she was well in her thirties, his sister was so naive, so sheltered and he slowly shook his head from side to side.

"I'm afraid they would babe and not bat an eyelid over it. I need to get off now, if mum remembers and kicks off again when she wakes up, tell her I'm trying to sort it out for her."

With that Andy stood up, kissed his sister on the top of the head and then reluctantly set off for the Crown & Two Chairman. As predictable as ever, Konstantin sat at the end of the bar on his stool, a stool that anyone in the know wouldn't dare to sit on. It was now the lull between the lunchtime drinkers and the Sunday night crowd, who were desperate to escape the house after being forced to spend the whole day with their families. A master at reading expressions and just by taking one look at Andy's face, Konstantin knew something was very wrong. Stepping from the stool he headed towards the backroom and without a word being spoken Andy followed closely behind. Not until the door was firmly shut behind them did either man speak. Konstantin took a seat at the table but Andy continued to stand as he nervously began to explain.

"I have some really, really bad news."

Konstantin lifted his open palms upwards

signalling for Andy to continue.

"I have to start at the beginning so that you will understand how dire the situation is. I've never shared this with you but my mum has early onset but very progressive dementia, Alzheimer's. Anyway, we were told that her brain needs to be stimulated as much as possible so I bought her a laptop and my sister signed her up to a social media account. Things appeared to be going well and whenever mum was on the computer it gave my sister some respite."

Konstantin yawned and glanced at his watch and Andy knew he was waffling too much but he needed the Russian to try and understand why this mess had happened.

"Sorry, I know I'm being a bit long-winded. Anyway, seems some bloke contacted mum and told her he was her son, don't ask me why she believed him. Somehow she got access to my papers and has given him all the numbers to the Cayman accounts. I've just checked and we've been cleaned out Konstantin. I know your bosses will blame me but please don't hurt my family, they know nothing about my business dealings and apart from the actions of an old woman who is losing her marbles, are innocent in all of this."

Andy waited for some kind of a response but there was none. What he didn't know was that

in his mind, Konstantin had gone into panic mode. This was his worst nightmare come true but after what seemed like an age he at last spoke and Andy was shocked at how calm he seemed, not to mention the lack of anger.
"Bring me your mother's laptop. It's a long shot but I have a tech man on the books that may be able to tell us where the scammer is."
"She ain't going to like that Konstantin."
The Russian stood up and headed towards the door.
"It's either that or you and me are toast, you saw what they are capable of and I have witnessed far worse. They will hold me equally responsible. I expect to see you back here in an hour, now I have some calls to make."

Andy returned to Chudleigh Street and thankfully Ruby was still sleeping. Shirley and Aida were seated at the table but the dishes had now been cleared away. When she saw him Shirley smiled with relief.
"What did they say, Andy, the people whose money it is?"
"It hasn't been dealt with yet. I need to take Mum's laptop."
"But you can't, she will go mad when she wakes up."
"It's that or you don't see me again and it won't

be my choice. Tell her it's broken and that's why this Colin geezer can't contact her. Tell her I am getting it mended for her."

Shirley got up from the table and grabbed the laptop. Handing it to her brother she told him to go before Ruby woke up.

Konstantin was waiting in the back room when Andy arrived and he wasn't alone. A tall, slim man stood beside the Russian and the first thing that Andy noticed were his long gnarly fingers. Handing over the laptop the stranger briefly smiled revealing teeth that seemed to be far too big for his mouth.

"Andy, this is Serge and he's going to do his best for us but it will take a couple of days. Go back to your family and find out as much as you can about this scammer, there might just be something that he has slipped up with and don't talk to anyone else. We can't risk this getting out or believe me; we won't be given a chance to sort it."

Andy glanced at Serge and once again Konstantin read his mind.

"Serge has been with me for years and is loyal to the core. Now go and if you want any hope of getting out of this unscathed, you will bring me something back that Serge can work with."

CHAPTER SEVENTEEN

Wearily, Andy made his way back to Chudleigh Street and he didn't have a clue how he was going to get his old mum to open up. As if they were made of stone, Shirley and Aida were still seated at the table and they both looked up and smiled when he walked into the front room. Just then Ruby began to stir and sitting up she yawned widely. Glancing around the room they knew she was looking for her laptop but Andy didn't give her the chance to kick off.
"Don't start fretting mum, I've taken it to be repaired. It's broken and that's the reason you haven't heard from Colin."
Ruby smiled at the mention of her son's name.
"Can I use yours, Shirley?"
Her daughter was quick off the mark for once and her reply even shocked Andy.
"It doesn't work like that mum. Colin won't know about mine so his computer can't send messages to my computer."
Ruby accepted the cock and bull story without question and when Andy assured her she would have it back in a couple of days she seemed happy.
"Nan, are you okay to watch her for half an hour only me and Shirl need to pop out."
"Okay but if she kicks off there ain't much I can

do."

"Don't worry; I'm going to lock the doors so she can't get out and if it gets too much for you just go up to your room. I wouldn't ask Nan but this is important."

A few minutes later, when they were sitting in his car, Andy, turned to his sister and his face was grave.

"I need you to tell me anything you might know, I realise it won't be much but you never know it could help us find the robbing cunt."

Shirley slowly closed her eyes and then opening them, stared at her brother. She hated lies, always had and now it was time to come clean.

"I haven't been honest with you and I'm sorry but I didn't tell you in case it all just fizzled out. Mum had a child, a boy, about two years before you came along. Tanner wasn't the dad as she hadn't met him then. Anyway, Nan wouldn't let her keep him, it was shameful back then so she was forced to have him adopted."

Andy couldn't believe what he was hearing but he knew not to interrupt her flow as Shirley could go into shut down mode in a second if she felt threatened or was being put on the spot.

"Wayne saw something on social media from someone trying to find a Ruby Chilvers. He pushed me to reply and that's how I learnt about Colin and before you ask, yes it's true. I straight away asked Nan and she couldn't deny it so I contacted the person and it turns out it was this Colin's wife, Debbie. I met her Andy and she's lovely. They live in Cambridge and are a bit posh, I think he's done well for himself. Debbie was supposed to arrange a visit and they were coming to London to meet Mum but on the day he refused. Debbie still came and she met Mum but obviously Mum didn't know who she was. I ain't heard from Debbie for a few days but I guess you could go and see her but the thing I can't work out is, if he wouldn't come and see mum, then why has he been messaging her and has taken all of your money?"

"That's what I'm trying to find out sweetheart. Now I need to go and speak to Mum and don't worry, I'll take it slowly."

When they went back into the house Ruby was sitting and watching television. Aida was beside her and they were both laughing at some stupid comedy. Taking a seat next to Ruby Andy patiently waited until the programme had finished.

"Mum, can we have a little chat?"

"Is my machine fixed only I need to speak to your brother?"

"Not yet darling but you should have it back tomorrow. Tell me about Colin will you."

"When I was sixteen a boy took advantage of me

and…"

Andy couldn't help but laugh at his mother's naivety.

"No not that mum, tell me about now, why did he want all of that money?"

For a second Ruby looked shocked that he knew and was worried she was in trouble.

"I'm sorry Andy; I thought it was my money. He's in trouble but as soon as he's sorted it he's coming to visit, all the way from Holland!"

"Is he? That's nice. Well, I'd better get back to the grindstone my darling."

Kissing his mum on the cheek his mind was in turmoil and he now doubted that the Colin his mother was talking about and the one Shirley knew about were the same person but he had to find out before he reported back to Konstantin. Luckily Shirley had Debbie Montgomery's address and an hour and a half later he pulled up outside the house. It was impressive and all of a sudden he felt guilty, this was going to be a wasted journey. When Andy had left, Shirley had phoned ahead and warned her new friend, she hadn't gone into too much detail but Debbie was told that a large sum of money was involved. Peering out of the window she watched the handsome stranger as he walked up the path to the front door. Smoothing down her hair in the hall mirror and waiting until he'd pressed on the doorbell before she answered, Debbie was all smiles when she opened up and to say she was attracted to the visitor was an understatement.

"You must be Andy, my half-brother-in-law?"

"I take it you have spoken to Shirley?"

"Yes. Please come inside."

Leading him through to the kitchen, Andy took a seat at the breakfast bar while Debbie made tea.

"So Andy, I wish we could have met under better circumstances but that's life I suppose. I really don't think I will be able to help as Colin and I have separated and the divorce has just begun. He's shacked up somewhere with his secretary."

"I'm sorry to hear that."

"I'm not and besides, you haven't driven all this way to hear about my woes."

There was no denying the chemistry between the two and while they talked Andy couldn't stop gazing at the most gorgeous hazel eyes he had ever seen.

"Shirley mentioned some missing money but as much as my soon-to-be ex-husband is a complete and utter bastard, there is no way he would ever have taken your money. He's a bank manager for God's sake."

"Look, I don't normally share my business with

strangers but time is of the essence so I don't have much choice. I have been looking after the account for some very unsavoury fuckin' geezers. If I don't get it back then I'm a dead man walking."

Debbie grinned at his words.

"Don't you think you're being a bit overdramatic Andy?"

"Sweetheart, you have no idea the circles I move in and there's nothing dramatic about it. We're talking over thirty million and they would blow my brains out for far less than that."

Now Debbie was scared and she went on the defensive for her husband though only God above knew why.

"As I said, I can't help you. At least you now know that crime doesn't pay."

He couldn't believe how high and mighty she was coming across but he knew better than to get arsey with her if he wanted her help.

"True as I have recently learned but I don't think you're grasping how fuckin' important this is! I will track that arsehole down but with your help, it could save a lot of fuckin' time!"

"Then I suggest you pay Colin a visit at the bank. If you leave now you should just catch him before they close. Would you like me to drive you, it will save time?"

Andy nodded and was heading for the door

before Debbie had even grabbed her car keys. On the way they talked some more and she began to realise just how far apart she and Colin were from the Chilvers family, not just in miles but in the whole way they lived. That said she liked Shirley and was starting to warm towards her brother. Andy was a year older than her, good looking and his smile was beautiful. Andy followed her gaze when she pointed across the street.

"It's just over there but it's better that he doesn't see me, so I'll be waiting around the corner."
As soon as he was out of the car and had closed the door Debbie drove off, the last thing she wanted was for Colin to know she was involved. Andy entered just as one of the cashiers, Mandy Dawson, was about to lock the door.
"I'm sorry Sir but we're about to close.
"This ain't business sweetheart it's personal and I'm here to see your boss Colin Montgomery."
Mandy gave him a strange look and then scuttled off down the hallway. A couple of minutes later and Colin appeared and he didn't look too happy.
"I'm sorry Sir but our hours of business are…."
Andy cut him off mid-sentence, something Colin hated and hardly ever tolerated.
"I'm here about Ruby Chilvers."
Almost instantly the colour drained from Colin's

face. He quickly turned towards Mandy who had been hovering in the background and told her everything was fine and that she could get off home now. Reluctantly doing as she was told Mandy gave a long hard stare at the visitor before she left.

"Look Mr?"

"Andy and I'm your half-brother."

"Look Andy I have made my feelings clear and I don't wish to have any contact with your mother."

"Is that why you cleared out her bank accounts?"

"I beg your pardon!!!?"

"Look Pal, I ain't here to play fuckin' happy families! The money belonged to some very unsavoury characters and if I don't get it back then they will be coming for me, my family, not to mention you and your soon-to-be ex-wife."

"How many more times, I haven't got the first idea what you are talking about."

Andy didn't have a clue how to go about extracting information, oh he knew how to knock a bloke about when needed but somehow he didn't think that would cut it this time. Luckily he knew a man that would be able to get the information.

"Okay, I've warned you so what happens next ain't down to me Pal."

With that, Andy walked out leaving Colin just standing there open-mouthed. When he was back in the car Debbie spoke before starting up the engine.
"So, what did he have to say?"
"Denied it, says he doesn't want anything to do with Mum and that he hasn't got a clue about the money."
"So what now?"
"Now I have to go back to London and do the one thing I didn't want to, tell Konstantin."
"That sounds like a Russian name; it's not dirty Russian money is it?"
For a second Andy looked in to those beautiful eyes again and then slowly nodded his head. Debbie could only stare at him, completely confused.
"Would you take me back to yours to collect my car?"
The return journey was taken in silence. Andy knew that once he shared the info with Konstantin there would be no going back and this Colin bloke most definitely wouldn't survive but if he didn't and they missed a chance to retrieve the money then he along with his family would be killed, of that he was in no doubt. Debbie was trying to think of what to do, she hated Colin, hated what he had done to her and their life together but now she was fearful about

what was going to happen to him. When they reached the house and Debbie had parked the car she invited Andy in for a drink and strangely, due to how tight time was and the need to get back to London, he accepted. As she waited for the kettle to boil he came up behind her and placing his hands on her hips he began to slowly kiss her neck. It was so out of character for both of them but the chemistry between them had been undeniable from the second she had opened the front door. As he moved his hands up and cupped her breasts she began to softly moan and a few seconds later they were pawing at each other's clothes. Sex happened there and then on the kitchen floor and Debbie had never climaxed in such an intense way in her entire life, for that matter neither had Andy and by the time it was over they were both breathless and glistening in sweat.

"Wow!"

Laughing at her words, Andy got to his feet and offered her his hand. As nice as it had all been he had to get back but now he was scared for her.

"I think you need to get out of here and sooner rather than later."

"This is my home Andy and no one is going to scare me out of leaving."

"Then you are either naive or very silly. These men will end your life in a second if you don't tell them what they want to hear and considering you don't know anything, well let's not go there at the moment. Why don't you come back to Mum's? If you're all together I have a better chance of looking after you all."
Debbie Montgomery couldn't believe what she was hearing; this was all so absurd, like something out of a movie but was she prepared to risk her life?
"I'm serious love and believe me they will be paying you a visit."
"Okay, but I need to pack."
"And I need to get off but I'll give our Shirley a ring on the way and let her know you're coming to stay."
Andie then kissed her, a long lingering kiss that sent shivers down her spine and when he stopped she looked into his eyes and smiled. If this was all a dream and the Russians were not coming, she still hoped she'd never wake up because in the last hour and for the first time in her entire life, she felt alive, really alive!

CHAPTER EIGHTEEN

When Andy got within a couple of miles of home he phoned Shirley and explained that in the next couple of hours, there would be a house guest coming to stay. Still traumatised at her brother's revelation regarding the missing money, she didn't ask too many questions. After the brief phone call ended Andy then continued on to the Crown & Two Chairmen. He wasn't looking forward to it, knowing that once he shared the information with Konstantin Colin was as good as dead but it was a choice between a stranger and his family and it was something he just couldn't keep to himself. Entering the pub he was surprised to see that the Russian's stool was empty and walking up to the bar he asked where the boss was. The barman didn't look happy so Andy guessed that either something had occurred while he was away or Konstantin was in a strop. It was probably the latter and Andy could understand why. Told to head towards the back room, the barman then used the wall phone to inform his employer of Andy's arrival. Knocking, Andy didn't wait to be invited inside. Konstantin was sitting at the table which was bare, with no papers, no alcohol and for the first time since they had met, Andy could see fear in the mans eyes. He looked up

but didn't speak so Andy took a seat opposite.
"I have some news and it's not great."
"I gathered that."
"It's a long story but I made a visit to Cambridge to see a bloke who is supposedly my half-brother. Mum has been in contact via Facebook with a bloke who says he's her son but I'm not sure they are the same person. Anyway, he's a bank manager so I went to where he works but he's denied any knowledge."
"Well, he would the cunt!"
"I'm not sure that he knows anything Konstantin, I mean a bank manager for fucks sake!?"
"They are the worst kind, always scheming. Right, we need to pay him a visit."
"There's no point until tomorrow as I don't know where he lives, we'll have to leave it until the morning and see him at his work."
Konstantin didn't look too happy about it but he nodded his head in agreement.
"Be back here by nine. We'll let him settle in and then we can catch the cunt before he goes on his lunch break."
Andy sighed heavily; he didn't want to be a part of any of this but had Hobson's choice in the matter. Pulling up outside Chudleigh Street he saw Debbie's car and his heart missed a beat, an emotion that was alien to him and one he then

dismissed immediately, for God's sake he'd only just met the woman. Walking into the front room he was greeted by the sound of raucous laughter a sound he hadn't heard in the house for a long, long time. Ruby and Debbie were seated on the sofa and were watching Shirley who was standing in the middle of the room attempting what Andy could only imagine was charades. The two women were red in the face from laughing so hard and even Aida who was sitting at the table had tears of amusement streaming down her face.

"Well glad to see no one is as fuckin' worried about all of this as I am."

The three women all looked in the direction of the door but now their faces were solemn.

"Can I have a word, Debbie?"

Walking into the kitchen, Andy closed the door so that they couldn't be overheard.

"I know we've only just met but things are going to get nasty and I'm sending Nan, Mum and Shirley out of the country so that they'll be safe. I will join them as soon as I can. Do you want to come with us or take your chances here?"

She stared at him and in that moment knew he was the sort of man she had always dreamed of, handsome, kind and a little dangerous.

"Andy this is all so crazy. Twenty-four hours ago and I was in the process of a divorce and living a relatively normal life, now, well now I feel as if I'm on the run!"

"You will be and I'm sorry we have brought you into all of this but I'm trying to save your life. I have to go and see your husband again tomorrow but I don't think Konstantin will be as friendly as I was."

"He's my soon-to-be ex but is he in any real danger, Andy?"

Andy Chilvers lowered his head as he nodded. "If you're thinking about warning him you're wasting your time as they will find him wherever he goes."

"So, won't they find us?"

"Not if I can sort out new Identities for everyone. So, will you let Colin know we're going to Cambridge?"

"No, Colin is arrogant and wouldn't take any notice of me anyway."

Andy decided not to go into any more detail, he knew what was going to happen to the bloke and it wasn't something he wanted her to hear.

"Where are you thinking of going?"

"I haven't decided yet and in any case, I have to get everyone passports and documents."

"None of you have passports?"

Andy smiled at her naivety.

"Of course we do, Debbie but if we travel, no matter where, under our real names then they will find us. Everyone will have to have new identities and that's for the rest of their lives. Are you prepared to do that?"

"You're scaring me now but yes, I will come with you and we could go to Thailand."

"Thailand?"

"I have a holiday home there that I inherited from my parents. It's still in their name so not associated with me and it's big enough for us all to live there."

He couldn't believe what a spot of luck her suggestion was.

"That sounds fuckin' brilliant. Thailand it is then. I'll sort the papers as soon as I can and hopefully, we won't have to wait too long. Don't say anything to Mum or Shirl yet, they tend to talk too freely at times."

"What about photo's?"

Andy walked over to the dresser and opening the drawer found the spare images left over from when Aida and Ruby had applied for bus passes. There was also one of Shirley and another of Andy that they had taken for fun when out on a shopping trip. Turning around he was about to tell Debbie she was the only one without a passport picture when she opened her purse and pulled out a small thumbnail image.

"I needed it for a job application."

Andy smiled, he really like this woman.

The sleeping arrangements were agreed, Debbie would have Andy's bedroom and he would sleep on the couch. Things didn't turn out as planned as neither of them was able to sleep and two hours after turning in for the night, Debbie heard her door quietly open and then close. In the darkness Andy heard a whispered voice.
"You took your time."
"You are a loose woman Mrs Montgomery!"
"Ms if you don't mind."
Debbie giggled as she pulled the bedclothes open so he could get in. This time their lovemaking was slower and tender but they both still experiences fantastic orgasms. Laying in each-other's arms they eventually fell asleep.

At just before six the following morning and before he went to meet Konstantin, Andy set off to see Harry Richardson. The two had remained friends since Andy had supplied the man with cigars years earlier. Harry was now semi-retired but he was still connected to several underworld firms and had always told Andy to get in contact if he needed help. Taking the North Circular and due to the time of day, the drive to Richmond would take just over an hour. Harry Richardson had moved out of the City a few years earlier and now resided on Dunstable Road. The area was expensive, the houses were large and Andy was worried that Harry wouldn't like him calling at his home. He couldn't have been more wrong. As soon as the front door opened, his old friend greeted him warmly with an embrace. Andy was invited inside and over several cups of tea he explained all to Harry and he didn't leave anything out. This was no time for secrecy; he needed all the help he could get if they stood any chance of surviving.

"Fuckin' Russians, I hate the bastards. You should never have gotten involved son but hindsight is a wonderful fuckin' thing."

Harry had a contact in the passport office and the details used were all of real people, people whose ages were matched to those of the applicant and who were paid handsomely for their details.

"Right, this is going to take a couple of days. Is that going to cause you any problems?"

"No that should be fine but if they can make it any quicker it would be better. Thanks, Harry, you're a lifesaver and I mean that literally."

"No thanks needed. Son, you're a good sort and I'm glad to help but take my advice, tell no one until you have to. Those Russians are tricky bastards and will go to any lengths to try and track you down."

The men shook hands, there was little more to be

said as both were aware just how dangerous this could turn out to be. Andy was back in Soho by ten to nine and driving to the back of the Crown & Two Chairman he stayed in the car until a minute to nine as he now hated being in Konstantin's company any longer than he had to. As soon as he walked into the back room, the Russian was out of his seat and after grabbing a small canvas wrap from a shelf and a can of spray paint; he headed towards the rear door with Andy following closely behind.

Colin Montgomery was late for work for the second day in a row. Tracey was insatiable and wanted sex every night and it was wearing him out. After dropping her on the High Street so that they didn't both arrive at the same time, he continued and parked his Mercedes at the rear of the bank. Entering through the back door he saw that Tracey and Mandy Dawson were about to open up and not speaking to either of them Colin entered his office. Konstantin had put his foot down and when his Range Rover pulled up a street away from the bank, their journey from London had taken just over an hour. Walking a short distance he crept around the outer walls of the surrounding shops until he was standing underneath the closed circuit camera which was situated above the rear door of the bank.

Shaking the aerosol can he reached up and sprayed directly onto the lens and then made his way back to Andy. Driving the car into the bank's car park the dash clock read ten thirty.
"That must be the cunts car, well we'll soon see if it is or not."
Konstantin pulled on a pair of gloves and then banged hard on the side of the Mercedes. Instantly the alarm went into a high-pitched siren mode. A few seconds later the back door flew open and Colin ran outside. The door, on an automatic closer slammed shut behind him. Pressing the key fob he glanced all around and when he was happy that it must have just been a glitch, he used the security keypad to let himself back inside.
"That's him."
"Good. Now, I'm going to stand beside the door so when he comes out I can grab him, you hit the car again. Well go on then you twat!"
Andy got out and as soon as Konstantin was in position Andy banged hard on the car roof. The alarm burst into life and within seconds Colin came out for the second time and he didn't look too happy. As the door closed behind him, Konstantin stepped forward and pushed the barrel of his pistol into the small of Colin's back.
"Fuckin' move you cunt or you're a dead man."
Colin raised his hands in submission and was

about to offer his car fob thinking it was a car jacker when he suddenly spied Andy.
"I told you yesterday that I haven't got a clue about contacting your mother or about any money. Why won't you believe me?"
Konstantin pushed him forward and opening the rear door to his Range Rover; he shoved Colin inside and at the same time threw his keys to Andy.
"You drive."
"Where to?"
"Just head out of the city and take the A1303 and then the A428, head towards Bourn Airfield."
Colin had been silent up until now and with Konstantin's gun pressed into his side it didn't make for conversation but when he heard the airfield mentioned and knew that it was only now used at weekends he became scared.
"Look chaps, can't we sort this out somehow?"
Konstantin pushed the barrel even harder into Colin's ribs and he winced in pain. At the same time, he felt the warmth of urine as the front of his silver-grey trousers became darker in colour.

Constructed in 1940 as a satellite airfield Bourn has seen its fair share of violence. Subjected to four air raids in 1941, there were no injuries but two de Havilland Mosquito planes were damaged. By 1948 RAF Bourn had been decommissioned and large sections were sold off in 1961 for agricultural use. Today part of the old runway is used at weekends by the Rural Flying Corps and the previous evening Konstantin had carried out some research, the place they were heading to would be perfect. In the back of the Range Rover, he had bolt croppers in case they needed to gain access, rope to tie the victim and his trusty canvas roll of torture tools. As they neared the locked gates he told Andy to stop while he got out and cut the chain. While this was being done, Colin tried desperately to plead for his life.

"Look Andy, I didn't touch your money. For fucks sake we're half-brothers. What do you think Mum would say if she could see you now?"

The words hit a nerve and Andy spun around in his seat.

"Don't you fuckin' dare mention her you cunt. Debbie's told me what an arsehole you are and besides, it's out of my hands. Tell him what he wants to know and you might just survive."

"But I don't know anything, pleeeeeeease!!!"

As Konstantin got back into the car Colin began to cry and not quietly but it made no impact on the Russian, Konstantin actually saw it as a weakness.

"Head over to the hanger."

Again he got out of the car, snapped the padlock and when he'd slid the large door open Andy drove inside before the door closed again. Bundling Collin out of the car onto the concrete floor, Konstantin bound the man's hands and feet before placing tape over Colin's mouth. Andy just stood there staring, worried about what would happen next. Unravelling the canvas wrap Konstantin removed the bradawl that had been sharpened to a fine point. As he slowly drew it down Colin's cheek he spoke.

"Now this can be relatively quick or very, very painful, the choice is yours. So where is the money, where did you move it to?"

Colin shook his head as he tried to say that he hadn't had anything to do with any money but his words were muffled. As Konstantin pushed the bradawl straight through his cheek and into his tongue Colin began to gag. There was so much blood that couldn't escape because of the tape. Bending down Konstantin sharply removed the tape and blood spewed from his victim's mouth. Forcing a dirty rag into Colin's wound to help stem the flow, Konstantin continued with his assault.

"You have two more chances my friend and then it's over for you."

Konstantin drew his finger a crossed his throat indicating death.

"So, where is it?"

Now frightened for his life, Colin again began to shake his head as tears streamed down his face but it made no difference. With one swift hard movement, Konstantin thrust the bradawl into Colin's thigh forcing him to scream out as he pushed the rag from his mouth. Konstantin sighed heavily in frustration and Andy was now beginning to feel physically sick. He wanted this to stop, it was clear that Colin didn't know anything and maybe Konstantin was now just venting his own frustration and fear.

"I think you've gone far enough, he ain't got a fuckin' clue about the money."

Konstantin spun around on his heels and the look on his face was manic and frenzied.

"He has one last chance and that's it. You are so naïve Andy; if I let this cunt go he would go straight to the Old Bill no matter what he pleads. So you cunt, what's it to be?"

Realising it was over, Colin accepted his fate, this was the end and he was helpless to stop it. For the last time, he slowly shook his head and at the same time, he closed his eyes and waited. Konstantin brought the bradawl down and plunged it into Colin's stomach several times. The screams were bloodcurdling and it took all of Andy's resolve to hold inside the vomit that was so desperate to escape.

"Right, let's go."

"We can't just leave the poor sod here!"

"He'll be dead within the hour or would you rather we took him with us, maybe dust him down and drop him back at the Bank? You soppy cunt, get in."

The hanger doors were once again opened and the Range Rover drew away. Andy was unaware that before they had even left London Konstantin had placed a magnetic false plate over the original registration number. A few miles into their return he pulled over and removed them.

"So, what's the plan now?"

"Now we go and pay Serge a visit and pray to God that he has some news for us."

CHAPTER NINETEEN

Born in London, Serge Benton was the son of a Russian woman named Natalya Vinogradov and a British man known as Donald Benton. He was always thankful that he didn't have to carry the absurd name of his mother or visit her homeland. He always found Russians to be obnoxious, though that didn't stop him from dealing with them when he set up his own small business. A computer wizard, Serge had excelled in his education and had soon learned the art of hacking. His small terraced house on Eagle Street in Holborn was filled to capacity with all manner of computers, wires and electronic components. Konstantin's Range Rover drew up outside and as he and Andy made their way to the front door it opened before they had a chance to knock. Serge had spent the last couple of days trawling through Ruby's Facebook account and he had some interesting news to share. Excited, he was also incredibly nervous as what he had to tell Konstantin was in no way good news.
"Do you have anything for me, Serge?"
"I do indeed but it's not what you want to hear."
Turning to face Andy he spoke and his tone was lowered as he did so.

"Your mother was indeed hacked but not from anyone in this country."

Andy felt sick and asked to use the bathroom. Running to the top of the stairs he only just made it in time as he wretched up all that his stomach contained. Splashing his face with water he stared into the mirror above the basin and he didn't like what he saw. For God's sake, they had just killed an innocent man. Oh, it was Konstantin who had carried out the act but Andy knew he was just as guilty and he didn't know if he could live with it let alone look Debbie in the face. After he managed to compose himself he re-joined the others downstairs. Serge had obviously been waiting for him before the details were given.

"It appears that the scammers have used proxies or VPNs."

Both Konstantin and Andy looked at their host as if he was speaking in a foreign language.

"Let me explain. If an IP address is used it's relatively easier to locate that address. Good scammers, use a proxy VPN or in layman's terms a Virtual private network. These services allow users to mask their IP and location. They are so sophisticated that they can easily fool fraud detection and conceal a user's true location. I've known VPNs to be bounced all over the world which can make tracking them down very difficult."

"Fuck, fuck, fuck!!!!"

"Hold on Konstantin I haven't finished yet, it's not all bad news. As you know, I am exceedingly good at what I do. After all, that's why you use me. Under normal circumstances it would be extremely hard work had your scammers used a reliable VPN service but they didn't they used a poor quality one and I have managed to get a location. There's just one hurdle, it's in Lagos City."

"Nigeria?!"

"I'm afraid it's all too common these days my friend. The people are poor but not unintelligent and will do anything to line their own pockets" Serge handed Konstantin a piece of paper containing the address of Babak Madueke's office.

"I have given you the location but that's about as much help as I can offer. It will be down to you or your bosses to locate the actual culprit and that won't be easy. Nigeria is a dangerous country at the best of times and when you add millions of pounds into the mix, well it doesn't bear thinking about the lengths these people will go to."

"Then you will have to come with us."

"Lagos!? Not a chance."

"Then you can tell my Bosses that in person

because neither of us is technically minded so even if we find the cunts we won't be able to do anything with their computers."

Serge knew who he was dealing with and as much as he hated to fly, he would hate being subjected to the wrath of the Russians even more.

"Let me know when and where."

Konstantin was not a man to talk excessively but on the way back to the Crown & Two Chairman his quietness was more noticeable than usual.

"You okay?"

Konstantin took his eyes off the road for a few seconds and looked blankly in Andy's direction.

"I have to inform my bosses about what's going on."

"Why? Why can't we go to Nigeria and try and sort it out ourselves? I know it's a long shot but it's at least got to be worth a try hasn't it?"

"It doesn't work like that, once I involved someone from outside of the firm, namely Serge that was it as far as keeping it a secret. Now if I don't tell them and they find out, which they undoubtedly will, my death will be unimaginable, yours too probably. When we get back to the pub I want you to go home and wait. When I hear back I will let you know."

Andy didn't go home instead he went to Chudleigh Street. Sitting everyone down, he slowly began to reveal all that had occurred, well, all except Colin's violent demise and also what was about to happen.

"I'm in trouble, big trouble and the men who will be after me are the sort who will hurt my family without a second thought if they think they can get to me. A lot of money has gone missing and they will want it back."

"Is it the money I gave to my boy?"

All eyes were suddenly on Ruby and Andy didn't have the heart to tell her this was indeed all her fault. Hugging her close he winked at the others and the pain was etched on his face.

"No sweetheart it isn't but we have to go away, all of us to a different country with new identities and we leave as soon as I can make it happen."

"Hold your bleedin' horses boy, I ain't fuckin' going anywhere and neither is my Ruby."

"Nan! Have you not heard a word I've just said? They will do terrible things to find out where I am and I ain't on about a few slaps here and there, they will slit your throat as soon as look at you."

"I've heard you loud and clear sunshine but for Gawd's sake, I'm eighty-three years old and not long for this mortal coil anyway and your old mum? Well she don't know what bleedin' day of the week it is let alone where you will be

living. We will be fine darling but I understand why you have to leave."
"Please, Nan?"
"No that's my final word so don't waste your breath."
"Shirley?"
"I'll come with you Andy and I promise I won't tell a soul not even Wayne. Our relationship was never going anywhere and a fresh start will be good but I wish you two would come with us."
Aida just shook her head and they all knew that once the old girl's mind was made up there was no budging her. Andy looked over to where Debbie sat. She hadn't said a word so far and this must all be a complete mind fuck but deep down he wanted her to go, she was the first woman, sexually wise, that he had ever had any real connection with.
"I'll come too. When do we leave?"
Just then Andy's phone began to ring; it was Harry Richardson informing him that the passports had been rushed through and were ready to be collected. He didn't tell Harry that he no longer needed two of them, instead, he told the girls to pack and then he set off for Richmond. After collecting the documents he requested Harry to carry out one last favour. Handing over a small stamped and addressed

Envelope, he asked his old friend to post it in a month's time. Realising what was inside Harry agreed without question. The two embraced and when they parted Andy was sure he could see tears in the older man's eyes.
"Good luck son."
"Thanks, Harry; I need all the luck I can get."
Setting off he made a quick stop at Simpson's travel agents in the Quadrant. The shop was far enough away that they wouldn't be able to trace him and he paid in cash so there would be no paper trail. Andy purchased tickets for Shirley and Debbie but not for himself, he needed to wait to hear from Konstantin first. Their flight was later that night and he was heading back to his mum's when his phone rang again.
Switching it to speaker he heard Konstantin on the other end.
"They want to see us. I don't know if that's a good thing or a bad but we leave tonight at nine."
With that the line went dead and Andy knew he had no choice but to join the Russian for the trip, whether he would return was another matter but he had to make sure the girls were safe. Racing back to Chudleigh Street he took Shirley and Debbie into the kitchen so his mother and grandmother couldn't hear what was being discussed.

"You two need to go tonight, I will join you as soon as I can. A cab will be here in an hour to take you to the airport so I suggest you pack as much as you can, and take this for any excess luggage charges."
He handed Debbie a wad of notes and then turned directly towards his sister, his face was solemn as he spoke.
"Shirley I know you said you wouldn't but I can't stress how important it is that you tell no one and that includes Wayne. Can you do that for me, sweetheart, can I trust you not to let me down?"
Shirley nodded her head and he had no choice but to believe her. Handing the two women their new identities Andy told them to memorise who they were, date of birth etcetera. Going into the front room he kissed Ruby and his Nan tenderly and held them both for several seconds more than he usually did before rushing back home to pack.

The taxi arrived at six thirty and it took another five minutes of hugs, kisses and tears before the women at last left the house. Shirley and Aida were sobbing; Ruby didn't know what was happening but wept as well, and even Debbie who hardly knew the family shed a tear. Finally, when the cab driver sounded his horn for the

second time and Debbie grew concerned that he might leave without them, the women came out of the house. As the cab pulled away Shirley turned in her seat and waved to her grandmother for what she knew would be the last time. Tears streamed down her face and Debbie handed her a tissue to wipe her nose.
"You okay darling?"
"No Debbie I'm not but what can I do about it? Stay here and wait for those men to come in the hope that they won't hurt us? I don't think so, Andy is a good brother and would never knowingly lie to me, he looked so scared Debbie and you know something? I've never seen him scared before."
Debbie hugged her half-sister-in-law and gripped her hand tightly.
"It's all going to be fine my darling, your brother won't let us down."
Trying to lighten the mood she told Shirley all about the house, about the servants they had and how big the swimming pool was. Usually, words like this would have had Shirley Tanner so excited, she'd waited years to have a holiday but now all she felt was empty and the longing for her mum and Nan had already begun.

Back at Andy's flat, he began to pack a small cabin bag for his trip to Russia and two large

bags for when he returned. Maybe it was wishful thinking but that was all he had left. Emptying his desk drawers he stashed fifty thousand inside the floor safe along with some very confidential papers and his notebook. The amount of cash had also been matched and placed into an envelope that he would send to Harry Richardson with a note again asking his friend to post it, though this time it would be to Thailand and to delay doing it for a couple of weeks. Another ten thousand was put into an envelope and also contained another small stamped and addressed envelope. This was to his grandmother as he now realised that the original money he'd given to Harry wouldn't be enough but ten grand and with both of their pensions, it would now see them alright for at least a year. If he survived all of this then he would look at sending them more money in the future. He then put twenty thousand into his flight bag just in case anything unforeseen happened. Slowly closing the front door, Andy wondered if he would ever see his home again. Walking towards the street door he suddenly stopped and made his way over the concierge's desk and handed Simeon the envelope.
"See this gets in the post will you?"
"Certainly Mr Chilvers and have a nice evening."

Parking behind the pub he was surprised when he saw that Konstantin already waiting in his car. This was unusual and Andy realised that the Russian must be wound up and worried about the trip. Strangely Andy had somewhat resigned himself to his fate. If he did return then it would be a bonus. Opening the back door he slid his case onto the seat and then got in beside Konstantin but there were no words exchanged between the two. Serge had agreed to meet them at the airport and Konstantin was praying that he wouldn't let them down.

The flight turned out to be as smooth as the previous one and when they touched down in Russia it felt to Andy like he had been doing this trip for a long time. Taken to the same hotel, they were instructed to wait in their rooms and a car would be sent to collect them the following day. Surprisingly Andy slept well but the same couldn't be said for his associates. An identical dull breakfast like the last was served in his room at eight that morning and after eating just a few morsels, he showered, dressed and then lay back on the bed ready for whatever the day was going to bring. An hour later there was a knock at the door and grabbing his phone Andy thought it was time to leave but when he answered he saw Konstantin just standing there.

The man had dark lines and bags under his eyes from lack of sleep.

"We need to go over exactly what we are going to say to the bosses."

"Why don't we start with the truth? We have all been robbed and we are doing our best to get the money back. Why don't we go for a walk and talk about it?"

Konstantin smiled as he slowly shook his head.

"You really don't have a clue who you are dealing with Andy. If they think the cash has gone forever they will make examples of us just to save face."

"Then that's why we need to convince them to let us go to Lagos."

Before Konstantin could comment his phone began to ring and Andy could see the Russians' hands were shaking as he answered. Saying only 'Da' the Russian for yes, Konstantin ended the call.

"Time to go my friend."

Serge stayed in his room and didn't even know Andy and Konstantin had gone out. As the two men slowly and silently walked down the hotel corridor ready to meet their fate, whatever that might be, Andy could feel the onset of nerves begin to build.

CHAPTER TWENTY

Thirty minutes after Andy's flight had left England, Shirley and Debbie boarded Thai Airways flight TG6383 to Bangkok. Cramped and tired neither of them enjoyed the eleven-and-a-half-hour flight. By the time they touched down at Suvarnabhumi International Airport it was three in the afternoon local time but they still had to get through customs and then there was another two-hour coach journey to reach the Naklua beach house in Pattaya. Built in the late seventies, Haven House was one of only four residences ever to have building permits granted at the end of the peninsular. The stonework was exquisite, painted white and all of the window shutters were a vivid shade of jade green. Debbie's parents were only the second owners and had made her promise to never sell their little piece of heaven but Colin hated the place so much he refused to visit. Luckily the outgoings and staff were cheap enabling Debbie to keep it going. Pulling down the long sandy drive, the taxi at last came to a stop outside at six that evening and Shirley sighed with relief, she felt grubby and knew she had bad breath. She was desperate for a shower and sleep, the plane had been cramped, noisy and all in all, it had been a downright horrendous trip. The housemaid

Kannika was waiting for them with open arms on the veranda. Ushering them inside, the maid was a little taken aback when Shirley declined the meal Kannika had lovingly prepared for them. In Thailand it was taken as rudeness, something Shirley most definitely wasn't but lack of sleep can make a person act in strange ways. Shown to her room she took a quick shower, got into bed and a few seconds later was snoring softly. Debbie stayed up for another hour as she hadn't seen Kannika for over five years and the woman had worked for the family for so long she knew it wouldn't be polite if she didn't spend a little time with the maid. Kannika told Debbie how sad she was when she found out Debbie's parents had passed away and how fearful she had been that she may lose her home and only source of income now that her daughter Lawan had started at the local college as money was tight and employment was thin on the ground.

"Please don't worry Kannika that won't ever happen. I've moved here permanently now. My husband and I have separated and the woman you met fleetingly is my half-sister-in-law but that's a long story for another time. I would like to add that she's great and not rude at all even if she did come across that way. Shirley had never been on a plane before let alone travelled for

hours and hours. I'm sure in the morning she will be as bright as a button. I've only met her a few times myself but I like her very much."
Kannika, who spoke remarkably good English, still looked confused.
"It's complicated but once I've caught up on my sleep I will explain everything. Now I need to go to bed my dear friend before I collapse in a heap on the floor."
Kannika embraced her employer.
"It's so good to have you back, Miss Debbie."
"And it's good to be back Kannika."

When Shirley finally woke at ten the next morning sunlight flooded into her room and she had to take a few moments to adjust to where she was. After yawning and stretching her limbs she got out of bed, drew back the curtains and couldn't believe what she saw. A fantastic swimming pool was right outside her terrace doors and beyond that was a beach with almost white sand and the most beautiful turquoise sea. Andy was going to love it here and she just wished he would hurry up and arrive. Walking down the long hallway that had several doors leading off to various bedrooms she managed to locate the kitchen and the aromas coming from it were mouth-watering. Kannika had prepared a fantastic-looking spread and even though it was

a world away from her usual Weetabix, Shirley's mouth began to water. Debbie was already sitting at the table and smiled warmly when her guest walked in.
"Morning sweetheart, sleep well?"
Shirley smiled, yawned again and then nodded her head.
"Take a seat and I'll talk you through all of these dishes."
Suddenly Shirley felt lost and was missing her mum and Nan but unlike the previous evening, she wanted to be polite so did as she'd been asked.
"Right, first we have Kaho Tom. It's boiled rice with egg. I know it doesn't look that appetising but believe me it's very moorish. That's a Thai omelette and the other dish is Khanom Pang Na Moo otherwise known as fried bread with minced pork."
Kannika smiled with joy that after so long Debbie had remembered the dishes but Shirley ended up only having the omelette as it was the only thing she knew or had ever eaten before. It was delicious and she vowed going forward to try the strange foods on offer as this was now home, at least for the time being.
"You okay darling?"
"It's just all a bit strange and I'm missing my mum."

"I know you are love and it will take some time to adjust but just look at it as a holiday and take one day at a time."

After breakfast, Shirley was given a tour of the house and grounds and then the two women took a stroll along the beach. It was breathtaking and everything Shirley had ever dreamed of.

"I wish Andy was here."

"He will be soon. Now how do you fancy a trip to the local market?"

Shirley beamed from ear to ear; shopping was her favourite pastime and the money Aida had pressed into her hand before she left was now burning a hole in her pocket.

That night Andy and Konstantin were again taken to the Aurora nightclub. They had decided that it was best to leave Serge at the hotel, he had no part in the money going missing and the less he knew the better. On their arrival at Aurora and unlike before, they were immediately ushered down the stairs and along the corridor to the stone room. Remembering his last visit, Andy could feel the knots as they tightened in the pit of his stomach. He nervously looked at Konstantin for some kind of reassurance but the Russian just continued to stare straight ahead. When the doors were

opened the only thing in the room was a table where the boss, Lev Baranov was sitting. This time he was not accompanied by the other bosses but was flanked on either side by two heavies, men who spent many hours in the gym bulking up muscle. Konstantin walked straight up to the table but Andy knew that this show of confidence was pure bravado and he stood back letting the Russian do all of the talking.
"Good evening Mr. Baranov."
"Konstantin. I hear you are having problems."
"Yes Mr. Baranov, unfortunately, some idiot has dared to take your money but we are working hard on the situation and hope to retrieve everything stolen as soon as possible."
"I hear they are from Lagos?"
Konstantin wasn't sure how his boss knew these details but he also knew better than to ask.
"Yes, Sir and we have a location."
Suddenly Lev's face took on a menacing appearance, a look Konstantin had seen many times before but up until now he had never been on the receiving end of.
"You will go to Lagos. On landing you have 48 hours to locate and eliminate those responsible and it goes without saying, to also get my money back."
Andy stepped forward and was about to protest but stopped when he felt Konstantin's hand on

his arm.

"We have also brought a tech wizard with us. I'm sure he knows very little regarding this firm but will be able to assist us if we have to search through any technical records."

"Good. Vladimir and Mikhail will be joining you as well, just in case you have any stupid ideas of disappearing."

Konstantin didn't argue, he didn't dare and instead just nodded before turning and heading upstairs. Andy was fast on his tail; he didn't want to remain alone in the room not that it would have made any difference but also he couldn't wait to have it out with the Russian. Unfortunately he would have to wait until they were back in the hotel as their two escorts were following closely behind. When they were at last in Andy's room, he turned on Konstantin and for once he didn't mince his words.

"What the fuck was all that about? Who the hell are Vlad the Impaler and Gorbachev?"

Konstantin couldn't help but laugh at his friend's reference to the two henchmen who would now be watching their every move.

"Very violent men who are accompanying us to make sure we don't go missing. Come on we need to get some sleep as we've got an early flight tomorrow."

Up and out of the hotel early, the three men and their minders, whom Serge felt continually intimidated by, headed to the airport at six am. Their eight-and-a-half-hour flight left at nine on the dot but there was nothing luxurious about the trip. The Aeroflot cabin crew did their best but the food on offer was well below par and the inflight entertainment was in Russian so Andy couldn't understand what was being said. He had tried to sleep but the seats were so uncomfortable that it was almost impossible. He at last breathed a sigh of relief when the plane finally touched down at Murtala Muhammed airport. It only took thirty minutes to get into the city but to say Andy was disappointed with the accommodation was an understatement. By the time they checked into the Lustro Serviced Apartments, it was three thirty in the afternoon local time. The accommodation was so basic that there was just a sink in their rooms with a communal shower and toilet at the end of the hall. Set up for backpackers, it was clean but not what either of them was used to. Sege didn't comment he'd backpacked around India a few years earlier and compared to that this was luxury. Konstantin and Andy didn't even bother unpacking they just dropped their luggage and set straight off for the financial district before the offices started to close for the day. Vladimir

pointed to a car that had been sourced by one of their contacts and reaching down he retrieved the keys from the driver's side wheel arch. Time was ticking and they had to find their target soon. Parking up close to the address they continued on foot. Vladimir and Mikhail stayed a few hundred yards behind but never let the three men out of their sight. When the BM Tech Company offices came into sight Konstantin couldn't stop the grin from appearing on his face.
"Well, at least the first step has been accomplished."
Noticing that a sign on the door stated the place closed at four, they all quickly made their way up to the office. Entering they found the desks had all been vacated for the day and about to leave, it was Andy who spotted Babak Madueke sitting at his desk with the office door open. Andy nudged Konstantin and they marched over with Serge following quickly behind but the two heavies waited at the exit so that no one could leave. Babak looked up and frowned when he saw his visitors and it wasn't due to the late hour of the day. No one apart from employees ever came here and least of all foreigners. Suddenly his heart began to sink and standing up he walked around the desk.
"I'm sorry gentlemen but we are not open to the

public."

Konstantin pulled out his gun and for a second Andy marvelled at the fact that he had been able to get it into the country but he didn't ask how.
"Sit!"

Fear was evident on Babak's face as he did as he was told and Konstantin walked around the desk until he towered over the Nigerian.

"You have something that belongs to my Bosses and they would very much like it back."

Babak raised his open palms and smirked.

"I have no idea what you are talking about Mr?"

While the questions were being asked Serge had already turned Babak's computer around to face him and after changing the language from Nigerian to English he began to scan the files. There was no mention of money but as he tapped in all of the information he had, the name Ruby Chilvers popped up onto the screen.

"Bingo!"

Turning the screen in Andy's direction he indicated for him to take a look at the monitor.

"That's mum!"

Konstantin again asked where his bosses' money was and again Babak denied any knowledge.

Raising the gun in the air Konstantin brought it down onto Babak's head and the sound of his skull cracking was audible to all. Andy rushed to his side but by Babak's staring cold eyes it was obvious that he was dead.

"For fucks sake, Konstantin!"

"Maybe I did use a bit too much force."

Andy glanced into the main office and luckily it didn't look as if Vladimir and Mikhail had noticed anything going on.

"A bit too much fuckin' force!? You've killed him. Well you'd better hope that Serge comes up with something or we're fucked."

"Bingo again!"

They both looked at Serge desperate for any information.

"It seems that the villain actually dealing with your mother goes by the name of Obi Adamu. There's no mention of the actual money but there is a home address."

Serge scribbled down the details and was about to stand up but stopped when he saw Vlad standing in the doorway. When he noticed Babak's lifeless body he glared at Konstantin but didn't say a word. He didn't need to as Konstantin was only too aware that in the next few hours, word would have gotten back to Lev Baranov.

"We need to go."

Andy was the last one to walk out of the room but not before he'd noticed the small memory stick in the side of the laptop, he couldn't believe that Serge had missed it. Pulling it out he stuffed it into his pocket and quickly upping his pace he caught up with the others. The men all left the building and climbed into the old Toyota Sienna. The seven-seater vehicle much to Konstantin and Andy's displeasure, could accommodate them all, so there was no chance of meeting this Obi man on their own. Vladimir then turned to Serge and told him he wasn't needed and to make his own way back to the hotel. He didn't need to be told twice and within the hour Serge was on his way to the airport. He didn't know where he was heading, he couldn't return to London in case they came looking for him. Maybe it was time to do some more travelling, anywhere so long as he got out of this Godforsaken country and away from the Russians as soon as possible!

CHAPTER TWENTY ONE

When Konstantin, Andy, Serge and their two minders had boarded their plane to Lagos; Lev Baranov was worried and so he decided to send two henchmen to England. He had little faith that the Nigerian trip would produce anything and wanted to explore every other avenue to get his money back. Konstantin had to answer to him but in turn, Lev also had bosses who were yet unaware of the fiasco that had happened. Losing that much money would make the firm look like amateurs and someone would be made to pay and pay dearly. In Russia, it was all about appearances, violence and making money and to lose millions would enrage the top men. Instructing the two henchmen to do whatever it took, he also told them to leave no loose ends.

The house on Chudleigh Street had been quiet for the last two days, far too quiet and Aida was beginning to regret her decision not to leave. She wasn't scared, she'd been through too much in her life for anything to scare her but she just missed them all so badly. The house had always felt so alive even if it was Ruby going into one or Shirley playing her music loud and of course there were the family Sunday lunches which would never happen again. Aida loved her

grandson dearly but she couldn't help feeling angry with him now, he had caused all of this and they were all being made to suffer because of his stupid business dealings. Even Ruby knew that something was wrong and continually asked for Shirley and it was driving Aida mad. If she asked once she asked a thousand times and Aida was beginning to realise just what her granddaughter had been forced to put up with since the advancement of Ruby's illness.
"I want my girl! Where is she?"
"She ain't here."
"But I want her, I want my Shirl!"
Aida got up from the table and with the aid of her brightly decorated walking stick, a present from Andy last Christmas; she hobbled over to the sofa. With a heavy thud, she dropped down onto the cushion beside her daughter.
"I know you do my darlin' but they've all had to go away. Now don't you worry, Andy will take good care of them."
"He's a good boy."
"Yes, he is sweetheart, now how about I do us both a nice bit of tea?   Smoked mackerel fillets and a lovely little salad?"
"I've never had them."
"Of course you have we always enjoyed mackerel, it was our Saturday night treat."
Ruby just stared vacantly at her mother.

"You used to love 'em with a bit of black pepper."
Ruby just continued to stare into space and when Aida had finally managed to haul herself up from the seating, the sofa was far too low; she wearily shook her head as she walked towards the kitchen. Filling the pan with water and placing it on to boil, she was just about to drop in the boil in the bag fish when there was a knock at the door. Glancing up at the kitchen clock she saw it was gone six. Who on earth would be calling now? Whoever it was wasn't giving up and continually knocked so Aida turned off the gas and slowly made her way down the hall.
"Hold your bleedin' horses; I ain't no spring chicken you know."
Opening up she came face to face with Wayne and never having liked him, Aida wasn't pleasant.
"What do you want?"
"Nice to see you too Aida. Is Shirley home only I have a few things to show her on the inter…."
Aida didn't let him finish his sentence, there was just something about him that made her skin crawl and what on earth her granddaughter saw in him was beyond her.
"She's gone away and won't be back."
Wayne looked confused. He had always had

complete control over Shirley and she would never go anywhere without checking with him first.

"I don't believe you."

"I don't give a flying fuck what you believe sunshine but I'm telling you she ain't here. Now fuck off before I call the Old Bill."

Wayne turned and began to walk down the street but would come back later; the old bat must be losing her marbles like Ruby. Returning to the kitchen, Aida continued to cook the tea and was just about to cut the bags open when there was a second knock at the door.

"Jesus Christ! Will anyone let us have our bleedin' tea in peace?"

The sound of the knock was somehow different this time, harder and louder. Tottering along the hall she was well and truly pissed off and whoever was on the other side was going to get the sharp end of her tongue. Opening the front door just enough to see who the caller was she gasped at the size of the two men standing before her. In Aida's words, they were both built like brick shit houses and looked so out of character for the area. She tried to close the door but wasn't quick enough and the bigger of the two instantly placed his boot against the frame.

"I need to speak with you."

Now Aida was scared, Andy had warned her

but she really didn't think anyone would actually come to the house and definitely not so soon. The two men towered above Aida's now frail body but she was made of strong stuff and puffed out her chest as she spoke.

"I don't know who you are and I have nothing to say to you now take your foot out of my bleedin' doorway before I call the Old Bill."

With one hand he swiftly leaned heavily on the wood and Aida wasn't strong enough to stop him. The door flew open pushing her hard against the hall wall. Once inside the two men closed the door.

"My name is Viktor and this is Boris. We have been sent here to ask you some questions and it can go easy or you can make it difficult. I would prefer this to be quick but my friend Boris likes violence so he would prefer the latter. So, what is it going to be lady?"

Aida slowly nodded her head and turning, began to walk in the direction of the front room. Ruby looked up when she saw they had visitors and standing up she began to dance around the room much to the surprise of the Russians.

"This is my daughter Ruby but take no notice of her, away with the fairies most of the bleedin' time."

"Hello."

"Hello Ruby my name is Viktor. How are you

today?"

Ruby danced over and grabbing Viktor's hand tried to pull him into the centre of the room. "I'm happy, oh so happy that you've come to visit. Please dance with me."

Victor heard Boris snigger and turning sharply gave a look that instantly wiped the smile from Boris's face. Suddenly he'd had enough of being nice and roughly pushed Ruby. She fell onto the sofa with a thud, her face full of fear. Aida was furious and waved her stick at him as she shouted.

"You bastard, how dare you do that to my girl! You should be bleedin' ashamed………"

Aida was cut off mid-sentence when Viktor lashed out again, knocking her to the ground. His gold ring had caught her on the side of the mouth and she could taste the iron in her blood as it seeped into her mouth. She was scared and now realised how naïve she'd been, these men didn't care about hurting two defenceless women. Aida had always been aware that Andy didn't exactly work inside of the law but he'd never been known for violence, not that he couldn't take care of himself if a row broke out but the men in her house were henchmen and through all the troubles in her life the only real experience she'd had of violence was at the hands of her husband. Her hip was hurting and it entered her mind that maybe it was broken, at her age it could easily happen and she prayed that wasn't the case. Again waving her walking stick in the air she tried not to show how worried she was.

"What do you want from us?"

Viktor grabbed her arm and with one swoop pulled her back onto her feet. His grip was hard and her skin was so thin that she winced in pain.

"Sit!"

Doing as she was told Aida walked over to the table just as Ruby started to cry. The sound was like that of a child and the two men just stared and then looked towards Aida.

"What's wrong with her?"

"My daughter has dementia so she won't be able to tell you anything no matter what you do to her."

"But you will! You could make things far easier by telling us where the money is. Boris, search the house."

"I don't want you going through all my bleedin' smalls; it's none of your business what we have in our home and I honestly can't tell you anything!"

Viktor glared which immediately silenced Aida. Taking a seat opposite he continued to stare which made Aida feel uncomfortable. She wanted to go to Ruby and calm her down but

she was rooted to the spot. The wailing continued but she knew no one would come to their aid as Ruby's crying was a daily occurrence and the neighbours were used to the noise. As quickly as it started it stopped and Ruby stared straight ahead her eyes set like glass. It felt like an age had passed when Boris finally entered the front room. Looking in Viktor's direction he solemnly shook his head.
"There is nothing."
Standing up and without a word Viktor headed into the hall and the men left the house without another word. Aida breathed a sigh of relief but it would be short-lived as the men would be back. Hobbling over to where her daughter sat Aida took a seat next to her and as she placed her arm around Ruby's shoulder Aida began to softly cry.

Viktor and Basil made their way over to Andy's flat in Newham. As they entered the foyer the concierge, Simeon, eyed them both suspiciously.
"Can I be of assistance gentlemen?"
Viktor knew he couldn't say they were here to visit a resident as the flat was empty and when they gave Andy's name they would be turned away. Deciding that in this instance fear would be the best way of reasoning they ignored the question and headed towards the lift.

Immediately Simeon was out of his seat and followed closely behind with all the good intentions of stopping the two unsavoury strangers from going any further. As he placed his hand onto Viktor's sleeve Simeon was instantly pushed away and then violently shoved up against the wall. Viktor then grabbed the irritating little man by the throat.
"Don't! If you know what is good for you, you will return to your desk and forget you ever saw us."
Simeon nodded his head and did as he'd been advised. He watched as the two men entered the lift and wondered which resident they had come to see, whoever it was, Simeon didn't fancy their chances. Removing a leather pouch Basil took out a couple of small tools and set about letting them inside Andy's apartment. It didn't take more than a few seconds and they soon began to rummage through the man's personal belongings. Luckily, along with some cash he had taken his second passport in the name of Michael Peters, with him on the Russian trip. The two men ransacked the apartment but came up empty handed so it was now time to revisit the old girls and this time they wouldn't stop until they got some answers. Pulling up outside the house for the second time that day, Aida saw the car from the front room window

and her heart sank.

"Looks like our visitors are back Ruby girl."
Aida considered calling the police but old habits die hard and it had always been a definite no-no in the East End. Ruby didn't take any notice and her face was expressionless as she just stared into space locked in a world of her own where no one else could ever venture. Hearing the loud knock on the door Aida ignored it and taking a seat beside her daughter she placed her arm around Ruby's shoulder.

"No matter what happens now my little darlin', remember I love you so very much."

Moments later the door could be heard bashing against the wall as it was kicked in. Viktor appeared in the doorway and he didn't look happy.

"Right! We have not found anything at that cunts flat so now you will help us or you will both die."

Aida felt the lone tear as it dropped down her cheek but Ruby only continued to stare blankly at the wall. Boris grabbed Aida by the wrists and hauled her to her feet. The snapping of her feeble bones was audible and she screamed out in agony. Still Ruby didn't utter a word and for that Aida was grateful. Dropping her down onto the floor Boris stood over her but as she attempted to hold her wrist with her good hand but the pain was so intense that she wasn't able. Removing a gun from his chest holster he slowly screwed on a silencer and then pointed it directly at the old woman's forehead. Viktor stood behind him and Aida could hear him as his voice boomed out.

"I have wasted enough time on you old woman! You have one chance only, where is the money?"

"I told you, I don't know anything, I swear I don't."

Viktor sighed; he knew that if he killed her first that would be it. Instead, he nodded to Boris who bent down and grabbing Aida by her silver-grey hair he dragged her into the centre of the front room so that she would see what they were about to do in every gory detail.

"No please, please don't hurt my girl she's innocent and couldn't tell you anything even if she wanted to."

"Then save her, you have the choice."

"I said I can't! Honestly, I would tell you but I don't know anything."

Viktor only had to look in Boris's direction and seconds later the gun was pointed at Ruby's right kneecap and then he fired. The screams were horrendous as blood poured from the wound. Aida felt the pain in her chest as it began to tighten until she couldn't breathe. She had a strange feeling in her arms and felt like she would vomit at any second. Her poor girl, what were they doing to her but Aida couldn't help, she couldn't move. It was like someone was sitting on her chest and when her breathing became laboured and she felt dizzy she realised what was happening. Dropping her head onto the carpet her eyelids began to flutter and then suddenly she had gone. Viktor walked over and prodded her in the side with the toe of his shoe. "Well that's one bullet we won't have to waste. Finish her!"

Ruby was still screaming but the noise instantly stopped the moment Boris fired into her head. The hole was clean and unlike her knee, there was only a trickle of blood. The attackers felt no guilt as they proceeded to search and ransack the ground floor. Still unable to find anything regarding the missing money, the two men walked out of the house leaving the front door wide open.

Two hours later Wayne Andino returned to the house determined to see Shirley no matter what the old woman said. Entering through the open door the first thing he saw was the mess, chairs knocked over and draws pulled out with the contents strewn over the floor. Initially, it entered his mind that the family had been burgled until he saw the bodies. Aida looked okay but it was the sight of Ruby that forced him to vomit on the spot. Running from the house he fell against the wall as panic began to set in. All he could think of was getting away but if he ran and someone saw him they might think he was the culprit and he'd get blamed. For once in his life Wayne Andino did the right thing and within a few minutes, the police were at the scene. It took a while to explain all that he knew which in all honesty was very little but he did explain about the surface of the mysterious son on Facebook. The unit investigating knew it was probably a cyber-crime but it was highly unlikely that the case would ever be solved.

CHAPTER TWENTY-TWO

Andy, Konstantin and the two heavies sat in the Toyota car, close to the home of Obi Adamu. Obi was still unaware of what had occurred at the office and as far as he was concerned it would be work as usual the following day. Strolling back from the evening market, hand in hand with Chi-Chi he felt as if he didn't have a care in the world. Money was plentiful, his wife was happy and life was finally good. As the couple entered the house, Konstantin nudged Andy's arm.

"We need to wait until dark or we will stand out like sore thumbs, I mean, how many white faces have you seen?"

Andy didn't reply he was still in utter shock after seeing Babak killed and sitting in the back pushed up against the door by Mikhail, he was starting to feel claustrophobic. He made a promise to himself; if he ever got out of this alive there was no way he would deal with the Russians again. It seemed like hours until darkness fell but in reality was less than one.

"Andy, go and knock on the door and then get back here."

"Why me, why can't you do it?"

Suddenly he felt a prod in his side and looking down, spied the barrel of Vladimir's gun.

"Okay, okay, whatever you want."
Stepping from the car he cautiously walked up to the door, rapped hard and then legged it back to the Toyota. By the time he closed the car door; Obi had opened up and was peering out into the night. After looking around he shrugged his shoulders and then closing the door, went back inside.

"Vlad, Mikhail? Go and stand either side of the door and when he comes out again, grab him! Andy, go and knock again."

Doing as he was told, a few seconds later they were all in position and again Andy rapped on the door and then fled back to the car. Obi opened the door slightly aggravated. The local kids often played pranks but this was the first time he'd been made to suffer. Seeing no one there he stepped outside to have a quick look around. Within seconds Vlad and Mikhail had thrown a canvas bag over his head and together lifted him off of the pavement and quickly carried him kicking and screaming to the car. Vlad swiftly secured his prisoner's hands with a plastic cable tie and after opening up the boot, Obi was thrown inside and the door slammed shut. He couldn't see anything and began to panic. When the car started up and drove away he knew he was in serious trouble. A few minutes later Chi-Chi called out to her husband as she was ready to serve the evening meal. The roast chicken was cooked to perfection and the jollof rice needed serving immediately. Chi-Chi had even made her husband's favourite dessert of homemade doughnuts in an attempt to sweeten him up. Recently there hadn't been anything happening in the bedroom and she was desperate to get pregnant so had gone to extra lengths tonight. When Obi didn't reply Chi-Chi threw down the tea towel in frustration and marched into the living room but it was empty. Tapping on the bathroom door she expected a response but there was nothing. Stepping outside she looked around the dimly lit street but there was no sign of him. Well, the meal would be ruined if he didn't come back soon and if that happened she would make him pay dearly. The car was driven away from the city out towards Snake Island. With only ten inhabitants it was the perfect location and Vladimir knew there was little chance of them being disturbed. Before leaving Russia he had researched the area and had foreseen what was about to happen and committing murder in a densely populated area in a foreign country was tantamount to suicide so this location was perfect. As the terrain became rough and the car bounced around on the unmade road, Obi began to kick out at the lid of the boot but it did no good. At last, the car came to a stop and the engine was switched off. Obi pressed his ear to the side of the metal but because of the canvas bag on his head, all he could hear was muffled voices. Suddenly the boot was opened and he was hauled out and then marched along a dirt track. Obi stumbled and fell but the men holding his arms were strong and he was soon back on his feet. Moments later he was pushed to the ground in a kneeling position. The bag was swiftly removed but when he looked up he had to squint as a torch was being shone directly into his eyes.

"Where is the money?"

Obi began to panic, for a start he didn't know which of the scams he had pulled off the men were referring to.

"We know it was you, your boss was very forthcoming with the truth."

Babak would never reveal anything, not unless they had tortured him. That realisation pushed Obi over the edge and he began to cry like a baby. Andy stepped forward and he was ragging. He wanted answers and not about the missing money, he wanted answers about Ruby.

"You snivelling little bastard! You played my poor mother like a fucking fool. Remember Ruby? Ruby Chilvers, the woman you made believe was your mother?"

Now Obi knew exactly what scam they were talking about and the amount of cash involved. "Please, let me explain. I only work for Babak. I get a wage but he keeps all the real money, he's the one who has what is yours, not me. Please let me go, I promise I won't let him know you have spoken to me."

"Too late sunshine, he's dead!"

Seconds later Vlad removed his gun and shot their hostage straight in the back of the head. The force propelled Obi's body forwards and into the mud. Andy's gasp was audible to all but when the gun was then pointed at Konstantin Andy began to run. His heart was beating so hard that he thought it would burst and then he heard Konstantin pitifully pleading for his life.

"What the fuck are you doing!? The boss will kill you for this!"

Vladimir grinned.

"This is Mr Baranov's wish. You have lost him a great deal of money and now I am sure that it cannot be retrieved, so you are now surplus to requirements and need to be disposed of."

"No, please, we can talk about this, I can get the money back just please give me a chance."

The last thing Andy heard was a single gunshot as Konstantin's life was terminated. Andy didn't hear the bullet with his name on but when it hit

him in the lower back he dropped to the ground. Still alive, he knew better than to try and get up. Playing dead was his only chance of survival and lady luck was shining on him that day. As Vlad and Mikhail began to walk towards him a dog suddenly started to bark and a strange voice was heard as it called out to the animal.
"Hambo! Here boy."
The dog ignored its owner and began to sniff around Konstantin's body. Vlad and Mikhail didn't know if the man was alone so it was too risky to hang around. In agreement that there was no way Andy would survive, especially being this distance from the city, they ran back to the Toyota and seconds later the car sped off. Chimezie Kalu, a local farmer and owner of the dog cautiously approached. First, he knelt beside Konstantin but as soon as he felt for a pulse and there was none he walked towards Andy. Unaware of who was kneeling beside him and thinking that it might be the Russians Andy continued to play dead. Chimezie again felt for a pulse and when he realised the wounded man was still alive he ran as fast as he could back to his small farm. Chimezie was a fourth-generation farmer on the land that no one else wanted. Growing coconuts he didn't earn much but it was an easy way of life and brought in just enough to get by. The old Isuzu pickup

was over twenty years old but she still had a lot of life left in her. Jumping into the driver's seat he retrieved the keys from the sun visor and started the engine. Driving over rough terrain the headlights soon picked up Andy's body, he had tried to move but his legs wouldn't work. Chimezie jumped out and somehow managed to drag Andy to the back of the van and haul him on board. Glancing around to make sure he hadn't been seen he then slowly drove back to his farm. Once inside the one-roomed hut that he called home, he laid Andy on the floor and rolled him over so that he could inspect the wounds.

"Can you hear me, my friend?"

Andy was able to nod his head, he was in excruciating pain and the beads of sweat on his forehead shone in the dim light.

"They will find your friend's body in the daylight and if I take you to the hospital they will know you are involved. We have basic medical care in Nairobi but there is nothing basic about gunshot wounds. Do you have money my friend and I mean lots of it?"

Andy shook his head and in any case, what he had was back at the hotel.

"In that case, I can assist you with the old ways if you will allow me?"

Again Andy nodded, what choice did he have?

Chimezie disappeared for what felt like hours but in reality, it was less than one. When he returned he carried an armful of various herbs and greenery.

"I have not done this for a very long time my friend but it is your only option. Handing Andy a bottle he told him to drink as much as he could. When the bottle was empty and his head felt as if it was swimming, Chimezie turned Andy onto his stomach and handed him a piece of wood to bite down on.

"This is going to hurt like nothing you've ever felt before but I have to remove the bullets or you will die. I can't risk you crying out so do your best and be strong."

In the dim light Andy's saviour set about cutting into the flesh and each time he inserted a pair of tweezers into the wound he felt Andy's entire body tense up but not once did he cry out. Finally, the pain became so unbearable that Andy passed out which was a blessing as it allowed Chimezie to continue without resistance. Luckily he was able to remove the bullets and though no expert, he didn't think any damage had been done to the major organs. By the looks of things, one of the bullets might have taken a nick out of Andy's spine so whether the man would ever walk again remained to be seen. Stitching up the open wound Chimezie then made a poultice with the greenery and packed it tightly onto Andy's back. A fever came and went and two days later Andy finally woke up. Looking at Chimezie who was sitting on the floor beside him he smiled.

"I'm Chimezie Kalu but people who know me just call me Chimezie.

Andy had to stifle a laugh.

"Pleased to meet you Chimezie and thank you for saving my life. The other man?"

Chimezie slowly shook his head, no more needed to be said and Andy remained silent for a few minutes.

"Where did the two men go?"

"I don't know. They drove off when Hambo started to bark."

"Chimezie, I know you have done so much for me already but I need to ask another favour. My passport is still at the hotel."

Chimezie nodded and at the same time handed Andy the items he had taken out of Andy's jacket pocket. The room card was still there and Andy breathed a sigh of relief. Passing it to Chimezie he then gave the address of the hotel.

"I will go after dark, it will be safer then."

Andy must have drifted off to sleep because when he woke he was alone and it was dark outside. Chimezie must have already left but whether he would return once he'd looked in

Andy's possessions was another matter but there was Hobson's choice so Andy just had to hope for the best. Chimezie Kalu drove into the city, parked a few hundred meters from the hotel and for a while he sat and watched for anything unusual. The two gunmen could still be inside but after two hours had passed he knew he had no choice but to risk it. Luckily the reception desk was empty as he walked inside so he headed straight up to the second floor via the staircase. Nearing Andy's room he stopped when he saw a door open and two men emerged carrying cases. Tall and well-built, it was obvious that they weren't locals and his assumption that they must be the gunmen was right. They must have waited to see if anyone came back to the hotel in case Andy wasn't dead. After hanging around for two days, Vladimir and Mikhail were confident that they had fully carried out Lev's wishes. Chimezie didn't stop at Andy's room; instead, he continued walking down the hallway until he heard the lift door close. Giving it another couple of minutes just in case they returned for some reason, he then let himself into the room. Andy's bag was still on the bed and glancing around he collected up anything he thought belonged to his new friend. Walking from the hotel he didn't relax until he was back in the cab of his van. This had all been exciting but it was excitement he could do without. When he walked back into the hut Andy smiled and he was even happier when he saw that his bags hadn't been opened. Trying to stand, he momentarily screamed out in pain and in seconds Chimezie was by his side.

"My friend you have not yet healed. Injuries like you have will take months to heal, you must be patient."

Reaching inside his bag Andy grabbed a handful of cash, more money than Chimezie had ever seen.

"I want you to take this. Not only have you saved my life and cared for me but it looks as if I will be here for quite some time. Now, it's in sterling so you will have to get it changed but I ask that you don't go on a spending spree which will get people, your friends, asking questions."

"Who said crime doesn't pay?"

"I didn't say it was criminal money."

Chimezie smiled and nodded and they both let the matter drop but he had no intention of spending the money yet. When this was all over and when Andy was well and had left Nigeria, Chimezie would find a way to leave Lagos as well and he would do so as a wealthy man.

CHAPTER TWENTY-THREE
2 Months later

In Thailand, things were going well for Debbie and she had found work at a local advertising agency. Even after all of her visits over the years her Thai was still very basic so they used her skills with all the English companies on the books. The same couldn't be said regarding Shirley. Every day she would sit on the front porch waiting for her brother to arrive and every evening she would come inside with tears in her eyes. Debbie hadn't got the heart to tell her that it was more than likely he wasn't coming. After their two-night-only sexual encounter, Debbie hadn't fallen in love with Andy, she liked him well enough and under different circumstances, they might have made a good couple but she was a realist and knew that he was either dead or had found a better life somewhere. Either way, she was happy to forget about him but it was becoming increasingly harder by the day with how Shirley was behaving. Shirley missed her family terribly, she hated the excessive heat and even though she had vowed to try the different foods on offer they all turned her stomach when she looked at them and she longed for a plate of good old English fish and chips. They did serve it at the bar on the beach but it was nothing like home and the fish tasted funny and she was sure it wasn't cod.

At the Agency, it wasn't long before Debbie caught the eye of a fellow employee. Niran Suwan was been born in Thailand but his parents had crossed the border from Vietnam when war had broken out in nineteen fifty-five. He had studied hard and was now the second in command at the agency and spoke fluent English. Initially, Debbie hadn't been interested but Niran didn't give up easily. Finally, she relented and invited him to dinner and Kannika prepared a fabulous meal for the couple. Shirley was in a strop and refused to attend the dinner, she had hoped that when Andy got here the two of them would get together. When Niran knocked at the door it was Shirley who answered and to say she was rude to him was an understatement. Kannika had been close by and she'd heard the exchange and immediately told Debbie. Secretly Kannika was over the moon that Debbie was with a Thai national, she didn't want to jump the gun but if they ended up together then Debbie would never leave and she didn't want Shirley to spoil everything. After greeting her guest, Debbie then grabbed Shirley by the arm and dragged her outside.
"And what was all that about?"
"All what?"

"Why were you rude to Niran?"
"I don't like him and besides, I thought you were waiting for Andy?"
Now Debbie felt guilty, not because she was being disloyal but because it was obvious Shirley was hurting so badly and missing her family.
"Sweetheart, I think it's about time you accepted that he isn't coming. He told us how dangerous it was going to be and in all honesty and I know you don't want to hear this but I think he might be dead."
Shirley began to cry and when Debbie tried to take her in her arms to console her, Shirley roughly pushed her away and ran off into the darkness. Back in the house, she told Kannika what had happened and the maid said she would go and look for the young woman.
"Is everything okay Debbie?"
"I'm so sorry about this Niran but my friend thought that I was waiting for her brother. We had a very short fling before I left the UK and she's got it into her head that we were going to be together."
"And are you?"
"Am I what?"
"Waiting for this man?"
"No. Sadly, I think he's probably dead but that's a long story for another time."
Niran took her in his arms and hugged her.

It felt good, it had been so long since anyone had made her feel wanted. The meal was a hit but throughout Shirley was on Debbie's mind and she only relaxed when Kannika and Shirley finally walked into the house later that night. Shirley refused to speak to anyone and instead, she stormed off to her room. At least she was safe and tomorrow would be soon enough to talk and try to sort things out.

The next morning at breakfast and you could cut the atmosphere with a knife. As soon as Kannika had placed the food on the table she disappeared back into the kitchen. The two women had to sort out their differences and for that they needed privacy.

"Shirley we need to talk."

"Do we? You seemed to have made yourself perfectly fucking clear last night. Do you want me to move out?"

"Don't be so silly of course I don't. I know you were hurt by what I said but we have to be realistic; we have to move on with our lives my darling."

"I know but it's so hard for me."

Shirley wasn't being truthful, she was still angry and last night she had hatched a plan, she was going home, at least for a visit. Later that day she found her passport and logging onto the computer, booked herself a one-way ticket to

London. Her documents were in her new name so she travelled under Sally Monroe but thankfully no one called out to her as she wouldn't have answered. It wasn't until the end of the day when Debbie came home from work that she realised Shirley was missing. Initially, she panicked but after searching the history file on the computer she found out about the flight. It was too late to stop the woman as the plane had already taken off; all she could do was pray that Shirley was safe and would remain so.

In London, the first port of call for Shirley Tanner had been Chudleigh Street. Getting out of the taxi she walked up to the front door and was about to knock but was stopped when she saw the yellow crime scene tape across the door. Her heart sank as she remembered what Andy had said about the men who were after him, how dangerous they were. Next, she headed for Bethnal Green Road in the hope that Wayne was at the Café. At first, she was hesitant to go inside but she couldn't just stand on the pavement all day. Walking up to the counter she rang the bell and when Mrs Andino emerged from behind a beaded curtain, she took one look at Shirley and then disappeared. In the past, the little Greek woman had never been overly friendly with her son's girlfriend but she had at least always said hello. A few seconds later the curtain parted again and Wayne appeared. Almost running to the other side of the counter he flung his arms around her.

"I've missed you so much, babe, where on earth have you been?"

Shirley began to cry so leading her over to a table in the corner where he knew they wouldn't be interrupted, he told her to take a seat.

"So, you didn't answer me. Where have you been?"

"It's a long story but Andy got into a bit of bother and some men, really bad men, were looking for him so we had to leave the country." Shirley was still guarded and never said what country they had gone to.

"Anyway, me and Debbie, that's another long story but we left and Andy was meant to join us but he never showed up and Debbie thinks he's dead. My Nan wouldn't come so she stayed home with mum but when I went to the house there wasn't anyone home and there was bright yellow tape over the front door. What on earth has happened to them, Wayne?"

Wayne felt a knot in his stomach, she didn't know about her mum and Nan. It was strange, after all the mean things he'd said and done to her but when she wasn't around he had really missed her. Wayne Andin wasn't a very nice person and because of the way he was, he had no friends. The only one who had ever stuck around was Shirley and he was going to make sure that from now on he treated her with the love and respect she deserved.

"Sweetheart I have some really bad news and it's going to break your heart."

Shirley's eyes were open wide and almost pleading with him not to say what she knew deep down he was going to.

"Your mum and nan were killed just a short time after you left. I went around to the house to see you and I found them."

"How, how were they killed?"

"Oh Shirl, you don't need to know the gruesome details, sweetheart. What good would it do?"

About to protest she thought better of it. If they were made to suffer in some terrible way then she would never sleep again. Suddenly she broke down sobbing and Wayne gripped her hand tightly.

"I'm so, so sorry babe. Look, you can stay here for a while it's no trouble."

Instantly she was on her feet and heading towards the door.

"I need to get out of here; I need to get my head around all of this."

Shirley was far more street-wise than anyone gave her credit for. She knew she had to get as far away from here as she possibly could. Deep down she realised she should never have returned and the only place she had to go to and the only people she had now, were in Thailand. Arriving back less than two days after she had left, Debbie was overjoyed to see her. Shirley revealed the news of her Nan and mum's death and the two women shared a day of tears. Debbie hadn't known them well but they had taken her into their home and kept her safe and for that she would always be grateful. Remembering when her parents had passed and how devastated she had been made her stay close to Shirley but strangely the woman seemed to have accepted her loss well, maybe too well.

The next month passed in a whirl and Niran was at the house more than he was in his own home which pleased Kannika. He was handsome and polite and it wasn't long before Debbie started to fall for him. He soon introduced her to his parents and within a month he had proposed. Shirley hadn't been overjoyed when she was given the news but she knew they all had to move on so she reluctantly congratulated the couple. There was just one problem, Debbie started to be sick every morning and when Kannika had heard the retching for the third day in a row she confronted Debbie one morning as she served up breakfast.

"Are you pregnant?"

Debbie was shocked; she thought she had hidden it well but obviously not.

"Excuse me?"

"You heard me well enough and there's no use burying your head in the sand you must deal with it."

"I'm not sure but if I am then I'm scared. It isn't Niran's and I know he will leave me when he finds out. I had so much unhappiness in my marriage to Colin and then Andy came along and it just happened."

"Why don't you tell Niran it is his?"

"I can't Kannika as we haven't slept together and even if we had I could never do that to him."

"When you get to work buy a test. Invite Niran over tonight and if it's positive you can tell him. If it's not then no harm has been done."

Debbie nodded her agreement but she wasn't looking forward to it and all day she was on tenterhooks. When she reached the house at just after five, Kannika was waiting for her. Debbie went straight to the bathroom. After peeing on the wand she sat on the toilet and waited. The three minutes felt like a lifetime and she could see her hands were shaking when she picked up the small stick, a stick that could possibly change her life forever. Carrying it through to the kitchen she handed it to Kannika.

"I daren't look."

The two lines were clearly showing and Kannika slowly nodded her head.

"Oh no!"

"Well at least we know, what time is Niran getting here?"

"Any minute. Well, I just have to get it over with I suppose."

A few minutes later there was a knock at the door but when Debbie opened up she looked sad and didn't place her arms around his neck like she normally did.

"Are you okay?"

"No, I'm afraid I'm not. We need to talk."

Grabbing his hand she led him over to the sofa and after taking a seat she looked deeply into his eyes.

"You're not going to like what I have to say but it still has to be said."

Niran went to interrupt but she stopped him, if she didn't continue now she didn't think she would ever be able to tell him. Maybe it would be easier not to, maybe it would be best just to end things but she owed him the truth no matter how much it was going to hurt.

"You remember I told you about Shirley's brother? We only slept together twice and it wasn't love, just two lonely people needing someone. Anyway, I'm pregnant."

Niran turned away for a second so that she couldn't see the tears in his eyes. He had waited so long to find the one and now his future had been torn apart. Suddenly he turned to her and took both of her hands in his.

"I will raise this child as my own. We will tell no one our secret and we will be happy Debbie I promise you that."

"Kannika knows and I have to tell Shirley as the baby will be her niece or nephew and besides, after what she has just been through it will help her to heal. Apart from those two, I swear it will never leave this house but are you really sure about this?"

"I have never been more sure of anything, I love you Debbie and always will."

The following morning Debbie asked Shirley to join her for a walk. The sun was shining brightly as they headed down towards the beach. Only a few days ago everything had been good in her world but now it felt as if she was on an emotional roller coaster.

"Let's take a seat on the sand as I need to tell you something, Shirley."

Shirley Tanner didn't know what was going to be said but she imagined that Debbie might ask her to leave the house after she got married and panic was evident in her eyes as she waited for Debbie to speak.

"I'm pregnant and it's Andy's child."

Shirley threw her arms around Debbie's neck and sobbed until she didn't think there were any more tears left. Slowly she pulled away and looked at Debbie.

"What about Niran?"

"I told him last night and he still wants to marry me. He wants to raise the child as his own."

Shirley took a moment to think. It should be her brother, not this man but what choice did Debbie have, be a single parent?

"Okay, I understand. One more thing, aren't you still married?"

Debbie laughed, this was all so absurd.

"In the eyes of the Law yes but Andy told me that Colin was dead and as we have no plans to ever return to England I can't see what difference it makes. You are certain you didn't tell anyone where we are living?"

"I promise. Wayne asked but I didn't tell him. Oh Debbie what a fucking mess! This news should have been the icing on the cake but now it's tinged with sadness."

"Maybe it is but only for a while. We have to stop looking back at the past and make a future for ourselves and the little person who will be joining us in just a few months. Come on let's go back, we have a wedding to plan."

CHAPTER TWENTY-FOUR
LAGOS

After the shootings, Vladimir and Mikhail returned to Russia and went straight to the club to explain everything to their boss. Well aware of how Lev would react, the two men had drawn straws to decide who would reveal all and Vlad had lost. He slowly walked into the room with his hands nervously held behind his back and his fingers crossed.

"The money was nowhere to be found Mr. Baravov. We tortured the men involved but they couldn't or wouldn't tell us anything." Vladimir didn't mention the fact that Konstantin had killed the main man before they could get anything out of him. Lev would have blamed his men for letting it happen in the first place.

"And Konstantin and the Englishman?"

"Dead just as you ordered."

"I said kill them when you had my money!"

"I'm sorry Sir. I shot Konstantin in the head but the other one ran. I managed to hit him in the back and I think he was dead but we got disturbed."

Lev Baranov was now irate. These men were muppets and he was now in fear for his life because when his bosses were told the truth the blame would lie squarely at his feet and the top

men wouldn't look favourably when informed that they had lost more than thirty million.
"What the fuck do you mean think!? Go back and check, I cannot have any loose ends."
"But Mr Baranov we….."
"I said go back! That's unless you want the same fate as Konstantin?"

Four days later Vladimir and Mikhail returned to Lagos and scoured every hospital in the city but no one had been admitted who remotely answered to Andy's description. After liberally greasing the palm of a local police sergeant, they were told that the body of a foreigner had been found on Snake Island and as yet the man hadn't been identified but there was no mention of a second victim. Vlad wanted to ask and about to speak, he was nudged by Mikhail. To mention a further body would bring suspicion on them and that was the last thing they needed. Booking into a hotel they spent the evening planning what to do next. The following day they headed down to the street market and began to ask around the locals. As soon as Vlad opened his wallet he was surrounded, now everyone wanted to help them.

On Snake Island, Andy was still struggling and every day Chimezie had made him stand up and

try and take a few steps but it was proving difficult not to mention very painful. The Lagos branch of the Red Cross, without any questions, had provided a set of old crutches, in Nairobi people got hurt all the time and few had money for medical expenses. That wasn't true for Andy but he didn't dare go to a hospital just in case somehow word got back to Russia. His worst fears turned out to be true when Chimezie returned from the market one day with frightening news. Russian men had been asking if anyone had seen an injured white man in the area. A reward was on offer but thankfully Chimezie had told no one about his guest. People were poor, dirt poor and would do anything for money to feed their families and he was worried. A couple of days later Chimezie was about to head out to buy food but when he opened the door he saw a white car approaching.
"Andy, hide!"
The only problem was the hut had just one room so lifting the old mattress he climbed underneath and Chimezie piled blankets and clothes on top. Walking from the hut as if he didn't have a care in the world, he made out he was about to get into his old van when one of the men called out. Stopping he smiled.
"Can I help you, Sir?"

Vladimir walked over and Hambo took an instant dislike to the visitor and began to bark. He was a good guard dog and an even better judge of a man's character but luckily for the Russians, he was also chained up.

"Quite Hambo!"

"We are looking for someone and are going from house to house on the island."

Chimezie smiled, it wouldn't take them long as there weren't more than five properties even if they were spread out and from the direction the car had come from he reasoned that he must be the second place they had stopped at.

"We don't get many people over here and I haven't seen anyone new."

Vladimir looked the man up and down, his clothes were dirty and torn and the place was a shambles. In his mind, he decided that there was very little chance that the Englishman would be here. Chimezie then took a risk and tried reverse psychology.

"Can I offer you both a drink on this hot day? I don't have much but you are welcome to what I do have. Please come inside."

Vlad scanned the shanty building, it was filthy and he wasn't about to accept the man's hospitality.

"Thank you but we have to be on our way."

Handing Chimezie a piece of paper with a

phone number scrawled on it he told the man to contact him if he saw anyone. The offer of a reward saw Chimezie nod his head several times to look convincing. The car sped off and when it had disappeared from view he went back into the hut and lifting the mattress off of his friend, he hauled Andy to his feet.

"That was a close call."

"It would have been even fucking closer had they have taken you up on your offer. What on earth were you thinking?"

"Don't worry Andy, they took one look at this place and how I'm dressed and all they saw is dirt and decay. If I was dressed well and the place was smart they may well have accepted."

Both men began to laugh and Chimezie, out of the blue, suddenly hugged Andy to him.

"What is this for?"

"You are a good friend Andy."

"And you are an even better one, you saved my life and I will be forever grateful."

The next morning Chimezie went to the market again and after asking a few friends, he found out that the two men had left Lagos. Returning home he was over the moon when he walked into the hut and told Andy he didn't have anything to worry about.

"They will never stop looking for me; the only thing that would stop them is if Lev were to die."

Andy stared at his friend trying to judge a reaction but there was none.

"Did you expect me to be shocked? I have come to learn that in this life it is all about self-preservation and peace of mind and I understand that while this Lev man is still alive you will never have either. Shall we go to Russia and kill him?"

The sentence was said so matter of fact that for a moment Andy was dumbstruck.

"I don't think you know how dangerous these men are Chimezie."

"In my village, we were known as warriors."

Andy started to laugh but immediately stopped when he realised he had insulted his host.

"Thank you but no. When I am fitter I need to return to England and check on my family, after that, who knows?"

It was a lengthy recuperation and Andy would stay on the island for another seven months. Week on week his mobility had improved but he still walked with a limp and needed the aid of a cane. Accepting defeat, he realised that this was probably as good as he was ever going to get. Handing Chimezie some money and his fake passport, he asked his friend to go into the city and book a flight to the UK. Two days later his friend drove Andy to the airport and at the departure gate the two men embraced.

"Will I ever see you again Andy?"

Not wanting to offend but knowing it was highly unlikely, Andy pulled away so that he could look at the man.

"Who knows but I hope so. Leave Lagos Chimezie and make a new life for yourself with the money I gave you. As soon as I get home I will write to you at the municipal post office and give you my phone number. Thank you for all you have done for me, you are the best friend anyone could wish for."

Chimezie handed Andy a scrap of paper.

"Don't write Andy, it takes too long. There is an internet café in the business district. I have an email address; you can send me your number that way."

For a farmer from a rural area, this surprised Andy and he couldn't help but laugh.

"Okay my friend."

As he turned towards the gate, he saw Chimezie wipe his eyes and it brought a lump to Andy's throat. In the world he lived, it was highly unusual for anyone to do anything for free but this man had gone beyond that and it was something Andy would never forget.

When his flight landed it was grey and overcast. Rain drizzled down and it was gloomy but Andy was glad to be home and couldn't wait to see Aida and Ruby. After a lengthy wait for his backpack, he hailed a cab and asked the driver to take him to Chudleigh Street. The police tape had now been removed and walking around to the rear of the house he located the spare key that they kept in the backyard in the peg bag. Letting himself into the kitchen he called out but there was no reply. The place was cold and a chill ran down his spine, usually his Nan had the heating on full blast but when he touched the radiator it was stone cold. As Andy made his way down the hall towards the front room he noticed all the sooty marks on the walls and doorframe, it was the residue left by the scene of crime officers in their attempt to lift any prints. Pushing the door open he could feel the nausea begin to rise and when he saw the dried blood on the carpet he couldn't stop himself and vomited on the spot. The Russians had paid a visit of that he was certain. Picking up a card that had been left on the table he read the details of detective Steve Barnard, stationed at Bethnal Green Nick. Lifting the receiver to the house phone there was no dialling tone; obviously the account had been closed. For several seconds he just stared around his family home not knowing what to do next. The only option left open to him was to call the detective, something he really didn't want to do but first he would have to purchase a new mobile. The house felt creepy but at the same time it was somewhere to stay and he very much doubted that the men would return, not after what they had done but what had they done? What if his mother and Nan were in the hospital? Walking to the high Street he purchased a phone and contract under his new identity. He asked the sales assistant if she would charge the battery for him and he would return in a couple of hours. The nearest hospitals to the house were The Mile End Road and The Royal London Hospital so Andy decided to start with the latter. When both places showed no admittance, he collected his phone, purchased a bottle of whisky and then headed back to the house.

The next morning and feeling dreadful due to the amount of alcohol he had consumed, Andy now accepted that he had no other option than to call Detective Barnard. Steve Barnard had been on the case from the moment the bodies had been discovered but the investigation had gone cold almost immediately. When a call regarding the case came through he couldn't believe what he was hearing. Andy introduced himself and asked the detective if he had time to call at the house. In seconds Steve was out of his seat and heading over to Chudleigh Street.

The seven-minute journey was completed in five and Andy was shocked when he heard someone knocking on the door. Cautiously he opened up just enough to see who was there.
"Mr Chilvers, Mr Andrew Chilvers?"
"Who are you?"
"Detective Barnard, we spoke earlier."
"Fuck me, that was fast."
"To be honest Mr Chilvers, this case was dead from the off so any information is helpful because at the moment it will soon be listed as a cold case and we both know what happens then."
Andy held the door open while the detective stepped inside and then checking that there was no one lurking about outside he closed the door and motioned for Steve Barnard to follow him through to the front room. Steve could immediately sense how on edge his host was, also Andy walking with a cane didn't go unnoticed and when his host took a seat at the table it was obvious he was in some pain. Steve sat down opposite. Pouring another glass of whisky for himself Andy offered one to his guest but Steve declined.
"As much as I'd like to join you, I'm on duty."
Andy nodded, took a sip of his drink and then began to talk.
"Before we start, can ask if my mother and

grandmother are dead?"

"You mean to tell me you don't know?"

"All I know is that I found a shit load of blood in here when I returned."

"Then sadly, I have to inform you that yes, they are both dead."

"So, have they been buried?"

"No. It's an ongoing case and no next of kin could be located so the bodies are still at the morgue."

Andy winced and Steve realised that his choice of words could have been put more sympathetically.

"Can I arrange the funerals?"

"Of course, an inquest was held a couple of weeks ago so there is no need to hold your mum and Nan any longer. Now, what can you tell me regarding what happened to them?"

Andy studied the detective as he removed a small tape recorder from his pocket, pressed record and then laid it onto the table.

"You can turn that bastard off right now!"

Steve Barnard grinned; it had been worth a try at least. Andy had never trusted coppers, in fact he had never even had a conversation with one but now it was time to break the rules of the underworld if he was ever to find any peace or justice for his family.

"It's a long story and everything I am going to

tell you is off the record, let's say hypothetical. It will close your case but no one will be brought to justice. The story will seem a bit farfetched and it's up to you to decide if it's true or not. Are we in agreement with that, if not this conversation is over."

Steve Barnard slowly nodded his head. It wasn't what he wanted to hear but he could tell that the man would not share any details unless he agreed.

"I'm going to use myself as the main character but in no way am I admitting to anything."

"Fair enough."

"From a young age, I began working outside of the law, nothing violent but it was most certainly illegal. Anyway, I somehow got mixed up with a Russian bloke who I thought was my friend but I ended up owing him a favour. They are slippery cunts and you get sucked in without realising it. I had been played and as you can imagine, that favour got called in pretty quickly. To cut a long story short, I ended up being a kind of banker for a Russian mafia group, I didn't want to but I had no choice. Around the same time my old mum was diagnosed with dementia. It was tough as my Nan wasn't very mobile so both of their care landed on the shoulders of my younger sister."

"So where is she?"

"Hold your horses; I have a long way to go yet. We got Mum a laptop, we tried anything we could to keep what brain cells she had left, alive. Unbeknown to us she struck up a friendship with someone on social media. The result? She was scammed by some cunt online who managed to get her bank details, Cayman Island bank accounts opened by me but in her name plus one in the name of my business. Over a short period of time that cunt almost emptied every one of them, money that belonged to the Russians and by the time I got wind of it all, there was just a few grand left."

Steve Barnard didn't speak but puffed out his cheeks in shock.

"So how much are you talking about, hypothetically speaking of course."

"Thirty-plus million."

Steve's eyes were now open as wide as saucers.

"Fuck me!"

"As you can imagine, I had no alternative but to come clean. I really thought they would top me but my so called friend wanted to try and trace the money before that happened. It took a while but the scammer was finally located in Nigeria. Me and my Russian friend, along with two henchmen, who were supplied by the Russian boss I might add, travelled to Nigeria. Needless to say, the money couldn't be located. The Mafia

didn't take kindly to the news and they shot my friend. I ran for my life and got shot in the back but thankfully with the help of a local farmer I survived. When the men were disturbed they scarpered but came back not long ago to find out if I was still alive. There was no record of me at any hospital and as far as I know, they returned to Russia. As for my sister, I got her out of the country as quickly as I could before I even confessed to what had happened."
"So what you're saying is that the Russians killed your mother and grandmother?"
Andy slowly nodded his head.
"I pleaded with Nan to take mum and go with Shirley but she flatly refused so I had no alternative but to leave them here. You know what old cockney women are like, hard work at the best of times and even worse if you try and make 'em do something they don't want to. My old Nan was a fighter in her youth and sadly in her eighties she still thought she could take on the fucking world and his wife. Anyway, the main man, or at least the one I was introduced to was called Lev Baranova but you wouldn't get within a mile of him. These men are fucking animals Detective but you will never locate them and even if you did, I would never testify. Who found the bodies?"
"Someone by the name of Wayne Andino, he

didn't give us much and I could tell he was reluctant to even give his name but I suppose I don't blame him after what he found. So this is it I suppose Mr Chilvers, the end of the line?"

"Like I said, there's no way I will ever give a statement."

"I'm sad about that but should you ever have a change of heart and wish to take things further, hypothetically of course, then please contact me."

Andy showed Steve Barnard to the door and after he closed it, leaned back onto the paintwork and looked up to the ceiling as he said out loud 'I'm sorry Mum, I'm so, so sorry'.

CHAPTER TWENTY-FIVE

After a restless night's sleep, Andy decided he would pay Wayne a visit and then make arrangements to lay Ruby and Aida to rest. Wearily he washed and dressed and then headed to the Athens Café on Bethnal Green Road. The place was rammed with breakfast diners and taking a seat he waited to see if Wayne was at work today. A few moments later Shirley's former boyfriend walked over to the table to take the order but when he saw who he was about to serve he stopped dead in his tracks.
"I haven't done anything Andy honest I haven't. She just ran out saying she needed some time and I never saw her again."
"What on earth are you on about?"
Wayne took a seat and placed his sweaty palms on his thighs.
"Shirl, she came to see me."
"When!?"
"A few weeks ago and I had to tell her about your Mum and Nan. She broke down then said she needed some air but she didn't come back."
Andy began to panic, what on earth was his sister doing back in London? He didn't have a clue where to look for her so his only option was to go to Thailand to see Debbie and find out if she knew where Shirley was but he had to

arrange the funerals first.

"I'll try and find her; if I do I will let you know Wayne."

The Greek smiled, for the first time ever, he was happy to be in the company of Shirley's brother. "Thank you, I know I wasn't the best boyfriend material but I did love her you know."

Andy nodded and then left the café. The funeral directors, T England & Sons were also situated on Bethnal Green Road but as he made his way there, out of the corner of his eye Andy noticed another café offering free internet access. Tapping his jacket pocket he felt the memory stick that he had pulled out of Babak's computer without anyone seeing. It was probably nothing and could even be password-protected but he decided it was worth having a look. Ordering a coffee he pushed the device into the side of the computer and couldn't believe what popped up on the screen. There was no need to log in, Babak must have been so confident his business was safe that he hadn't bothered with any protection. Every single pound that had been stolen from the Russians came up on the screen and Andy knew he had to move it before anyone else was able to find it. This was going to take time but it would have to wait until he'd made arrangements to lay his mother to rest. Before he left he pulled out a scrap of paper from his pocket and tapped in Chimezie's email address. Typing in his phone number, he also asked his friend to take a photograph on his phone and send it back. He gave strict instructions that it must only be a head and shoulders shot and Chimezie must not smile. Andy didn't explain what he wanted the image for but Chimezie wasn't stupid and Andy knew he would work out what it was all about.

Walking along to the funeral home, as he entered it gave Andy the creeps but worse was to come when old man England came through a set of crimson velvet curtains. He looked ancient and with a curvature of the spine it was like something from a horror movie.

"How can I be of help Sir?"

"I need to arrange a double funeral. I will not be attending and I don't require any announcement in the gazette. I want basic coffins with a single red rose on each and straightforward cremations. I want 'Abide with me' played as they are brought in, the Lord's Prayer said as the coffins are lowered to the furnace and that's it. Here's six grand to cover the cost."

"Where shall I send the invoice?"

"No need but be certain that if my requirements are not met then I will find out and you'll be the next fucking corpse going in the oven."

Andy then gave the bare minimum of details so

that the bodies could be collected from the morgue and left his number so that he could be sent a text with the date. With that he left leaving old man English visibly shaken but not so much that he would turn down the work. The cost to his business would be roughly two thousand so he stood to make a healthy profit. Rubbing his hands together he disappeared back behind the curtains.

In Russia, Vlad and Mikhail were now facing their boss and to say they were worried was an understatement. Again Lev was waiting for them in the stone room and his patience was wearing thin.
"So?"
"Nothing Mr Baranov but I do have one last idea."
"What?"
"I think we should return to London. The Englishman's family were wiped out and if he did survive then he's bound to have returned for the funerals."
Lev took a moment to think. It was at least worth a try and one last ditched attempt to save his own life couldn't be overlooked.
"Okay. Go tonight and don't return until you have some news."
Lev had ten days until he attended the six

monthly meeting with the heads of the Babanin family and not going wasn't an option.
Next on Andy's list was a visit to Richmond and the house of Harry Richardson. He had to hire a car as he didn't dare set foot in Soho to collect his own which he imagined was still parked at the back of Konstantin's pub. He used his fake passport and driving licence and less than thirty minutes later he sat behind the wheel of a relatively new Nissan Qashqai. Taking the A406 he headed for Richmond and an hour and a half later tentatively knocked on the front door of Harry Richardson's home. When his old friend opened up he couldn't believe who was standing on the step.
"Well bless my soul, didn't think I'd ever see your ugly fuckin' mug again."
Andy smiled as the older man warmly embraced him and then ushered him inside. Harry couldn't be off noticing his guests recently acquired limp but he didn't comment, knowing all would be revealed soon enough. After they were seated in his study and Harry had poured them both a scotch, he turned to Andy.
"So, what's occurred?"
"You're not going to believe this. After I left you, I got the girls out of the country. Mum and Nan wouldn't budge so I had no option but to leave them both behind. Anyway, I was made to

take a trip to Russia with Konstantin and some tech wizard by the name of Serge who had been able to track down the money to somewhere in Lagos."

"Fuckin' Lagos!?"

Andy slowly nodded his head and smiled. "Yeah, you couldn't fuckin' write it, Harry. So anyway, we rock up to this club in Moscow where Konstantin's bosses hang out and the one in charge, Lev, well he wasn't a happy bunny I can tell you. Made all of us, along with two of his fuckin' goons, fly out to Nigeria. It didn't take long to locate the two blokes who had scammed my old lady but Konstantin got carried away before we could work on the first one. Topped him right there in his office no less. So then went on to pay a visit to the second geezer, by this time Serge was back at the hotel so I think he must have legged it. Our minders drove us and the robbing cunt out to somewhere remote, killed the bloke when he repeatedly said he didn't know where the money was kept, and then they killed Konstantin and shot me in the back as I ran."

"Gutless cunts!"

Some local farmer and his dog disturbed them and they drove off. Chimezie, the farmer, took me in to his home and nursed me back to health although it's taken a long time. He's a fuckin' top bloke Harry, had my back from the off and he had no reason to."

"What, you're saying you didn't go to the hospital?"

"I couldn't Harry as I knew they would be checking. I know I could have died but I would definitely have been killed had I shown up at the hospital. They actually came back for another look just a few weeks ago so I know I still ain't safe. I had to fly home using my new passport, it was risky but I just had to check on me Nan and the old lady."

Suddenly Andy stopped speaking as his eyes filled with tears.

"They weren't home but when I walked into the front room and saw the blood on the floor, I knew they were probably gone. The cunts had killed them both Harry, fuckin' slaughtered them and they killed them before we had even landed in Nigeria."

"What!?"

"I know, I'm gutted and out for revenge."

"So, what you got planned?"

"That's where you come in my old friend and I won't be offended if you decline. When Konstantin was bashing the brains out of that guy I whipped a memory stick out of the side of the computer. At the time I didn't know what it contained but it was passwords and all the

accounts where the money was being held. I'm going to move it in the next few hours."
"How much are you talking about?"
"Minimum thirty million but that's only the Russian's money, who knows what other scams they pulled off."
Harry's eyes opened wide, this was big but dangerous.
"So, what do you want to do about it?"
"I want you to put me in contact with someone who will carry out a hit and I ain't talking about some wide-boy muppet, I'm talking about a professional. The money means nothing to me; I only came across it because my family were wiped out which was my fault!"
"I don't think it was…….."
"Please Harry don't try and make me feel better, if I hadn't got mixed up with those cunts then Mum and Nan would still be alive but that's my guilt and something I have to live with. The least I can do now is to seek out some kind of justice for them."
"And then what?"
"Disappear, maybe try and find my sister and Debbie. Oh, by the way, I will need another passport for my friend but I have to wait to get a photograph."
Harry nodded his head sagely.
"Leave it with me. I will need a few days but it

ain't anything I can't sort out. Are you really sure about the hit Andy, because once the ball is in motion there's no stopping it."
"I've never been more certain about anything Harry."
"I'm truly fuckin' heartfelt for your loss Andy."
"Thanks, you're a good friend Harry and I don't know what I would have done without you."
"Don't be a twat!"
"No, I mean it, you've gone above and beyond and when I sort this money out you won't be forgotten, my friend."
With that, Andy left Richmond and headed back to the house on Chudleigh Street, sure that tonight in his dreams he would be forced to face his demons. Taking a seat at the table he switched on Ruby's computer which had been returned to the house after the initial investigation and was surprised to see that Chimezie had already replied. The email contained a few pleasantries and a winking emoji indicating that he knew why Andy wanted the photograph. Getting out of Nigeria to come to the UK was near on impossible if you had a Nigerian passport, so if Andy could arrange a British one it would make Chimezie's dreams come true. If he decided that he wanted to leave Nigeria then possibly the two could meet up somewhere but Andy wouldn't put any pressure

on his friend. Leaving your homeland was a big ask, Andy knew the feeling all too well. Suddenly an image popped up and he smiled when he saw the face of his friend. Now all he had to do was hope that the old printer still worked and luckily it did.

It took Harry almost five days of contacting various people who knew of other people in the line of work he was looking for. Narrowing it down to two, he sought out the council of Cecil Craven. Cecil had been a Marine and a mercenary. He took on the more difficult hits for the firms in London and as yet, he had a one hundred per cent success rate. A meet was arranged for the weekend at Harry's house under the ruse of a barbeque. Anna, Harry's wife, would be away visiting her sister so it would be perfect timing. It had been relatively easy for Andy to open accounts in the Cayman Islands and moving the money had been simple. He had needed to use his original passport as identification but the Cayman's were known for their privacy and without the relevant passcodes; there wasn't anyone who could gain access to information. He's been surprised at the final amount transferred; it ended up being just short of fifty million.

It was a lovely sunny day when he arrived at the house and as he approached the front door he could smell the aroma of the barbeque coals. There was only Harry's car in the drive and Andy was thankful that he had arrived before the hit man but he was in for a shock when he was shown into the garden. Sitting at the table was a small balding man wearing thick black-framed glasses. He was nothing like Andy had envisaged and when Harry introduced Cecil Craven, the man politely stood up and offered his hand.

"Hello, I'm Cecil."

"Andy, Andy Chilvers, pleased to meet you, Cecil."

The man didn't offer his surname so maybe this wasn't the hired killer, maybe he was just a neighbour who had popped round. Whoever he was, Andy wasn't about to start talking of murder. The trio enjoyed a few beers and burgers and then suddenly Harry seemed to disappear.

"Right, let's get down to business."

Andy was a little taken aback because he had convinced himself that this wasn't the man he was supposed to meet.

"Let me tell you a little about myself. I was a marine for ten years and when I finished my time and work was thin on the ground I ended up joining a mercenary group. There aren't many countries I haven't worked in, don't get me wrong, I like the payment but I like killing even better. Sick I know but that's me."

"You just don't look like a contract killer, at least not my image of one."

"And that's where I have the advantage. I speak seven languages fluently and that includes Russian, don't worry, Harry already gave me the lowdown. Now, tell me in your own words what happened and don't leave anything out as it could be imperative, at least regarding my safety."

As he'd been asked, Andy revealed all and he left nothing out. By the time he'd finished, he felt drained and very emotional. Throughout his revelations, Cecil didn't utter a word.

"I'm concerned about the young people who will be at the club, innocent people."

"Don't be, I can assure you I will target only those who you have instructed. If a few of his men get caught up in it then so be it. What about the target?"

"Lev Baronov is the one who would have ordered the deaths of my family. He arrives most mornings at ten and always has at least two body guards with him. There is a stone lined room on the lower floor where he runs his day to day business as well as the torture of anyone who gets in his way. Apart from a cleaner, the club is usually empty until around seven at night."

"Good, that's helpful. Now I won't deny this will be a difficult mission, not to mention dangerous. I appreciate no cost has yet been mentioned but now we have to come down to the nitty-gritty."

"So, what am I looking at?"

"Three Mill. The one thing I will tell you is if you ever discuss this with anyone else, I will find you."

Andy nodded his head sagely.

"That's not a problem, give Harry, or better still send me your details and it will be paid tomorrow. All I ask is for you to let me know when it's done."

Cecil handed Andy a scrap of paper containing bank account details.

"I do not provide any contact details; it's safer for both of us. Give me your phone number and I will text you when I am leaving and then what TV programme to watch."

Andy didn't understand what Cecil meant but he nodded his head all the same. Scribbling down his mobile number he handed it to the stranger before thanking Cecil for his help. Shaking hands with the new acquaintance, Andy then said his goodbyes to Harry before making

his way home. Back in the garden Harry joined his guest and offered the man another beer.
"So, what did you think?"
"Seems a nice bloke Harry and the poor cunts been through it. I think I'm going to enjoy this one."

CHAPTER TWENTY-SIX

The following morning Andy transferred the agreed three million and then sat back to wait but it was almost a week later when he finally received an anonymous text of just two words which said 'Leaving tonight'.
Cecil Craven flew out of Heathrow with Aeroflot Airlines and when engaged in conversation, which he tried to keep to a minimum, it was always conducted in Russian. It helped him to blend in and also polish up his language skills. Travelling in a cheap nylon suit and tie and with his trademark horn-rimmed glasses topped off with a trilby hat, he looked like any average white-collar Russian, possibly returning home from a business trip. For the past week, Cecil had been planning everything down to the last detail. He had several contacts in the Russian capital, people who would do anything for money and though both parties involved in any deals had a mutual distrust, there was strangely also a level of respect. Cecil had set up a telephone answering account in Omsk where an agreed amount would be paid in advance for a woman to answer calls acting as a receptionist for some fake company, when the agreed time had expired the phone line would be disconnected with no trace it had ever existed

The contact had come via his arms supplier and he never met the contact face to face but was assured he wouldn't be let down. He also reserved a room at the basic Ibis Hotel under the name of Boris Petrov a travelling fire prevention officer. His underground acquaintances had already provided all the necessary components he needed but Cecil had been sure to use several different names for delivery. Together the parcels could raise interest regarding what he was up to but separately they were just miscellaneous items. The wiring and various electrical tapes were all left at post office boxes under different names and he planned to collect them over a three or four-day period. With each visit, he would either wear a selection of wigs or different glasses so as not to be recognised from the previous day. The final item he needed had to be collected in person and it was the most risky part of his plan. Oleg Volkov dealt in arms; there wasn't anything he couldn't acquire and he would sell to anyone at the right price. Known by many as the Butcher, Oleg was as sadistic as any human being could be. He wasn't part of the mafia and he didn't care who he sold to, that said, he would never reveal his client list which he memorized so that there was no paper trail. He had only been crossed once, leading to his one and only stint in Jail but after serving five years; he had hunted the grass down and inflicted a payback so gruesome that no one would ever dare to cross him again. The victim had been found in an abandoned warehouse two months after going missing. He had been skinned alive and left hanging from a chained hook in the ceiling and it was estimated that it took the victim three days to die in agony. Cecil had contacted Oleg a couple of days before his arrival and placed his order. The two had carried out business several times over the last few years and Oleg had come to like Boris Petrov. The man was trustworthy and polite, both things high on Oleg's list of priorities when doing business.

Within an hour of arriving and after checking in at the hotel, Cecil began the first of his collections and taking the item back to his room he began his task. The following morning he did the same before taking a stroll with his trusty camera. Snapping away, along with many other tourists, he was able to get three or four shots of the target building. He wanted to make sure there would be no hidden challenges and when he got back to his room he studied the images over and over again for several hours. On day three it was time to visit the home of Oleg Volkov. Cecil had chosen to walk the four-mile journey, a taxi would have left a witness and that was something he couldn't afford. In his hands, he carried two holdalls, one empty and the other containing the payment he was about to make. Cecil knew that the journey back would be tiring and he planned to walk as far as he could and then take the metro or as a last resort, a taxi. Arriving at his destination, he studied the building for a few moments. The house on School Street looked like many of the others in the area, run down and in dire need of external decoration but Cecil guessed the neglect had been done on purpose. Knocking on the door he was greeted warmly by Oleg, a small, grey-haired man who appeared as inoffensive looking as Cecil did and it was a good cover. The two made their way down into the cellar and entered a room through a hidden door. Cecil always enjoyed this part of his visits as the arsenal of weapons lining every spare inch of the walls was fantastic.

"So, how are you, my friend?"
"Good thanks Oleg, always busy it seems."
"By your order, you are planning something big my friend?"
"You could say that."

Cecil would never discuss his assignments with anyone and Oleg laughed, on every visit he had tried to get Cecil to talk about his work and every time the man had declined and it was becoming a bit of a ritual between the two of them.

"Here you go, twenty-five pounds of the best grade A explosive on the market."

Nodding his thanks, Cecil began to place the packages into the holdalls and after Oleg had checked the payment for the merchandise, Cecil set off on the return journey. He managed to get quite a distance from Oleg's house before his arms began to ache so glancing all around he reasoned that it would now be safe to catch the metro. It stopped not far from his hotel so all being well he would soon be able to put his feet up. Cecil never tired of this mode of transport, set out like the London underground that was where any similarities ended. These endless tunnels were stunning, almost works of art with the vast columns, ornate tiling and gilding and Cecil never tired of looking at them. When he was finally back in the relative safety of his room, he set to work. First, he wired up the explosives and checked everything several times and once he was happy he then dismantled the device and packed it away in a workman's bag. Next, it was time to change his appearance. Removing a set of hair clippers he began to shave the hair in the centre of his head to give the impression that he was balding. Cecil would add a moustache and different glasses in the morning. Climbing into bed he drifted off immediately, it had been a long day.

Up with the larks Cecil showered and dressed in slacks and a shirt and tie. After securing the moustache he checked his paperwork which he'd brought over from the UK. The document looked official and bore the name Omsk Electrical Technicians and included the Soviet government stamp. The name on the form was Aurora's Nightclub. Tucking the paper into his briefcase, he pulled on his anorak, picked up his work bag and headed out of the hotel. It was just after nine a.m. when he knocked on the club's front door and it took several minutes before someone answered. At last a disgruntled-looking man appeared and pushed open one of the double doors.

"Yes?"

Cecil politely tipped his trilby just long enough for the man to notice his hair and balding pate.

"I am from Omsk Electrical and I have come to check out your wiring for safety."

Ivan Popov, one of the doormen, had been napping in the office and wasn't best pleased at being disturbed. He took a step forward and he towered over the man before him but it didn't faze Cecil.

"You can't come in we are closed."

"I am a government official, do you wish me to

call the Politsiya? I am legally entitled to enter and inspect these premises and you have to allow me access. I work to a tight schedule so if you don't let me in then my bosses will not be happy."

Cecil pulled the official-looking paper from his briefcase and thrust it towards Ivan's face. Knowing how bad Lev's mood had been of late Ivan didn't want to upset his employer any further by getting the police involved.

"Okay, okay. Will it take long?"

"Less than an hour but I have other premises to visit today, so I will need to return tomorrow to complete the inspection."

Hopefully it wouldn't be necessary but if something went wrong or the device didn't detonate for some reason, he had bought himself extra time to return and hopefully rectify the problem. Ivan stood aside to let Cecil pass and while the inspector began to look around Ivan went into the office and phoned the number on the sheet of paper. Just as she'd been paid to do, the woman in Omsk answered in a professional voice.

"Omsk Electrical, how may I help you?"

Ivan asked if Aurora's Nightclub in Moscow was due an inspection and after being put on hold for a few seconds, the appointment was confirmed. In the basement, Cecil glanced all

around and couldn't be off noticing the blood on the rear rock wall. It made him think of Andy's mother and grandmother and something hit a cord. He had always loved killing but this time it felt personal which was strange. Quickly assembling all the components from his bag, he looked for somewhere to hide the bomb until the next day. Sitting at the back of the room was an old pallet. It contained boxes of wine glasses and by the look of the dust on the cardboard; it hadn't been touched for a very long time. Opening up the centre box he removed a few of the wine glasses and then placed the device inside. Careful not to forget the glasses that now stood on the concrete floor, he put them in his bag and a few minutes later was on his way to the foyer. He did a double take as he passed Lev Baranov entering. This was all he needed but Cecil kept his head down and Lev had too much on his mind to take any notice. As soon as Lev was inside Ivan was quick to inform his boss of the visitor.
"About the man who just left."
Lev took off his hat and stared at his employee.
"There's no problem Boss, I checked the bloke out and it's all above board."
Lev looked his employee up and down and momentarily wondered where all these muppets came from.

"What bloke? What's all above board?"
"The man, who just left, he was here to do an inspection on the electrics and make sure they are safe."
"And?"
"Well, I just wanted you to know that's all."
"Ivan, I have a fucking mountain of shit going on at the moment, do you think I'm interested in some government official coming to check out the electrics!? Find yourself something useful to do and I am not to be disturbed."
With that Lev stormed down to the lower level, leaving Ivan feeling a fool.

Back at the hotel, Cecil began the next and final part of his plan. Sitting on the bed he got out one of the mobile phones and tapped a message to Andy.
'Watch the Russian news channel MOSKVA 24 after eight tomorrow morning London time. Stream it via Cyber Ghost.'
With that, he ended the text, removed the memory card and cut it into tiny pieces. He would go out for a stroll later and dispose of the phone, he couldn't leave a stone unturned, this was a very dangerous country. Deciding to place everything onto the bed to take stock in readiness for his departure, Cecil then went out for dinner, careful to still be dressed as Boris

Petrov the electrical man. When he returned to the hotel he paid up his outstanding bill informing the receptionist that he would be leaving very early the next morning. Back in his room, Boris laid out his clothes for the next day. Jeans, a cashmere sweater and loafers would be topped off with a long camel coat. Removing the black nylon cover from his suitcase, he revealed the expensive Louis Vuitton logo. Next, he completely shaved his head and he was finally ready to return home. After doing a double check to make sure all his belongings were accounted for he climbed into bed. Sleep came easily for Cecil but the same couldn't be said for Andy back in the UK. It wasn't the fact that the planned act was sitting uneasily with him because it wasn't, what he was concerned with was whether the man he'd paid would be successful or not.

The following morning Cecil didn't eat breakfast, he'd learned over the years that it was best to stay hungry, and there would be time for food when his mission was complete. Taking his time to get dressed, he now looked expensive and classy and with his outfit topped off with a new brown fedora hat and designer sunglasses he bore no resemblance to the occupant of room 122. Taking the lift down to the reception area

Cecil just strolled outside and flagged down a taxi. At the Aurora Nightclub Ivan Popov hovered around the main entrance in anticipation of his boss's arrival, for some strange reason he always seemed to be in Lev's bad books, well not today, today he would be ready and waiting to open the front door. As usual, Lev was punctual and at three minutes past ten his chauffeur-driven car pulled up outside the club. On the opposite side of the road on one of the many benches situated along the bank of the river Moskva, Cecil Craven sat patiently waiting. Holding a newspaper up as if engrossed in its content he regularly glanced over the top. Checking his watch he breathed a sigh of relief when he saw Lev Baranov arrive. He gave it a few minutes for the target to go down to his office and then standing up he held out his arm in an attempt to hail a taxi. It was only a few seconds before a Hyundai Solaris pulled up to the kerb. When Cecil was seated inside he informed the driver that he would like to be taken to the airport and as the car passed the club, Cecil removed his mobile and tapped in 333. Suddenly there was a loud explosion as glass flew out of windows and the driver put his foot down, not wanting to wait around to find out what had happened.
"What on earth was that!?"

Cecil's act of confusion and interest was played out well and the driver shrugged his shoulders. "It's best not to get involved. The Politsiya will be here soon and they have a habit of grabbing anyone in the vicinity and blaming them."
Cecil didn't reply but inside he was smiling.

In England, it had taken Andy a while to locate the news station on the internet but now he sat almost glued to the screen. Watching the time tick by, he hadn't moved an inch since getting out of bed an hour earlier. He couldn't understand the language but he'd luckily been able to locate the subtitle tool on the taskbar. It wasn't needed as at ten minutes past ten the news station began to report on a huge explosion in the capital. Captured on a mobile phone by a couple of tourists on honeymoon, the sound of an almighty explosion burst through the computer's speakers and Andy could only stare wide-eyed as Aurora's Nightclub seemed to disappear before his eyes in a veil of dust.

CHAPTER TWENTY-SEVEN

Andy woke when the sunlight from a chink in the curtains shone into his eyes. He had sat almost glued to the computer screen the previous day and after drinking heavily he must have fallen asleep because the computer was still beside him on the sofa. Standing up he tried to stretch but every muscle in his body ached. Deciding to go and make a cup of tea he mulled over what had happened in Moscow as he walked towards the kitchen and it didn't make him feel good, oh he had avenged his Mum and Nan's deaths but it wouldn't bring them back and now he had been the instigator in the death of others, did that make him as guilty as the Russians? Andy Chilvers had been in many scrapes over the years, some of them violent but he had never taken a life before and it didn't sit well with him. True it was Cecil who had blown up the club but that wouldn't have happened if he hadn't paid for it to be carried out. Suddenly he felt the bitter drawing in his cheeks, always the precursor before he was about to vomit. Running, he luckily made it to the kitchen sink just in time but very little exited his mouth. He hadn't eaten in over twenty-four hours and knew that the sudden onslaught of nausea was guilt pure and simple. Wiping his mouth with

the tea towel he stared out of the kitchen window for a few seconds before his daydreaming was brought to a halt by the sound of his mobile ringing. Racing back into the front room he snatched it up thinking that Cecil might be trying to contact him for some reason.
"Yeah?"
"Hi Andy, it's Harry. That little package has arrived."
"That's good, is it okay if I pop over this morning?"
"Sure. See you later then."
Consuming the hot tea and after forcing down a couple of slices of toast, he waited to see if the food would reappear, when it didn't he knew it was safe to have a shower. Twenty minutes later and still dwelling on the explosion, he headed off to Richmond.

Harry opened the door as soon as he saw Andy's car pull into the drive. He wouldn't mention Cecil or inquire if there was any news as he knew Andy only too well and realised that the man would be feeling bad for what had happened. Harry had always liked his friend but Andy Chilvers never did have the stomach for hard-core villainy. Leaving the door on the latch he walked into his study and poured two glasses of scotch. Andy soon entered and without waiting for an invitation, took a seat on one of the leather Chesterfield armchairs. Harry handed over the crystal tumbler of golden liquid and then walked over to his safe and removed the package. Handing the fake passport to his friend Andy then opened it and smiled warmly when he saw Chimezie's photograph.

"Thank you, Harry, I don't know how I will ever be able to repay you but I've put a gift in your bank account in the hope that it goes someway to showing you my gratitude."

"I don't need payment or thanks Son, you've always been a good friend to me and friends help each other."

"I don't suppose you know what's happened?" Harry pursed his lips and slowly shook his head.

"I had the Russian news on yesterday and a massive bomb went off. It blew that cunts entire club to smithereens, with him in it. I haven't heard from Cecil but I know it was him."

"You won't ever hear from him unless you require his services again and I sincerely fucking hope you won't."

"I feel like shit about it all but I couldn't let it go Harry, I just couldn't."

"Of course you couldn't, we're Londoners and when someone hurts one of ours there is a price to pay. In the East End, it's how we are brought up and it will always stay that way. So, what now?"

Andy sighed heavily and then shrugged his shoulders.

"Try and find my sister I suppose but it's going to be like looking for a fucking needle in a haystack and to be truthful, I don't have the first clue where to start."

"I thought she'd left the country?"

"So did I but it seems she came back and then disappeared again."

Andy savoured the warmth of the last drop of his scotch and suddenly he was incredibly tired. Placing his glass on the side table he shook his friend's hands and told Harry, who was still seated, that there was no need to see him out. Andy set off for Chudleigh Street via a stop off at the post office and as his car disappeared from view down the drive, Harry was now overly inquisitive to find out what his friend had put into his bank. Logging online to his account, he sat back in shock with his mouth wide open as he saw that his finances had risen overnight to the tune of one million pounds. Stopping off at the post office on Richmond High Street, Andy placed Chimezie's passport into an envelope along with a scribbled note of his address and then paid the postage. He was giving his friend the chance of a new life but whether Chimezie would take it would be down to him. There were still a few days until the funerals so for now he planned on going back to the house to sleep and deep down a little part of him hoped that he wouldn't wake up. Parking the car at the bottom of Chudleigh Street so it had no association with the house, he again made sure to use the rear entrance.

Andy spent the next two days alone and kept all the doors and windows locked with the blinds and curtains drawn. He was becoming paranoid that someone might be watching and getting drunk and thinking about his family only exasperated his anxiety. On the morning of the funeral, he felt lower than he'd ever done and the ache in his heart was getting bigger by the day. The cremation was set for eleven and by ten he was dressed and on his way to the East London Crematorium and Cemetery in Plaistow. Parking up he walked for quite a while and then got into a black hackney, it was safer than driving his car any further and he would be able to scan the area without being seen. Andy had visited the Crematorium a few days earlier, he wanted to be there but not to be seen but that was going to prove difficult as the chapel only had one room. There was a small door at the rear that led to a tiny office and that was the only spot he would be able to use. Now the day had come and hiding behind one of the gravestones, he watched as a large black van pulled up and the coffins of Ruby and Aida were pulled out and taken inside. About to head towards the rear of the chapel he stopped when another car drove to the front of the building. Mikhail and Vladimir got out and as they did so a shiver ran down Andy's spine, Cecil might have gotten rid of Lev but his two henchmen were still on the warpath but hopefully, they would soon be called back to Russia. When the chapel doors at last closed he made a run for it and then slipped in through the backdoor. Putting his ear to the wood he could hear his Nan's favourite hymn and when he thought of all that they had gone through and all because of him, Andy felt the tears that he couldn't stop, as they rolled down his cheeks. With no real service to mention, the funeral was over in less than fifteen minutes but he stayed where he was until he heard the footsteps of the crematorium director approaching. Slipping out of the door he cautiously edged along the outer wall until he reached the front of the building. All the vehicles had gone and Andy breathed a sigh of relief. He didn't return directly to Chudleigh Street knowing that the Russians would probably pay one final visit so instead he made his way to the old warehouse in the hope of seeing Rob Winter his trusted former employee.

As he approached the first thing he noticed was that the main gates were wide open and there was a 'To Let' sign on the front of the building. It was obvious that Lev Baranov had cleaned out his stock in a pitiful attempt to recoup some of the lost money and Andy just prayed that Rob was okay and they hadn't harmed him but it would be too dangerous to try and contact him. With his hands in his pockets and his head hung low, Andy slowly walked back towards his car.

The next few days were spent much the same as the last with Andy swinging between great sadness at the loss of his family and being so drunk that all he did was sleep. He didn't have the first clue where to begin looking for Shirley and it hadn't crossed his mind that she would have returned to Thailand. Deciding to call on Wayne again to see if he had heard from her, Andy drank copious amounts of coffee to sober himself up. The visit was a dead end as Wayne hadn't heard a word and he again asked for Andy to contact him if he found anything out.

In Thailand, it was the day of the wedding and the house was filled with flowers and laughter. Debbie wore a traditional Thai Sabai wedding dress of white and red with gold sequins and she looked stunning. Kannika was in tears and it took all of her resolve to stop but when she saw Shirley and Lawan emerge from the bedroom in their beautiful cream bridesmaid dresses the waterworks started all over again. The ceremony took place outside on the large patio with the couple's friends and work colleagues and with Niran's parents and family, there were over a hundred guests. It was a happy day although there were a few private tears shared between Debbie and Shirley when they took a moment to think about Andy but those thoughts were soon pushed to one side as the dancing and eating began. Debbie and Niran spent their honeymoon in a five-star villa with a pool and private chef and it was so magical that Debbie never wanted it to end. Niran was the perfect husband; he was kind and attentive to his wife and now, thankfully, got on well with Shirley.

The months passed quickly and it was soon time for Debbie to give birth. Niran had returned from work to find her in labour with Kannika going from fussing over her dear friend to panic mode. He phoned for an ambulance and within four hours, at Niran's insistence, Andrew Suwan came into the world kicking and screaming. When the couple returned home, Shirley was over the moon to meet her nephew and taking Niran to one side, couldn't thank him enough

for naming the baby after her brother.
"You are welcome Shirley and to give the boy, my son, his father's name is an honour and I promise to always love Andy and raise him to be a kind little boy just as I imagine his father was."
"Yes, he was Niran, my brother was the best and you would have loved him."
Shirley was in floods of tears, life in Thailand had turned out to be okay and even though she thought of her Mum, Nan and Andy every day and cried often, she knew that her life was now here in Thailand with her new family. She had accepted that Andy was dead but this was a new beginning and she had no alternative but to embrace it but it was still so difficult at times. By the time little Andy turned two months, the family had settled into a routine and Shirley had even found a boyfriend though it had taken her a while to accept that not every man would treat her like Wayne. Kasem was a colleague of Niran's and although it wasn't a burning love affair, the couple got on well and Shirley was enjoying the attention, attention she had never received before. To be taken care of instead of being a carer was new to her and without question, she was enjoying it.

CHAPTER TWENTY-EIGHT

After the explosion, Andy had spent the next few months hardly leaving the house, he was also in a deep depression. He now had more money than he could ever spend but deep inside he knew he had absolutely nothing. He went from being sober for a few hours to being inebriated in alcohol the next. The latter was the only way he could cope with the loneliness and loss of his family.

He still hadn't found out where Shirley was or even if she was still alive and that thought he couldn't bear, to have lost all of them all would be worse than death but as hard as he tried not to think about it, whenever he was sober the thoughts started to creep into his mind. One morning he woke up and realised that he couldn't continue living like this, he had to move on and make some kind of life for himself. Showering and dressing, something he hadn't done for many days, he set off for Margaret Street in the West End. Having passed Savills many times over the years Andy had always told himself that if money was no object, he would buy a house through this company. Taking his new passport as identification he walked into the office determined to purchase a Property.

"Good morning Sir, how can I help?"
"I want to move out of the city, somewhere rural."
"Certainly Sir, my name is Gerard, now what type of property would you be interested in and what is your budget?"
Andy had to take a moment; he hadn't given much thought to what he wanted.
"The budget is unlimited but what I want, well…."
"Maybe Sir would like a coffee and to take a moment to decide what you're looking for?"
Andy felt relieved and taking a seat on one of the plush sofas, the agent handed him a notepad and pen.
"I always find it helps if one writes down the key factors and to be honest it makes it much easier to eliminate unsuitable properties."
Andy began to write down a list which seemed to grow by the second. He wanted somewhere spacious and set in private grounds, maybe a minimum of five acres. There had to be a pool in case Shirley ever came back, his sister loved to swim but in the past, it had only ever been down Mile End Park Leisure Centre. Having no close neighbours was a must and he wanted the place already done, he wasn't much good at DIY and he really didn't fancy having hordes of builders walking around the place. Lastly, he thought

about what period he wanted and settled on something older, the new builds always seemed too cold and clinical. Finishing his coffee, he handed the notepad back to the agent, who then took a seat at his desk and began to tap away on his keyboard. Within five minutes Gerard came back over to Andy with the details of three houses and Andy looked disappointed.

"Please don't worry Sir, our system takes into account everything you have asked for and rejects anything that falls short. We have hundreds of properties on our books but these three have everything you have requested."

"Okay and enough with the Sir, please call me Michael, Michael Peters."

"Thank you, Michael. Please take your time and make a note of anything you don't like about each of them."

Andy looked through the documents and the one which stood out the most was situated a few miles from Maldon in Essex.

"I like the look of this, when can I view it?"

Gerard took the leaflet and smiled when he saw the choice.

"That certainly is a magnificent property and it's vacant so we could drive over there this afternoon if you wish?"

Andy grinned, it was perfect as once he'd set his mind on doing something he hated delays.

"Might I enquire if you will need a mortgage, Michael?"

The estate agent's eye lit up when he was informed that it would be a cash sale. Arranging to leave at one and when Gerard said he would drive, Andy then headed over to the Pink Flamingo on Wardour Street. He had a hankering to see his old friend Bobby Richmond. Keeping his head down and now wearing sunglasses and the navy cap that he kept in his coat pocket at all times, Andy wanted to stay as invisible as possible. It was only a ten-minute walk but not wanting to take any chances he hailed a cab and asked the driver to take him to the rear of the club. Climbing the metal fire escape he banged hard on the steel door.

It was unusual for Bobby but he was up and dressed before noon and when he looked through the spy hole, he couldn't get the door open quickly enough.

"Well bless my soul, the wanderer has returned. Come in, come in Andy."

Andy took a seat on the old sofa while Bobby poured them both a scotch.

"I must say I didn't think I'd ever lay eyes on you again mate.

So, what's been occurring?"

Andy took a sip of his drink and then slowly recalled all the events of the past few months.

While he talked Bobby didn't utter a word but his changing expressions spoke volumes.

"You poor cunt and what complete and utter bastards those Russians are. I knew Konstantin was shady but not capable of that, well he got what he deserved but I'm heartfelt sorry about your family."

Andy had left a few things out of his revelations, he hadn't mentioned Thailand, Chimezie or the possible new house. It wasn't that he didn't trust Bobby but if those maniacs decided to visit him, Andy knew his old pal wouldn't be able to bear the pain they would inflict and would spill his guts in an instant.

"So, what now?"

"Now I leave the country and just hope they don't find me.

If they visit you I would appreciate you telling them that you haven't seen me."

"Goes without saying Andy, goes without saying."

Finishing his drink, Andy Chilvers then embraced his friend knowing this really would be the last time they would meet, the embrace was reciprocated as Bobby was thinking the same.

"You take care Andy and get as far away from this fuckin' shithole as possible. It's been a pleasure knowing you my friend."

"Likewise Bobby."

Andy then headed back to the Estate Agents. He wasn't sure if the viewing would come to anything but a drive out to the country would make a nice change. When he arrived, Gerard was waiting for him and as it turned out, the house was everything Andy was hoping for and more. The rooms were light and spacious and he knew the pool area would have Shirley screaming in excitement, that's if he ever saw her again.

There was a bonus, the security system was top of the range and had only recently been installed. When Gerard informed him that all of the furniture, very expensive-looking furniture, was also negotiable, it was the icing on the cake. In the next hour, the deal was agreed and using Savills's in-house solicitor and the fact that Andy didn't want any searches carried out, the completion date was set for one week later.

Returning home, Andy's spirits had been slightly lifted. He decided to pack up any of his family's possessions that he wanted to take but in all honesty, there wasn't much except for some old photographs. Waiting until dark, Andy then set off for his flat. It was risky but he wanted some of his stuff and there was no way he was just leaving it. For a start, there was a hidden diary detailing all of his contacts and deals, something the Old Bill would love to get their hands on. Entering the foyer, he was pleased to see that Simeon was on duty and as soon as the concierge spied Andy he almost ran over.

"Oh Mr Chilvers, I am so pleased to see you. Two men were here a while back and they scared the life out of me. They went up to your apartment but I don't know if they took anything."

Andy placed his hand on Simeon's arm and smiled reassuringly.

"It's fine my friend, I know all about it. I need to collect some items and then I will be leaving for quite some time. Keep an eye on the place for me will you and should those men ever return, I have not been back, okay?"

Andy winked and Simeon smiled, he liked Andy, the man had always been so polite and generous financially, especially at Christmas time.

Andy made his way up to the flat and even though he was expecting it, was shocked at the state of the place as he let himself inside. It had been ransacked and running through to his study he lifted the plant pot and was pleased to see that they hadn't located his floor safe. Emptying the contents he then filled a couple of holdalls with clothes. Taking one last look around Andy closed the door and knew it would be for the last time.

As he walked from the foyer, he stopped and pressed a wad of notes into Simeon's hand. "There's a number here as well that you can text me on, enter it in your phone under an assumed name and then destroy the paper. I will see you again sometime and remember, not a word to anyone."

Simeon winked and then watched as the best resident he had ever known, exited the building.

On the day that Andy was to collect the keys to his new property, there was a slight feeling of excitement. He had already packed all of his belongings into the car and was enjoying a final cup of tea using Aida's favourite blend of teabags when there was a knock at the door. For a second he froze, were they back, was this the day it would finally all come to an end? Cautiously he pulled the net curtains to the side and through a small gap, he could only see the back of a lone caller. Andy was sure that they wouldn't come back single-handed so he guessed that he was safe to see what the person wanted. Opening the front door Andy immediately broke into a wide grin as he almost lunged forward and took Chimezie into his arms.

"You came! I'm so pleased to see you old friend

but a few minutes later and your trip would have been for nothing."

Chimezie Kalu just stood there looking confused and uncomfortable in his new suit that by British standards was of low quality and poorly made but one that the Nigerian was over the moon with. At his feet were two large suitcases and Andy realised they contained his friend's entire worldly goods. Andy resisted the urge to laugh, it would have been an insult and he wouldn't hurt the man for anything.

"Come in, come in, I have so much to share with you, my friend."

Chimezie was glad to be out of Nigeria but on his arrival in London it had scared him, so many strange people and skyscraper buildings.

The seven-hour flight had been exhausting and travelling on a fake passport had only added to his anxiety.

With the door closed he could now relax and Andy thought he could see a lone tear run down Chimezie's face as he drank his first cup of English tea.

"I'm so tired Andy, I need to sleep, my friend."

"And you will but not now and not here, it isn't safe. I have just bought a new house and was about to go there. Come on, let's get going."

On the two-hour drive to Maldon, Andy relayed all that had happened and this time he left nothing out. He trusted his friend with his life and had done so in the past.

When they pulled up outside the house, Chimezie's mouth hung open in awe.

"Is this really all of yours Andy?"

"It's ours my friend, a fresh start and a new life for both of us, well if you want it that is?"

Chimezie beamed from ear to ear and couldn't stop nodding his head.

The next few weeks passed by in a flash as Andy taught Chimezie all the things that were expected of him in England. They dined in good restaurants and the food was a cultural shock much like it had been for Shirley in Thailand but the pair were enjoying each other's company. That said, Chimezie saw sadness in his old friend's eyes that no amount of money could lift. Having lost his own family many years ago, he knew what Andy was going through but there was nothing he could do to ease the pain. On a walk along the prom one sunny afternoon, Andy started to talk about his sister and Debbie when suddenly Chimezie stopped and grabbed his arm.

"You must travel to Thailand and find this woman, see if you still have feelings for her and maybe she will have some news on your sister."

For a moment Andy stared at his friend as he

took in the enormity of what Chimezie had just said. He had thought of going many times but something and he didn't know what it was, had always stopped him.

"But she might not be interested in me anymore and I'm sure Shirley wouldn't go back there not after coming back to London?"

"Maybe not but unless you seek her out you will never know.

I have yet to find a woman who wouldn't be swayed by the size of your bank balance."

"And how would you know?"

The remark was cruel as Chimezie had always been poor until he met Andy. The show of hurt was evident on his face and Andy wished he could take back the words.

"I'm sorry my friend I shouldn't have said that, please forgive me."

"Unlike in the West, in my village, wealth is measured in different ways and I did have my fair share of women whether you believe me or not.

Now as I was saying, a life of crime did pay off for you this time and I guarantee that you will return with her and if you're lucky, your sister as well."

Andy spent the next few days mulling over all that his friend had said and his emotions went from there and then wanting to go and book a flight, to thinking it was a stupid idea. His mood towards Chimezie had improved and every time he was about to bite the man's head off for some meaningless inane thing, he stopped himself from saying something he knew he would regret. Finally, when he couldn't stand his swinging emotions any longer he came to a decision.

"I'm going to Thailand."

Chimezie smiled broadly, whatever the outcome, it was time for his friend to start over and to do that he had to get some answers.

"I think it's for the best Andy, one way or another at least you will know. Would you like me to accompany you?"

Andy thought for a moment, he would like the company but then again if it was bad news he didn't think he could stand Chimezie continually trying the cheer him up.

"No, it's fine. I intend to go there and come straight back once I've found Debbie.
Stay here and relax, you deserve it."

Two days later the Emirates flight left Heathrow Terminal 3 at two in the afternoon. Andy had decided on first class and he wasn't disappointed. His seat turned into a bed so unlike his sister, the flight was relaxed and somewhat enjoyable and on his arrival, he felt fresh and ready for the day ahead. Exiting the airport, again unlike his sister, Andy didn't take the bus and opted for a taxi to take him to Nakula Beach. It was nine am local time so with luck on his side he could be there before noon. Nerves had begun to set in, he so badly wanted Shirley to be there but he was also excited about seeing Debbie again.

The taxi driver spoke little English and apart from asking if Andy would like to meet a girl or boy if he preferred, the journey was taken in silence. Wearing a baseball cap with a camera hanging from his neck he resembled any other tourist and knew the fare would be hiked up because of how he was dressed. He was still coming to terms with having so much money and for a moment he thought about asking in advance what the charge would be. When the car neared the house and the driver informed Andy that they were almost there he asked the man to pull over. Getting out he studied the surroundings. It was a beautiful place, the sun glistened on the water and he knew if all went well it was somewhere he could see himself living. About to get back into the car he stopped when in the distance he noticed someone come out of the front door. Zooming in with his camera, Andy couldn't believe what he saw and his face broke into a huge smile when he realised it was Shirley but she wasn't alone. A handsome Thai-looking man had his arm around her shoulder and she looked so happy, the kind of happy he had never seen on her face before. Seconds later another man emerged with a baby in his arms and for a fleeting second Andy was confused until Debbie walked out and placed a kiss on the man's cheek and then another on top of the baby's head. The tears flowed freely down Andy's face and then suddenly he could feel the familiar acid fill his cheeks and bending over to vomit, he had to place his hand on the car roof to steady himself. This was it, it was all over. The feeling of utter despair and emptiness was overwhelming. How could he just barge in and break up what looked to be a loving and happy family? His heart was broken and wiping his mouth, Andy wearily he got back into the car and told the driver to take him back to the airport. There wasn't another flight until the following afternoon so after spending the night in a local hotel, Andy at last set off for his return journey.

To say Chimezie was surprised to see his friend so soon was an understatement and he could tell by the look on Andy's face that things hadn't gone well. Chimezie didn't pry that wasn't his way and he knew Andy would eventually reveal all that had happened when he was ready. Later that day and after downing several large tumblers of scotch, Andy began to talk. He told his friend all about what he had seen and as he did, tears rolled down his cheeks.

"I wish to God that I had never gone there Chimezie."

"And that would have just left you wondering for the rest of your life. Sometimes it's better to know the truth even if it isn't the truth you wanted. Now? Well, at least you know."

"And knowing has left me with no one in life to love or care about."

"You have me, my friend, always. I may not be related by blood but I am still your brother."

Andy slowly nodded his head and smiled. The tears flow and for a while, he actually sobbed so he couldn't speak. Chimezie didn't say anything or try to console his friend, Andy needed to release his hurt before he could hope to move on. After what felt like an age to Chimezie, Andy dried his eyes and then with an expression of total defeat he looked at his friend.

"Yes you are and once again I owe you everything. Chimezie, can you remember once saying to me that crime does pay?"

"I do indeed Andy, you only have to look around us at all the beautiful things."

"Well, Chimezie Kalu, I can tell you that it most definitely doesn't, I am living proof of that!"

The End

Printed in Great Britain
by Amazon